I0707590

Dreamer

Dreamer

Krista Vanden Bosch

This is a work of fiction. All characters and events were created in the mind of the author.

Dreamer

ISBN: 979-8-9888563-0-6

Content Warning

This story may contain elements that some readers find distressing. The following list may contain spoilers. Content warning for emotional and physical abuse, blood and gore, violence and death of a child.

Chapter 1

I was riding the train. Riding with no destination in mind. Two small light fixtures, not even bright enough to illuminate a closet, were the only sources of gloomy light in the windowless car. Taking in my surroundings as best I could in the dark space, I found the little car to be dingy and dirty.

Some of the bench seats were cockeyed and torn, making me think there had been an accident of some kind in the recent past. Instead of fixing it up, the train people had just thrown the car back on the tracks, made sure it moved, and called it good. The walls were grey with dark smudges here and there. It was too dimly lit to tell if the smudges were remnants of smoke damage or something much worse.

I'd never been on a train in my life before this, but in my inexperienced opinion, this car looked too old and dilapidated to carry passengers. Yet here I was. Me, Rose Russo, stay at home mom and wife, was on the run from my increasingly abusive husband. This piece of junk train was apparently all I could afford. But it was taking me away and that was all I could ask for right now.

Brakes screeched as the train prepared to stop, the sound reverberating in the tight space of the car. When we stopped completely, the engine sighed not far from me. The door opened automatically with a whoosh, filling the little car with cold winter air. The bitter chill made me shiver as I realized, in my haste to leave the house, I had forgotten a coat, even in the dead of winter. I huddled down, trying to block the cold breeze using the seat in front of me, and rubbed my exposed arms vigorously with my hands.

A man stepped into the dusky car. Or not so much stepped in, as floated in on a cloud of exhaust that swirled in behind him. His dark appearance spelled trouble, and with it, a feeling of foreboding hit me like a ton of bricks. He wore black pants with a tucked-in black shirt under a long black coat, topped with a black homburg hat. His style reminded me of working men from the early twentieth century. All he needed was a newspaper in one hand and a briefcase in the other to complete the look.

Maybe this was a magic train that had taken me back in time. That would certainly explain the oddly dressed man and the car that looked like it had gone through WWI. Or, more logically, I had gone cheap on the train ticket, and this guy was on his way home from a funeral. For all I knew, he worked at a funeral home. No matter where he came from, his unusual entrance held me transfixed. I honestly tried not to stare, but my eyes were drawn to the figure like he was a diamond in a pile of coal.

I sat captivated in the back corner seat, on the complete opposite end of the car from the new arrival. Either he was exceptionally tall, or the car was unusually small, because the poor guy had to bend his hat-clad head forward to keep from bumping the ceiling. He paused at the front of the aisle. With his arms crossed over his chest, he looked tall, dark, and devious.

The brim of his hat obscured his face, leaving me wondering what he might be hiding. Was he scarred from cheek to chin? Was his nose crooked from being broken a few too many times? Just as mysterious as how many licks it would take to get to the center of a Tootsie Pop, I didn't think I'd ever know.

The train felt as if it were locked in a kind of stasis, waiting for Mr. Devious to take his seat, just as I was. I physically jumped when he suddenly started moving forward, moving down the narrow walkway, passing all the open benches. Right toward me. Power ebbed from every movement he made. Movements that were graceful and calculated, controlled and sensual. Not quite human. But most certainly masculine. Desire tingled through me, a feeling I hadn't experienced in years. I tried to look away, but he was stunning to behold.

I sat frozen, unable to move, unable to run. Even if I could, there was one manly—I mean, massive—problem. The only way out was blocked by Mr. Devious' large form. I considered jumping over the few benches that stood between me and the open door. Way easier than jumping the man who spanned floor to ceiling.

As if in tune with my thinking, the door whooshed closed, the engine coughed, and we lurched forward. I was jostled in my seat by the unexpected movement, but Mr. Devious held steady. Within moments, I heard the wheels speeding along the tracks and knew we were moving at quite a clip. That door no longer meant safety. Now, it was more like certain death. At the very least, a disfiguring, painful landing. The question was, would it be the lesser of two evils? Mr. Devious was just a couple steps away from me now.

Stopping in front of me, he lowered himself down until he was more on my level, anchoring himself with a hand on either side of me. His face turned up to mine, and I gasped. Blood-red strands of hair poked out from under his hat. Eyes, the same shade of red as his hair, met mine. His face was the color of obsidian, with what looked like veins of molten lava snaking from his scalp and disappearing beneath his shirt. Dread rocked me as I realized I was locked on this train with a demon. Possibly even the devil himself.

I gave the death door another look, contemplating my escape route and wondering if I'd even make it before this demon caught up to me. That's when I noticed I was unable to move, locked in my seat by invisible restraints. My head and eyes were the only parts of me with any freedom. I opened my mouth to say something. Anything. Ask what he wanted. Beg for my life if I had to. *Anything.* But somehow, he knew and covered my mouth with a finger. The universal sign to stay quiet. I took a deep breath to steady my shaky nerves, and with it, I caught a trace of freshly cut grass, fresh air, and all things summer.

If this really were the devil, I'd expect him to smell like sulfur and rotting flesh, death and decay, pain and suffering. Pretty much all things bad, but summer, absolutely not. His crisp scent enveloped my senses, helping me to relax. Slightly. I took another deep breath and gave him a weak nod, letting him know I wouldn't scream.

He removed his finger from my lips. We sat in silence. Staring at each other. Bumping along the tracks, not moving a muscle. Not that I could even if I wanted to. The lights overhead flickered before going out completely, plunging us into a darkness that was nearly unbearable. The tension, which had been on a steady decline moments before, made a U-turn and was nearing chart-topping records.

Time stopped, and the darkness stretched for ages. My heart was ready to pound right out of my chest, and my breathing was becoming erratic. I was on the precipice of having a nervous breakdown. Locked in a dark train car with God-knows-what creature, who wouldn't?

Heat radiating from Mr. Devious' body was the only indication he was still crouched in front of me, reminding me that I was not alone in this personal hell. I still wasn't sure if that was a good thing or not. Gentle hands cupped my face, a gesture that was surprisingly comforting. I squeezed my eyes shut, absorbing the tranquility that seeped through his warm hands. Our skin-to-skin contact soothed me, almost as if he was drawing my anxiety out through his fingertips.

It may have been seconds or it may have been hours that we sat like that before a faint light flickered from the floor. It illuminated only the two of us, leaving the rest of the car cast in darkness. I was stunned to see his appearance had changed drastically. The hat was gone, and instead of bright red hair, thick black hair was slicked back to perfection. I had an absurd yearning to run my fingers through it, ruffling it to give him a more human appearance. However impossible that might be.

Those chilling red eyes were now entirely black and set into a face chiseled from stone. Literally. His face looked like it was made of a light-colored marble, with a smooth surface and hard lines. Dark variegations ran where the lava once flowed. Power still oozed from every pore, and probably I should have been shaking in my boots, but I was feeling the total opposite. I had an overwhelming need to have him touch me. All of me. Now, I'm not the kind of girl to sleep with a stranger, but believe me when I say there was a bewitching eroticism about this man.

His hands, which were still perched on the sides of my face, pulled me in for a kiss. Slow and tender at first, then increasing in intensity, igniting a fire in my nether regions. Those hard lips, which looked like they would crumble to pieces if he ever smiled, were unexpectedly soft and sultry and perfect. Quite possibly, it was the best kiss I'd ever had in my thirty years of life.

I'd kissed my fair share of men in my younger days, back before I was married. For the last almost ten years, it had only been my husband, Marc Russo. *Crap, Marc will be so upset if he finds out about this.* I had to stop. I couldn't, though. I wanted more. A *lot* more. Shoot, I would have pulled him in closer, but I was still being held by those damn unseen restraints.

We sat with our lips locked so passionately that I thought I might melt. I was ready to beg for more when he pulled away. His hands were running down the front of my body, coming to rest at the hem of my shirt. My arms rose above my head of their own accord before he deftly pulled the shirt from my body and discarded it somewhere in the dark. My pants soon went the same way as my shirt. I held my breath in anticipation, not knowing what would come next now that I was nearly naked.

It was hard to tell what he was focusing on because he had no discernable pupils, but I assumed he was taking in my state of undress with the slight movement of his head down the length of my body. At five-foot-ten, with a slim body and curves in all the right places, I was used to men gawking.

My hair has always been long, except for a brief time when I experimented with shoulder length, and it's naturally a coffee-bean brown. Although it can be unruly and frizz up to five times its normal size in humid weather, I've always been happy with the finished result. Thanks to my mom, I have a cute button nose and deep brown eyes.

The black abyss of Mr. Devious' eyes made me feel a little insecure as they took in every part of me without a word of appreciation. Or disgust. His expression was inscrutable. I was about to scream at him for staring when he leaned in and started to nibble at my neck. Affectionate little bites that I didn't think possible from someone so hard. *Hard.*

He looked hard all over. That made me think of another part of his anatomy, and I wondered if that would be as rock-hard too. Heat rushed to my face. I swore I could feel him smile against my neck between bites. But I hadn't said anything. I moved my focus back to what was happening above his waist and that marvelous mouth.

With each bite, a shock wave flashed through my body, sending me closer and closer to orgasm. With each bite, he went lower, stopping long enough to release a nipple from the soft cup of my bra. His tongue swirled and caressed until it was hard enough to cut glass. Or his face. I felt another smile from him, and he carefully put the nipple away.

He must have had the same thought and didn't want to ruin his gorgeous complexion. The nibbles continued down my stomach, over to my hip bone. He was so close to my pleasure zone that it would have been game-over for me if he even looked in the general vicinity. A low rumble vibrated my skin, and I knew Mr. Devious was laughing. His train of thought was either like mine, or he was reading my thoughts.

"Okay, I have to know, are you—"

My words were cut short by a sharp sting before the sensation returned to ecstasy.

I'd read my fair share of vampire novels, watched movies and TV series based on the life and times of a vampire, and I knew that their bite could be quite the orgasmic experience. Was it possible that Mr. Devious was an actual vampire? From what I'd seen so far, there was a high probability. In books, the vampire was always described as looking human, check. They were pale, check as of right now. His initial appearance didn't fit the description, but that didn't rule anything out yet.

Without any windows, there was no light penetrating our little car, so I was unable to determine if he was photosensitive. Vampires were also described as dark and mysterious, double check. Last, but not least, they were powerful. Also, a check, if he was able to hold me locked in my seat with sheer willpower.

Straightening, his black eyes returned to my face, a spot of blood glistening on his lip. Alright, that sealed it; he was absolutely, positively, a vampire. I'd just had an encounter with a vampire. Just wait till Maiz heard about this.

Maiz and I had been besties for most of our lives. We met at daycare as tiny little babies and had pretty much been inseparable since, even going so far as applying to the same colleges and picking the one we were both accepted to. I told her everything. Almost. I'd been holding back on how bad things were at home lately. She'd been so busy with her successful interior design business that I didn't want to bother her with my problems.

Mr. Devious licked the drop from his lower lip with deliberate sexiness, sending tremors through my body at the sight of his tongue of torture. Taking my hands in his, he stood, pulling me up with him. Weak from whatever had just transpired, I wrapped my arms around his neck, using his stability to support me. He had to be well over six feet tall in this barely six-foot tin can. Way too much man for too little space.

He bent his head forward. The perfect position for looking down at me as I stared up at his exquisite face. There was a caring—dare I say loving—look on his face. It made him look almost human.

"Rose," his deep voice rumbled. "You have to wake up."

"What? No!" I pushed him away from me. "No, no, no, no, no. This can't be a dream. It just can't be."

He didn't confirm that it was a dream, but then he didn't have to. The slight tilt of his head and somber look about him told me everything. It should have been obvious from the start, but I'd never been good at reading people or situations. Of course, there were no hot demon vampires walking around seducing women on rundown train cars. *I'm such an idiot.*

I didn't want to wake up. I didn't want to open my eyes and see the depressing walls of my room.

The train had stopped moving. There were no screeching brakes this time. One minute it was hauling ass, the next it just stopped. In a blink of an eye, the ride was over, but I wasn't ready to get off. Well, I was, in a totally different sense of the word. Mr. Devious smiled at me.

You're reading my mind, right? Because, really, why else would you smile at the very moment I'm thinking something inappropriate? This is a dream, for heaven's sake. So, technically, you're a part of my brain and know everything that's going on in my head. I made you up. My thoughts are your thoughts. Somewhere, I should know what you're thinking, too. I just need to find it. Give me a minute.

I was rambling and not making much sense. Not even to me. To anyone else, I would have sounded like a complete lunatic. I was trying to prolong my time here. If the dream was over, I'd have to go back to real life, and I wasn't ready for that. Panic started to rise.

Mr. Devious wrapped his hands around mine and pulled me to him.

"We'll meet again," he whispered next to my ear.

The confidence in his voice tempered my panic. He placed a light kiss on my forehead right before the light on the floor flickered out, and I was swathed in darkness once more. His heat was no longer close against my skin. I reached for him, but he was gone. Somewhere in the distance, the train's whistle was blowing. It grew louder and louder, over and over, until my bones vibrated from it. Then, the floor slipped from under me, and I was falling.

I bolted upright, my heart racing and my body shaking. Back in my own bed, I double checked my surroundings, finding it to be the same as when I went to bed last night. Everything that had just happened was only a dream. I could still feel Mr. Devious' hands on my skin, his mouth on mine, and all the emotions he'd evoked in me. But he was really gone, back to being a figment of my imagination.

What an imagination it was, though. Reaching over to the bedside table, I grabbed the still-beeping phone and shut off the alarm.

"Bad dream, honey?" Marc mumbled from the opposite side of the bed.

"What? Oh, yes," I said, deciding that was better than trying to explain Mr. Devious and all the things he had done to me. "No more scary movies for me."

I tried to sound light and nonchalant, even though in my mind's eye, I could see a tall, handsome man, standing in front of me, the heat and sexuality rolling off him in waves. Oy, I had to get out of here and distract myself if possible.

"I'll go get breakfast started," I said a little too quickly, struggling to untangle myself from the sheets.

"I told you to stop watching that crap. All that dumb shit you watch. Maybe you'll listen to me from now on."

Marc Russo and I met on a muggy August night nearly ten years ago at the local bar. The humidity outside made it feel like we practically had to swim through the air to get inside. Between the car and the door to the bar, my hair had achieved eighties rock band status with its teased-to-new-heights look. After hours of dancing in close quarters, I was sweating buckets when a handsome man cut in to dance with me. Looking and smelling the way I did, I was flattered that he had chosen me over all the other beautiful women in the room.

He was a touch taller than me, his brown hair unkempt with shimmering pieces of gold that popped in the bar light. His nose was a bit narrow for his face, but he was still handsome. He had a confidence about him that I found incredibly attractive. I wouldn't call it love at first sight, but more like infatuation on the dance floor.

That was the night our romance started. I'd soon find him charismatic, sweet, and really good at making me feel wanted. Maiz, on the other hand, said there was something that didn't sit right. She thought he was vain and arrogant. Instead of listening, I blew off her concerns, figuring she was jealous that he had picked me and not her.

I should have listened to her. What I did, despite her concerns, was spend every waking moment with Marc. I felt all grownup having a boyfriend ten years older than me, and responsible enough to own his own house. On top of that, he was a successful accountant, moving his way up the business ladder. I was not a gold digger, but when you're surviving on ramen noodles and PB&Js, it's nice having someone who can afford a pantry full of groceries. Or take you out to a nice restaurant instead of the local dance bar with greasy food.

A little over a month into our relationship, I found out I was pregnant. Our unexpected gift sent our careless romance into overdrive, and we were married a month later. Seven months after that, we welcomed our baby boy, Lake.

He was the calmest baby any new mother could ask for, and over the years, he'd stayed that way. He never threw a fit about having to eat his vegetables, cried about having to do homework, or got upset about having to go to bed early for school. At only nine years old and in the fourth grade, he was testing in middle school curriculum. Marc had always wanted more kids, but we were never able to conceive again. A sign from above? Or a cruel joke from below?

In a way, I'd been okay with that. As they say, the better the firstborn is, the worse the second one will be. I don't know who "they" are, but they have an opinion about everything. By their standards, our next child would be an absolute monster.

Once Lake was born, we decided it would be best if I quit college to be a stay-at-home mom. That's when a change in Marc first started. I think he felt aggrieved that I wasn't bringing home the bacon. That I got to stay home and "sit around," as he'd say. That was, of course, far from what I did, but he didn't see it that way.

Years passed, and nothing I did was good enough or done right. It was like he was looking for reasons to start a fight. When this all first started, I would stand my ground and argue, but somehow, he would manage to talk circles around the issue, eventually coming back around to it being my fault.

"If you hadn't done this," or "If you hadn't said that", and the best of all, "You're crazy for being upset about this." He was so convincing that I always wound up believing him. I didn't know what was right or wrong, and I didn't know what was wrong with me.

These days, I don't waste my breath arguing with him. There was no point. He looked the same except for a few extra pounds around the middle, but he wasn't the man I'd married. I wasn't the woman he'd married either. I used to be fun, laid-back, and outgoing. Now, I tried to tiptoe over eggshells to avoid any unnecessary confrontation, causing me to be uptight and high-strung.

I looked nearly the same, except that my long brown hair was now a near-platinum shade of blond. Marc's choice, not mine. I figured he had a thing for Barbie growing up because that was who I saw when I looked in the mirror. Barbie wasn't unattractive or gross—she was someone all the girls wanted to be back in my childhood—but it wasn't me.

Through the years, I'd put up with it because that was my wifely duty, or so I thought in my love-muddled mind. On top of everything else, I had Lake to think about. I was raised by two parents, and that's what I wanted for my son. We both loved him, and that was what he needed. Lots of love. From *both* parents. So, I kept my head up and tried to keep Marc happy the best I knew how. Even if he was getting harder and harder to please, and his animosity towards me was increasing by the day. Until last night, I didn't think it could get much worse. Boy, was I wrong.

Earlier in the week, a cold front had moved in, keeping temps in the low thirties. Colder still once you factored in wind chill. This wasn't unusual for Pennsylvania, but it didn't happen all that often. That chill had crept its way inside our house and permeated my very soul. All I wanted to do was crawl back under the covers, light the fireplace, and stay where it was cozy and warm. That wouldn't be acceptable when there was work to be done. Marc expected a clean house, and I was the gal for the job. So, after he left for work, I turned the heat up to seventy from sixty. His body ran hot, just like his head, I supposed. Only yesterday, I had forgotten to turn it back down before he got home.

After Marc got home, the evening was agonizing. He went straight upstairs to change out of his work clothes before coming back down for supper. Lake and I were already seated at the table, waiting, and waiting, and waiting. I was about to tell Lake he could go ahead and start when I heard Marc's tell-tale angry stomp down the stairs, all the way over to the table and next to me. Out of the corner of my eye, I could see him staring daggers at me, and that's when I remembered the heat. That was one of his rules: never touch the thermostat.

My anxiety soared. I pondered my level of stupidity on this one. Idiot, moron, or had I hit completely lost-my-mind status? It wasn't until after I had put Lake to bed that Marc pulled me into the bedroom to "have a word." I knew it was going to be more than just a word; this was going to be an earful.

"I pay for *everything* in this house. That includes the *heat*. What made you think you could change it?" he asked, getting louder with each word.

"Honey, calm down, Lake will hear you," I said, looking at the door behind him.

"Calm down? *Calm down?* Who are you to tell me what to do? I don't give a shit if Lake hears me. Maybe he'll learn from my mistakes."

"I'm sorry, I just wanted to take the chill out of the air so I could get my work done. I just forgot to switch it back today."

Too late, I realized my slip-up. No, this was not the first day I had changed the heat, but it was the first time I'd forgotten to change it back.

He glared at me, like he was trying to bore holes through me. Maybe he was rethinking his choice of wife all those years ago. Whatever it was, I was squirming like a worm in the sun under his scrutinizing gaze.

"Please," I said, "say something."

He raised his hand. My eyes and brain were unable to work together to comprehend that it was arcing through the air toward my face, meaning I utterly failed to move out of the way in time. In my late attempt to step out of the way, I tripped over my own feet and stumbled to the floor. An intense burning lit up the whole left side of my face. Putting my hand to my cheek, I found it searing hot, and I looked up at him in total bewilderment. His face mirrored mine.

His hands balled at his sides. I wanted to believe that he wouldn't do anything more, but I couldn't quite convince myself. His expression looked confused, but his body language said he was still poised for a fight. Staying on the floor so as not to show defiance, I waited for his next move.

Without looking me in the eyes, he said, "Rose, I'm so sorry. I never meant to do that. I would never hurt you intentionally, but you made me so angry talking back to me like that." He looked defeated. Or he tried to, anyway. "I'm so stressed at work. With the new merger and the new employees and the cuts, it's been so hectic."

He extended his hand. The same hand that had just slapped me. The one that surely was outlined on my cheek in red, swollen skin.

I hesitated to take it, not trusting him or my legs to hold me up. My whole body trembled inside and out, but I took the assistance that was offered. He hauled me off the floor and pulled me close, wrapping me in a hug. I didn't, or more accurately, I couldn't return the gesture. His touch repelled me, and I wanted to run from the room. My throat choked with tears as we stood there, my arms limp at my sides, my mind screaming in anger.

Marc loosened his hold enough that he could lean back and look at my face.

"Please, please, please forgive me," he said, unshed tears in his eyes.

Oh, he was good. I wouldn't forgive him automatically, but he was still my husband, and marriage was about forgiveness.

"I know you would never deliberately hurt me," I said, my face burning with the anger of a thousand bee stings, "but I need time."

Putting my hands on his chest, I tried to push out of his arms, but he grabbed my wrists. Had it been my fingers in that vice grip, a couple may have snapped like twigs.

"Rose, I love you," he said. A touch of desperation in his voice.

Just like that, I was too exhausted to do or say anything more. I nodded at him, appeasing him for now. When his grip loosened enough, I pulled my wrists free and made my escape. I felt dirty, not in the sweaty, stinky sense of the word, but more like I had done something wrong. It must have come from breaking my values and allowing Marc to treat me like a ragdoll that he could toss around.

I wanted to shower, but I knew that wouldn't wash away the feeling, so I changed into a pair of shorts and a t-shirt for bed. In the bathroom, I started my nightly routine, skipping the face wash part. My cheek was still burning, and I was too damn tired to worry about mascara smudges and clogged pores.

I watched myself in the mirror as I brushed my teeth and wondered who that woman was who was staring back at me. She looked like a lost stranger. Tears poured from my eyes, and I knew if I didn't put a stop to them, I'd have a full-on mental breakdown. Before heading back to the bedroom, I gave myself a little pep talk, telling my reflection to pull it together and everything would be okay.

Marc was waiting on the edge of the bed, but I had nothing to say. Anything I said right now would be in anger. That wouldn't benefit anyone. I avoided eye contact and went straight to my side, curling up beneath the covers as close to the edge as I could get. The bed shifted when Marc got up to shut the lights off, shifting again as he climbed in next to me. He wrapped an arm around me, pulling me back against him, so we were spooning. He must have missed that I was practically falling off the side of the bed to get away from him. Or, more likely, he just didn't give a damn.

Something was pressing against my back. Anyone who's met a man knows what that something is. Sometimes, maybe even most times, it's welcome. This was not one of those times. I had to fight the urge to leap from the bed screaming and lock myself in one of the other four rooms. Preferably the one farthest from Marc. That would cause more problems than it would solve. All I wanted was to go to sleep and get this night over with.

"Rose," he spoke from behind me, "it's been too long."

"Not tonight. Please? My face still hurts, and I'm getting a headache."

"I should have known you'd use that excuse."

He gave a loud harrumph and turned away from me. The bed shook as he shifted his weight back to his side, giving me enough relief to drift off to sleep. Enter Mr. Devious in that weird, scary, wonderful dream. Words I never thought I'd use in the same sentence.

Last night felt like a dream. Not only the dream itself, but the altercation with Marc as well. But today was a new day. I tried my damnedest to put what happened behind me, chalking it up to stress, and I hoped Marc would stick to his word and never hurt me again. *He loves me, and I love him. Time to move on.*

Down in the kitchen, I started some bacon and scrambled eggs on the stove, put muffins in the oven, and cut up some fruit. Lake perched himself on a stool at the counter while I was whisking the eggs.

He was hunched over the sketchbook he had gotten for his birthday, drawing what looked like a dragon curled around a lamp post, the tip of its forked tongue poking out the side of its lips.

I playfully ruffled his hair, eliciting an exasperated sigh. So as not to break his concentration, his eyes never left the page as his hand came up to wave at me in a "shoo little peasant" wave. I grabbed his little hand, placing a loud smooch on his knuckles. A smile lit up his face, that adorable dimple popping. That dimple was going to melt the hearts of every girl in school one day. For now, it was his weapon to get whatever he wanted. It was my kryptonite. Anytime I saw it, I just wanted to go kiss-crazy on that cute wittle face. Don't even get me started on all the embarrassing baby talk it brought out. Embarrassing for me, of course.

As quick as the dimple appeared, it was gone, and he was back to work on his current masterpiece. I'd bet Maiz that he'd grow up to be an accomplished artist one day. The loser had to pay the winner one million dollars. For Maiz, that would seem like pennies, but as a stay-at-home mom, I'd have a harder time coming up with the money.

I wasn't worried, though. Lake put so much thought into every drawing, being meticulous with even the smallest details, and each piece came out vivid and lifelike.

Like my dream.

Never in my life had I been able to recall a dream in such detail. The smell of the old, musty train car we were sitting in. A hint of burning from the train's breaking shoes in the air. Mr. Devious smelling like sunshine and goodness. His velvet-soft fingers touching my body, and the uproar it caused when he put his mouth to my skin.

The plethora of feelings he aroused, my pure X-rated arousal for him. I ran my fingers along my hip bone, where Mr. Devious' nibble had nearly sent me over the edge to the land of magical orgasms.

Two symmetrical bumps scraped the bottom of my fingertips. They were warm and painful to the touch. Not exactly what I would have expected to find from something that happened in a dream. Was it possible that I subconsciously knew they were there and dreamt up a reason for them?

I'd have to make a run to the bathroom to have a looksee at what exactly I was feeling. Marc would be down any minute, so I'd have to make this quick.

I scooped out some eggs, a piece of bacon, and a muffin, and set the plate next to Lake's sketchbook. He was too focused on his drawing to notice anything other than what his pencil was doing. I knocked on the counter to interrupt his flow, pointing to the plate when he looked up at me, astonished I was still there.

The pipes above ceased humming with water from Marc's shower. My time was running out. I assumed my "stern mom" look and told Lake to eat or he'd lose his sketchbook for the rest of the day. When he knew I meant business, he exchanged his pencil for the fork, and I made my way to the guest bathroom across from the kitchen.

Closing the door as quietly as I could, I pushed my jeans down just enough that I could inspect the injury. There was no bruise, no discoloration of any kind. Just two evenly spaced dots. The kind you might get from a bite. From a vampire. Or a strange demon man.

There had to be a reasonable explanation. Maybe I'd knocked into something while vacuuming or scratched myself while I was putting laundry away. Or even when I'd tripped over my own feet and fallen to the floor last night. Maybe I'd dug in my nails during the dream, giving me the illusion of the bite and leaving marks. The possibilities were endless. Anything other than getting bit by a devious demon vampire in a dream. That part was only a crazy coincidence.

The floor creaked as Marc moved through the hall towards the stairs. Straightening my clothes, I moved quickly and quietly back to the kitchen. His plate was waiting for him by the time he finished clomping down the stairs. Marc pulled up a chair next to Lake.

"Good morning, Laker," he said, giving our son an awkward pat on the back.

That was usually the extent of their morning conversation. Now that I think about it, that had been the extent of their exchanges for the last nine years.

There was a frown on Marc's face as he looked at Lake's sketch. I could only imagine what he must be thinking. "What a waste of time," or "Such a smart kid, and he wants to waste his brain coloring in a book."

Back before Lake could understand, Marc had expressed his expectation that his son grows up to be a big, important banker, or lawyer, or doctor. Some profession that was going to allow him all the riches that came along with the job. Struggling painter was not on that list. Not that I believed he would be struggling with those skills, but his dad wouldn't see it that way.

"Sure smells good. I'm starving," Marc said, smiling at me. I set the plate in front of him along with the salt and pepper. His smile faded. "Scrambled eggs again?"

"They're Lake's favorite."

My voice sounded small.

"Yeah? What about my favorite?"

Huh. After all these years, I didn't know which breakfast food Marc liked most. I wasn't even sure he enjoyed eating because he constantly had something negative to say about everything I made.

"What about what I want?" he asked, stabbing at the eggs with his fork. "Is it too much to ask for you to mix it up a little more often? We have scrambled eggs six out of seven days."

Now come on. Eggs were Lake's favorite, with the plus side of being quick and easy, but I tried not to make them more than three times a week. Over fifty percent of the week, we ate something other than eggs. Ninety percent of the time, he made the same complaint, though not always with this much animosity.

"You should take a cooking class," Marc continued. "You have too much free time. If you took a class, that would benefit everyone."

As usual, I wasn't going to argue or make a big deal about it, even if I was steaming inside. Especially with Lake sitting within earshot. Marc knew darn well and good that I kept busy enough with housework, errands, and with Lake.

Years and years ago, when Marc and I had decided that I would be a stay-at-home mom, there had been an unspoken agreement that I would take care of all the housework while he brought home the bacon. Not actual bacon, because that was grocery shopping, which fell under my chore list.

My chore list also included vacuuming, mopping, cleaning toilets, dusting, laundry, taking clothes to the dry cleaners, picking up clothes from the dry cleaners, folding clothes, ironing everything (even the sheets), wiping down and oiling the cupboards, cleaning the stainless steel, conditioning the leather furniture, and taking out the garbage.

My list wasn't confined to the inside of the house; I was also expected to mow, weed the flowers, and, in the winter, shovel. We had a snowblower, but since it was the same size as me, it was hard to handle. It was much easier to break my back pushing a shovel from one side of the driveway to the other than risk chopping myself to pieces when the snowblower ran me over.

"I'll look into it," was all I said.

I felt as pathetic as I sounded. *I'm such a wiener.* I should have stood up for myself, but I was too tired. *I'm always so damn tired.*

"I'm sure. Or, like everything else, it will go in one ear and out the other." He dropped the fork onto his plate, like he was doing a mic drop. "You know what? I'll just grab something to eat on the way to work and take my coffee to go."

Oh. Shit. I forgot the damn coffee. The one thing I loved about mornings was my first cup of coffee. But on this particular morning, there were so many other things to think about. More accurately, one particular thing. Thinking about Mr. Devious had me out of my mind. Personally, I thought getting breakfast made in the amount of time I had with the amount of focus I had used was a win.

There was nothing I could do to diffuse the situation other than to be honest. "Sorry, honey, it slipped my mind. Give me a few minutes, and I'll have it ready."

Marc's face started to turn a concerning shade of red. He slammed his fist on the counter, making his plate clatter loudly.

Lake jumped in his seat, dropping his forkful of eggs to the floor. Marc looked down at the mess in disgust.

"Now look what you did," he said, turning his glare on me.

He pushed back his chair with such force that I expected it to fly across the room, but it only tipped back and caught on one of the dining table chairs directly behind it. Had that chair not been there, the glass-top table may have shattered into a million pieces. That obviously would have been my fault for not having his coffee ready after I'd made the horrible choice of eggs for breakfast.

He must have wanted it to fall loudly to the floor, because he turned and kicked at the chair, like it had done him a disservice for not doing as he expected. Better the chair than me. The metal leg of the chair caught his shin. Pain made him go rigid, but refusing to show any modicum of weakness, he turned and stormed out without another word. The slam of the garage door behind him reverberated through the quiet house.

Lake sat staring wide-eyed at his plate, his hands clasped in his lap. I walked around the counter, putting an arm around him to pull him close without actually coddling him like I really wanted to. Now that he was nine, he had made it clear that he was too old to be babied and didn't need all that mushy stuff.

It was completely off-limits when his friends were around to do any of that "lovey-dovey mom stuff." His words, not mine. I hadn't had to watch my p's and q's in a while, since his best friend Aiden hadn't come for a visit in almost a month. When I'd tried to ask Lake about it, he would only say they were still friends. I felt that it was safe enough to do a one-armed hug with no one else around to bear witness to a moment of lovey-dovey.

"Are you mad, too?" Lake asked.

"No, sweetie, I'm not mad at Dad. He's just stressed, and we're just stuck in the middle."

"Not at Dad. At me."

I was taken aback by such a crazy statement.

"What?" I turned him to face me. "Of course I'm not mad at you, silly boy. You've done nothing wrong. Why would you think that?"

"Dad doesn't like my drawings. They make him angry. He doesn't say it, but I see it when he looks at them. I thought they made you angry, too, because you don't say anything either."

Lake was more observant than I realized. I'd rarely caught the looks Marc gave the drawings, but I knew for a fact that my facial response did not even remotely resemble Marc's expressions when I looked at the sketches.

I may not have understood Lake's fascination with scary dragons, creatures, or other things that went bump in the night, but those weren't the things that worried me. And they certainly didn't make me upset. It was what he was captivated by—this was his passion, and I loved him for who he was. If I hadn't said it enough already, Lake was an extraordinary artist. I could only be impressed by him.

"Honey, your dad, he just wants what's best for you. It's not that he doesn't like what you're drawing, he just doesn't like that you spend so much time on it. You know what I mean? He doesn't *not* like it, but he doesn't *like*, like it. Make sense?"

"Mom, it's fine."

Lake struggled under my grip, and I knew I'd overstayed my welcome. I released him and gave him a quick and loud kiss on his cheek. He rolled his eyes, but I caught a hint of a smile before I bent to clean up the mess off the floor. A good floor mopping was on the list of things to do today anyway.

An hour later, Lake was at school, Marc's suit had been dropped off at the cleaners, and I was making my way through the grocery store. When I said I was making my way, I meant I was like a dang racecar driver zooming through the aisles, swerving around the patrons standing in my way. My list wasn't all that long, but this girl had places to be and details to Google on the computer, all before a certain someone got home.

After collecting all the items I needed in record time, I found an open checkout line, allowing me to blow through that candy stand in five-point-seven seconds. It was longer than that, but that was what it felt like. My unnaturally good luck followed me through my drive home, sending me all green lights the entire way. Someone was sure looking out for me today.

Monday was laundry day. So, after the groceries were put away, I started the wash, then dusted, vacuumed the entire house, mopped all the floors, then put a roast with carrots and potatoes in the crock pot. My first load of laundry was ready for the dryer, allowing me roughly forty-eight minutes of research time before I had to get back to my household duties.

I sat at the counter, my laptop set in front of me. In the search field, I typed "meaning of 'train' in a dream." There were only about one million results, but I felt safe assuming the top result would give me the answers I needed. According to dreams.com, the meaning could change depending on the type of train, if the train was moving or stopped, or even flying, and if there were passengers or not.

From what I could interpret, a train symbolized the direction of my life. In the beginning of the dream, the train was moving, which could mean my life was moving along as it should, in the right direction. Then something in my life happened, stopping the train on its tracks. That life-changing, train-stopping event would have been when Marc slapped me. Or it should have been, if I wasn't such a wiener and hadn't just brushed off his violence as a lapse of judgement.

Still working inside the dream library of dreams.com, I typed "demon" in the learn-your-mind-here search box. The meanings again varied depending on the situation with the demon. For example, if the demon turned human, it would represent my inner selfishness or secrets that I wanted hidden from the world. So maybe because he went from human to demon, he symbolized someone around me—*cough, cough*—*Marc*, bringing his true self out.

The website also stated that for married women, this could indicate problems within the marriage. *Well, that seemed obvious.* Another meaning stated that a demon could indicate a need to make a change in one's life or something one does not like about oneself.

I wasn't sure if Mr. Devious was really a demon, so to be safe, I also looked up vampire. *Now this one made sense.* A vampire represented a person in my life hell-bent on draining me of life. Someone who wanted to bring me down. To make me as undesirable as them.

Being bitten by a vampire characterized my time, energy, and life being drained from me by that same toxic person. If that wasn't the epitome of my life these last few years, I didn't know what else would be. Marc's demeaning attitude toward me had gotten worse and worse. As soon as I found a way to tolerate his verbal attacks, he changed his approach, leaving me to find a new way to endure.

Enough of that depressing subject. I changed my search to "sex." I found that sex, which I hadn't had in the dream, but had certainly wanted, could mean that I desired more of it. Well duh. I was human after all.

Over the years, the intimacy between Marc and me had dwindled. There'd been a time in our relationship when we couldn't get enough of each other, could barely keep our hands off each other. After we had Lake, our sex life started to fade. The next few years, we tried unsuccessfully for more kids. All the while, Marc blamed me for our failure. We never had any testing done because, heaven forbid, he should find out the problem was his.

He started pushing me away. Even rejecting me when I tried to flirt him into bed with me. He'd tell me that it was unladylike to come on to him. A girl can only be pushed away so many times before she stops trying. I'd left the initiating up to Marc since then. It was few and far between, but it did happen once in a blue moon. There was no more foreplay. No more big o's for me. It was wham, bam, thank you, ma'am, see you on the next solstice. I'd rather have more hanky-panky with the man I married than the person he'd become.

Next subject. I switched the search to "paralysis." This contained another obvious answer. The inability to move would imply a loss of control or represent a feeling of being trapped. That was exactly how I'd felt last night as I lay in bed with Marc holding on to me.

Even if I wanted to leave, I had nowhere to go. Marc and Lake were my only family. My mom died in childbirth. My dad drank himself to death a few years ago after his second wife died of breast cancer. I had a half-sister, but we were never that close. And because I had no job, my financial situation was less than nil. I could take Marc to court to get some monetary support, but he would fight me tooth and nail, causing a long, drawn-out battle and a fortune in lawyer fees that I couldn't afford to even put on retainer.

The most interesting dream I'd had in ages, and it turned out to be way more depressing than I'd anticipated. Damn, what a letdown. Here I thought it was a premonition of the good things to come. A train out of my personal hell. A man too gorgeous for words coming on to me. I'd felt happy and free, and so many other lovely feelings, only to discover the dream was defining my lonely existence.

***

Marc and Lake sat at the table, patiently waiting for me to finish putting the plates out.

"How was your day, darling?" Marc asked when I took my seat at the table.

"The usual. Busy." I didn't need Marc knowing I had taken an almost hour-long break to "play around on the computer," as he would put it, so I changed the subject.

"Lake got a nearly perfect score on his academic progress test. Isn't that fantastic?"

I gave Lake a wink.

"Good work, son, but that's not what I asked." Marc pinned me with a hard stare. "I asked how *your* day was."

Oh no, that was his upset tone. As hard as I tried, I couldn't figure out what I'd done. Even with my slacker time, I was still able to get all the laundry washed, dried, and ironed. Including the sheets that took forever and caused me to lose brain cells to sheer boredom.

"It was good," I said. "A usual Monday,"

"Let me rephrase that. What did you do all day? Because it clearly wasn't spent on preparing supper. A pot roast? Really?" He looked at his plate in disgust. "Yet another reason for you to take a cooking class."

"Monday is my busiest cleaning day. I thought it logical to do a crock pot supper so I could get the house the way you like it."

I plastered a caring smile on my face, trying to appease his rising anger, but it only made it worse.

"If you thought this logical after this morning's disaster, then we have some bigger issues." He looked at Lake, who was concentrating hard on his plate, steadily shoving forkfuls of food into his mouth. "We will talk about this later."

Crap. In my eagerness to do some dream searching, I had forgotten how poorly breakfast had gone. Had I remembered, I might have spent a little more time on supper. I should have waited till later in the week, anyway. Those details weren't going anywhere, and then I could have held on to the good feelings before they were replaced by pure depression.

Other than Marc's grumbling, huffing, and puffing, we spent the rest of supper in silence. Lake finished rather quickly thanks to his continuous food train. He politely excused himself, while I still had a full plate. The exchange had caused me to lose my appetite. I nibbled, biding my time, waiting for Marc to leave the table. He was eating slower than usual, torturing me by drawing out this awkward encounter.

When he finally left the table, he dropped the plate loudly in the sink, then went upstairs, stomping all the way, reminding me of the impending argument. I dumped the remnants of my plate in the garbage, then took my time washing each dish, scrubbing each speck of food with exceptional care. When I couldn't prolong the inevitable any longer, I made my way upstairs. Sluggishly.

"Close the door," Marc said when I walked in.

I did as he asked without question. I'd already stopped at Lake's room to say goodnight.

Our door was solid oak, a decent enough sound barrier so that Lake shouldn't be disturbed. Marc charged toward me like a raging bull. I may have been a timid little flower around him, but I credited myself for not flinching when he stopped a foot from my face.

"What else did you do today?" Spit flew from between his clenched teeth when he asked the question.

"I already told you. I did my usual cleaning today."

"You're lying. Something else happened today because you forgot my suit. The suit I need for my meeting with the owners tomorrow. Now what the fuck am I supposed to wear?"

I stupidly stood there, shaking my head, running through the day in my mind. I remembered dropping it off on my way home from the grocery store, and then—I'd never picked it up. I didn't know what to say. There was no good way to explain why I had forgotten it.

The blow to my face caught me by surprise. A pain so ferocious that I saw nothing but bright white light that made my head feel like it was about to explode. And then I was falling. A never-ending fall down a deep, deep abyss. I waited for the hit, or more accurately, the kersplat at the bottom, but there was nothing. I was falling, then I wasn't. My lungs began to burn, and my chest felt tight. In my fear of hitting the bottom, I had forgotten to breathe. I took a sharp breath to stop the burning which only made the pain worse.

My eyes flew open as I choked on the water that filled my mouth and lungs. Deep, dark, thick water all around me that was impossible to swim through. I was sinking, and there was nothing but a murky pit below that scared me more than the thought of drowning. Who knew what monsters might be lurking there, waiting for a juicy victim to pass by? There would be no coming back from that.

I tried swimming harder, kicking and pushing the water to reach the safety of the light above, but nothing helped. It was as if I was surrounded by liquid quicksand; the harder I tried to fight, the faster I descended into the blackness. There was nothing left for me to do but succumb. I closed my eyes, letting the darkness invading my vision overtake me. Everything faded away.

Without warning, sweet, fresh air filled my lungs, quenching the burning and pushing back the darkness that surrounded me. Water spurted from my mouth and nose as I was finally able to take in air. I had never been so happy to smell stuff. I took a loud, deep breath through my nose, then had to hack up the remaining water in my lungs. The ache in my chest was finally gone. My vision was clear, too. It took a second to figure out where I was. *Toto, I don't think we're in Kansas anymore.*

Not in Kansas. Not in Pennsylvania. Not any place in the United States that I was aware of. I was on a beach with the softest, whitest sand I had ever seen. Or felt. In front of me, a shimmering sapphire ocean stretched to the horizon. Behind me was a lush, green jungle. All the colors complemented each other, making it the most beautiful place I had ever seen. Something was off about it, though. I just couldn't place the source of my unease.

Then, when there was nothing else, the source of the oddity struck me. There was no sound here. No animal noises drifting out of the trees. No woosh of the waves hitting the shore. It was like I was inside a vacuum.

Sighing, I fell back on the sand, letting the sun warm my chilled body. Movement beside me made me turn. A deeply tanned man with ice blue eyes and slicked-back black hair sat watching me. He wore nothing but a pair of black camo board shorts.

Even though his arms were wrapped loosely around his bent legs, they rippled with muscles. My savior, I presumed. There was a familiar quality about him. Looking him over once more, I couldn't help but think about what it might feel like to run my fingers down those sinewy muscles as he thrust inside me.

"There's no time for that," he said.

"Huh?" His deep voice startled me out of my thoughts. "What do you mean by that? How do you know what I'm thinking?"

"I can see it in your eyes. They get this far-off, lusty look. Not to mention, you have a little drool there."

He swiped his thumb along the corner of my mouth.

"Crap, please tell me you're kidding."

Without a word, he winked at me as he wiped his thumb on his shorts. I didn't know this guy, and therefor making it difficult to decipher what that meant. Damn, I could die of embarrassment right here.

"You have to go," he said, pulling a piece of wet, plastered hair from across my forehead.

"But I just got here. Is it because I drooled? I can almost possibly guarantee that I won't do it again."

"We'll meet again."

"Wai—"

My protest was practically cut off before I could start it. I was back in my bedroom, Marc's face hovering over mine. He was sitting on the floor next to me, lightly rubbing my head. A thundering pain kept tempo with my heartbeat, preventing me from trying to sit up. The pressure in my left eye was building in intensity, like an oversized grape being squeezed until it pops.

"What happened?" I whispered.

"You passed out. You hit the floor pretty hard. Here, I got you an ice pack," he said, laying the pack on my head.

I'd estimate our ice pack weighed somewhere around two pounds, but on top of my head, it felt like fifty.

"Honey, I don't know what happened. It's all a blur. We were talking about what happened today. You gave me a look like I didn't know what I was talking about. And then—"

It was coming back to me now. "You hit me."

"I will never do anything like that again. It was an accident. I was blinded by my own dumb rage. Come on, let's get you in bed."

Hmm, I thought I'd heard words similar to that last night. Last night, though, he only slapped me. This was a full-on knockout.

Putting his arms under my neck and legs, he lifted me off the floor. The jarring movement made my head feel like someone was taking an ice chisel to it. I could feel the tears start to well up, causing the pressure in my left eye to join the thumping beat with my head. It was unbelievable that any of this was happening. I didn't know the man I'd married as well as I'd thought.

He grunted with exertion and laughed. "Geez honey, are you gaining weight?"

A fly on the wall may have thought he was trying to be funny, but I knew deep down he was being serious. After what had gone down tonight, there were no words. No way to answer that without being a total bitch. I wanted to be a bitch. I wanted to yell and scream and punch and tell him to take his hands off me, but I didn't. I stayed quiet.

"Wow. I'm kidding. Trying to make you laugh," he said, but there was no amusement on his face.

Not like my Dream Man when he teased me.

"My face hurts."

"Fine. You don't want to talk. Or laugh. I'll just leave you alone."

He set, or rather, dropped me on the bed. The ice pack bounced, nearly causing me to cry out with the additional smack to my already banged-up face. Giving me another irritated look, he turned and headed for the door.

Unlike me, he let it slam closed behind him, not giving a damn if Lake was sleeping or not. I stiffened at the sound. I should have been used to it by now, as often as it happened lately. My nerves were shot from the constant worry of saying or doing something wrong.

It was daunting to think about having to get up and change out of my clothes, but after my long day, I was dirty and stinky. Pain be damned, I carefully slid off the bed, taking slow, steady movements towards my closet to keep my head from bobbing. An etiquette teacher would have been proud.

In the closet, I slowly peeled off my soiled clothes, replacing them with my favorite oversized concert tee. The collar scratched the battered side of my face, sending a rush of pain, making me light-headed. I trudged, defeated, back to the bed before I took an unintentional nap on the closet floor.

Before I could climb into the mountain of a bed, I caught a glimpse of myself in the vanity mirror. My left eye was nearly swollen shut, and there were already little splotches of purple, signaling an incoming bruise. Swelling of my cheek and nose gave me a lopsided look.

I contemplated the pros and cons of taking some ibuprofen. Pro: It would help take down the swelling, so it wouldn't be so much work to hide from Lake in the morning. Con: If I had internal bleeding, it would make my blood thinner, making the internal stuff worse even as it made the outside stuff better.

Shoot, I had no idea what I was talking about. I wasn't a doctor. I should probably see one, though. Opting for only one pill instead of the handful I really wanted, I tucked my exhausted butt into the bed.

It took a minute to figure out the best position so that my face didn't feel like it would spontaneously combust from the burning pain. Sleep eventually overpowered my will to stay awake and figure out the future direction of my life. *Who am I kidding, anyway?* Nothing was going to change. The only difference about tomorrow was that I would have to add ten layers of makeup to cover up the bruising.

Chapter 2

I stood in front of my childhood home, back in South Dakota, hundreds of miles away from the house I shared with Marc. It was a cute little four-bedroom, two-bathroom, split-foyer house with not even half the square footage of my current house. That house might be nicer and more expensive, but that's all it was, a house. A place where I spent my time from day to day. Living with Marc was starting to feel more like a prison, and I was sentenced to life.

My childhood home was full of love, laughter, and family. Some days, I wished I could turn back time so that I could do things differently. I wouldn't have left home so early. I would have spent more time with my dad. Maybe even tried to nurture my relationship with my sister. A sister I could talk with would be nice right about now. At least I still had Maiz.

Checking out my current dream surroundings, I found them to be as elaborate in detail as the first dream, although it lacked color. Just like the train car, the world was tinged with shades of grey and bleakness. I could see what would have been the sun, high in the sky, being blotted out by thick clouds of acrid smoke. Smoke that filled the air around me, burning my nose, and making my eyes water. Everything around me exuded an intense sense of doom.

There were pops, bangs, and booms all around me. Gunfire. There was a battle raging somewhere nearby, but the street was deserted. No one was in sight, but I could hear screaming. Someone was dying a horrific death, judging by the sound. All the houses looked abandoned, so I couldn't figure out where exactly it was coming from. There was no immediate danger that I could see, but the pops were getting louder. Closer. Enough nostalgia for today.

I sprinted up the narrow walk and pressed my ear against the door, checking for any movement inside. Nothing. I tried the knob, but it was locked. Damn. My dream put me here. Why would it lock me out? I checked my pockets. Nope, no keys. Another gunshot rang out, closer yet.

I tried the door again—still locked. There was a slim possibility that I could have unlocked it with my mind. It was *my* dream, for heaven's sake, I should be the one to decide if I was locked out of my own damn house.

Well, this dream was turning out to be a bust. Maybe if I wished for it hard enough, I could get the damn thing to open. I pressed against the door, whispering a mantra of "please, please, please open."

The door opened, catching me completely off-guard. I began to fall inside, bracing myself to hit the floor. Instead, a pair of strong arms caught me, pulling me back up to my feet. The door slammed shut behind me. The sound reminded me of real life, and for a moment, I thought I had walked into a Marc trap. This couldn't be happening—dreams were my escape. My safe place away from Marc. He couldn't be here, too.

With the door closed, the windowless entryway was too dark to see the man's face. What gave him away was the pair of glowing, icy blue eyes looking back at me. *Thank you to whoever I need to thank for not including Marc in my dream.*

The man led me up the stairs and around a corner that opened into the living room. Because the drapes were tightly drawn, the room was dimly lit by candles on the coffee table. No wonder the house looked abandoned. I was sure all the houses in the neighborhood were sealed up, so whatever was going on out there, stayed out there. Any sign of life would only draw trouble.

This room looked the same as I remembered it, aside from the cold, empty feeling. Oh, and the exceedingly handsome man standing in front of me. The same man from the island, except for a few subtle differences. Instead of being neatly slicked back, his black hair was long, and in messy disarray. His whiskered face looked like it hadn't seen a razor in weeks.

I usually didn't like beards, but damn, he made facial hair look good. His dark-wash jeans were torn and dirty. That was saying something if I could tell in the low light that the dark jeans were dirty. His shirt probably used to be white, but now it ranged from light brown to dark brown. Probably from blood, sweat, and tears, both old and fresh.

"What happened to you?" I asked, breaking the silence.

"Nothing major. Just a zombie apocalypse."

He was so hard to read, I honestly had no idea if he was joking, being serious, or anything in between. This was a dream, and anything was possible, but why zombies? I had no reason to dream about zombies. *Zombies?*

"Oh, right, zombie apocalypse. I'm supposed to believe that, when I don't even watch any of that kind of crap?"

"It's your dream."

He had me there. If anyone would have an explanation, it should be me. Zombies must have had a deeper meaning, like monsters were creeping into my marriage right before the world imploded. Or something dark was spreading like a virus, and I needed to get out before it ate my brain. I didn't know the real meaning behind it, and really, I didn't care.

"What are we supposed to do now?"

"Again, your dream. What do you want to do?"

I shrugged helplessly. Had my brain put us back on that deserted island, I knew exactly what I'd want to do right about now. Given our current circumstances, though, I had no idea.

Technically, I supposed, we were safely locked inside a house with plenty of bedrooms and nothing else to do. His clothes may have been disgusting, but I could still make out his beefy body beneath. And that derriere was just asking me to grab hold—he must use some sort of buns of steel workout. This guy looked capable of protecting us should something happen while we were preoccupied.

Get a hold of yourself, Rose. There are zombies wreaking havoc outside, and I'm thinking about grabbing an ass.

Dream Man plopped down on the couch in the living room. A space I'd remembered as always being warm and bright from the sun shining through the large picture window in the front now felt cold and dreary. The clean white walls and salmon-colored carpet looked aged and worn.

I sank down slowly on the other end of the couch, pulling the afghan off the back. My own mom had crocheted the blanket before I was born. It always smelled of Avon perfume, as if the scent had been infused into the yarn, just as it did now. I wrapped the blanket around me, closed my eyes, and inhaled the flowery scent.

In my mind, I could see my dad, stepmom, sister, and me, all squished together on this very couch for Sunday movie night. All of us sharing this very blanket. My stepmom and dad cuddled close on one end. The love they felt for each other had dripped off them in what seemed like disgusting rivulets to my teenage mind. My sister, Raven, and I pushed together on the other side.

I loved my sister. I looked after her as best as I could, but she was five years younger than me, which meant we were never at the same school at the same time. We were total opposites. I was outgoing and rebellious while Raven was quiet and shy. She always got good grades, while I barely slipped by. Being older, I was always a step ahead on the maturity ladder. I tried to play it off as though I was too cool to hang out with a little kid like her, when the truth was that I was jealous of how flawless she was.

Even as a child, she was so beautiful. Her lustrous black hair was always silky smooth, and her long, dark lashes gave the impression she was already wearing makeup. She never had any awkward growing-up phases. No dorky child phase, no pimply teenager phase. She was just plain perfect, from her head to her toes.

I had intended to maintain a relationship with my family, but I'd had big dreams. As a kid, I'd always dreamed of traveling the world and seeing the beauty nature had to offer. To do this, I planned on becoming a famous photographer while working for a major nature magazine.

After high school, I moved away and went to the Art Institute of Pittsburgh. Three years later, my stepmom was diagnosed with breast cancer that had metastasized to her brain. The disease took her from us not even six months later. I flew back home for the funeral and could tell that losing his wife had torn my dad apart, but I didn't stick around to help either him or my sister. I knew they were hurting, but I was selfish and living my own life on the East Coast. At that point, I thought exploring my own opportunities was more important than what was going on at home.

Then came Marc, sweeping me up in a whirlwind romance. When we were planning our wedding, I invited both my dad and sister. By that time, though, my dad was already in failing health due to his drinking, and unable to travel. My sister, being the loving, caring person that she is, refused to leave him alone.

She said she would be devastated if something happened to him while she was away. He was my father, too, and I should have been understanding. Instead, I was pissed that neither of them came to support me during the happiest time of my life. Clinging to that anger, I refused to visit them after that. Even when Lake was born.

When my dad passed away a couple years later from cirrhosis of the liver and heart failure, he did so without ever meeting his first grandson. All my anger, all my selfishness, disappeared when I got that call. I flew home for the funeral but was too ashamed to say much to Raven. I had acted terribly, and I didn't know how to fix it. Marc didn't want me to stay, so I'd flown in for the funeral only and was back home the next day. Dad left her everything and she was legally an adult, there was no reason for me to stay. I'd regretted my decisions ever since.

"You okay?" Dream Man broke into my thoughts.

If Marc were here, he would have asked, "What's your problem?" His voice would have been tinged with irritation, not the concern I heard in Dream Man.

I opened my eyes, finding that we were still on the couch in the bleak living room. Exhaling, I let go of the past. There wasn't a whole lot I could do about it now. No use dwelling on the woulda coulda shoulda's, and no use dredging up all that drama with—this guy. Damn, I didn't even know my Dream Man's name. If he had one.

"Do you have a name? I've had multiple dreams with you now, and I don't know what to call you."

He was quiet for a minute, as if he was trying to decide whether he should answer or not.

"Lucian."

"Lucian. That's beautiful. Why did you hesitate to tell me?"

"Nobody has ever asked for my name."

"Really? What do they call you? Or do you just kick them out of the dream before they can get to that part?"

I said it trying to be funny. I didn't really think that he was in anyone else's dreams but mine. This man, Lucian, was created from my imagination.

"They call me whatever they want, or don't call me anything at all. I am there for them. In any capacity they want. That doesn't usually include asking my name."

I was caught off-guard by his answer. First, that was the most I had heard him speak. There was the slightest hint of an accent, although where from, I had no idea. The sound of his voice was deep and beautiful.

Second, what he said made it sound like I wasn't the only one to have him in my dreams, but I didn't know how that could be. He was my Dream Man, so how could he be with other people? Would that mean he was with other women? Doing the things that I wanted to do with him? He was irresistible, and he just said that he was with others in any capacity they wanted.

I was feeling a bit jealous when he reached across the couch to pull me next to him. No, not just next to him; suddenly, I was on his lap. My legs had wrapped around him, and the blanket had been moved to wrap around me from the back so that there was nothing but sexual tension between us. He may have looked like he hadn't seen a shower in years, but he smelled delicious.

"That was a neat trick," I said.

There was a playful look in his eyes. "I've been doing this for a long time."

"Don't do that," I said, putting a hand over his eyes.

"What? You don't want to play with me?" He moved my hand from his eyes to his hard—chest.

He smiled at me. His teeth were straight and white, and the teasing in his eyes nearly turned me to liquid fire.

"No. Yes. I mean, no, I do. There are a few things that need to be straightened out."

"You'd really rather talk right now?"

"I need answers. It'll drive me crazy." He didn't answer, only waited for me to continue. "I've dreamt of you a few times, assuming that was you on the train, so what do you mean nobody asks your name? You're *my* Dream Man, right?"

"Yours huh?"

"Like, it's my brain that came up with you, so you're mine. Other people won't have the same you. Or you at all. Right?"

"What do you know about Greek mythology?" he asked.

"I know that I failed that test in high school. What I do remember is that Zeus is the head honcho and throws lightning bolts. Aphrodite is the most beautiful. There is a master of the sea. Ummmm, Cupid shoots arrows into wannabe lovers' asses to make them fall in love. That's all I got. How did I do?"

Lucian sat smirking at me. Not a full smile, but a smile that said he found me amusing. Maybe he was thinking he should save some time and just eat me now.

"That was deplorable. Most people know more simply by watching one of the many movies or TV shows about our pantheon."

"Would you believe me if I said I was bad with names?"

He laughed, a deep, rumbling laugh that set my heart racing. That could be construed as a good or a bad thing. I was uncertain which it was at the moment.

"You were sort of correct. Zeus is, as you say, head honcho and has been known to throw thunderbolts. Especially when he's pissed. Aphrodite is the goddess of love and beauty, but that doesn't necessarily mean she's the most beautiful." He rubbed the back of his fingers down the side of my face. The side that would be bruised and battered in the morning. "Beauty can mean different things to different individuals," he said, looking me straight in the eyes, his own icy blues swimming with the flickering candlelight. "You were wrong about Cupid."

"I was not. I've been through enough Valentine's Days to know who and what he does."

"Wrong pantheon. Cupid is Roman. Eros is the Greek god of love, and he's not actually one of the dirty dozen."

"It's like you're speaking Greek to me right now. What's a pantheon? And what do you mean by dirty dozen?"

"Pantheon is the collective term for all the gods in a particular group. The dirty dozen refers to the twelve Olympians, the more popular ones you see in the movies or learn about in school. What you don't know is that it all started with the Primordials. First it was Chronos and Ananke, then came Chaos, Gaia, Tartarus, and Eros. Any of this sound familiar?"

"Yes, Eros is the Greek version of Cupid." Lucian only stared at me, deadpan. I blushed. "Sorry, my sister got all the smarts. She could probably recite all the Olympians and the premortals."

"You're cute." He booped my nose. It seemed so out of character for a big, scary demon vampire to boop my nose, but there it was. "It's primordial," he continued, "not premortal. The first, and most powerful of them being Chaos. Chaos created Nyx and Erebus, the gods of night and darkness. It was Nyx who created Morpheus, Phobetor, and Phantasos, the first of the Oneiroi."

"You're just making up words now." My ears were listening, but just like when Lake was a baby, all I was hearing was gibberish.

"It's a complicated history and I'm trying to make it as easy to understand as possible. You can do some research when you wake up. Not everything online is accurate, but it will help. The Oneiroi are the dream makers. Morpheus, their leader, is my father."

There was a pause. Apparently, he was waiting for me to say something about all the words he had just said. So many words. Words that I didn't understand. I couldn't comprehend how I had known them enough to even dream about them. This was a dream that my imagination had come up with, but it was so advanced that it was almost plausible that I hadn't come up with it myself.

"You need to break it down a little bit farther," I said.

"I'm a dream walker. I'm a four-thousand-year-old immortal being."

Once again, he stopped talking to give me a chance to say something. I could only give him the crazy stare. It had unlovingly been dubbed that because I looked like a total nut job. Usually, my head was slightly tilted, one eye was twitching, and the other was practically bulging.

"It's a lot to take in, I know," he said cautiously. "Do you need a minute?"

"Pfffff, noooooo." I stretched out the word, sounding like a word-slurring drunk person. "This is a dream. Just a whacked-out, messed-up dream with zombies, the house I grew up in, and now a four-thousand-year-old Greek god. I mean, really, how crazy-town is that? Marc must have hit me harder than I thought. Knocked around my brain a little. Now, it's bringing up all this weird, hidden information from my subconscious that I didn't know I knew."

Lucian stiffened at something I said. Closing his eyes, he was taking deep, steady breaths.

"What else did he knock loose?" I asked. "What else can you teach me?"

Lucian's eyes popped open. They were a deep, scary shade of angry red. It was my turn to stiffen.

"I'm sorry. Whatever it was I said, I didn't mean it."

He looked surprised. About as surprised as if I had slapped him across the face. He blinked, bringing his eyes back to their normal shade of icy blue.

"That really was you on the train. I wasn't positive since you look so different."

"Benefits of being a dream walker."

I took that to mean he could look however he wanted. Or I wanted. Not to mention I had dubbed him Mr. Devious without asking his name, like he said most people do.

"He, I mean you, were a demon. Or a vampire. I haven't been able to decide which one."

"Vampire? That's a new one."

"Hello? You bit me."

He was starting to feel too close for comfort. On one hand, I wanted to be close, but on the other hand, he was a vampire in sheep's clothing. He could throw off his guise at any moment and rip me apart. I needed some distance between us before he locked me in place again. I started to scoot off his extremely comfortable lap.

"Don't be afraid," he said, grasping one of my hands.

"I'm not." It came out a little too loud, a little too quick, and a little too obvious. "I'm worried about you. For you. I'm worried about what I might do to you. No, not like that."

Still holding my hand, he leaned in and kissed me, very effectively shutting me up. All my worries went up in smoke. Probably close to literally, because my body was now on fire. *Shit, I have the hots for a demon vampire.* A no good, quite possibly very bad, demon vampire.

I cleared my throat and said in an almost normal voice, "I'm not afraid. You're Lucian. I know you. It's all good." He raised an eyebrow at me.

"Rose, I would never hurt you."

"Good to know. I thought having a demon in all these dreams was a sign that I was gonna die or something. With all that's happening, well um, never mind." I stopped myself from saying more. I didn't want to upset him again.

"You don't need to watch what you say around me. Also, I may look like a demon with my eyes, face, and wings, but I'm not. Or a vampire. Or a combination of the two."

"Wings? I didn't see those. Vampires can have those. I think."

"I'm not a vampire."

"If you're not a vampire, why did you bite me? I don't mean those sweet little nibbles you started with, I'm talking about the bite on my hip that left a mark in real life."

His eyes started to change again. This time to black.

"You didn't like it?" he asked, looking at my lips. "I tried to make it as pleasurable as possible, so you didn't notice the pain."

I remembered the intense pleasure. My body was basically convulsing for more. The way he was looking at me said he could eat me up—not in a demon vampire kind of way, but in a sex god kind of way. I wanted more.

"Does that mean you were only doing that to distract me, not because you wanted to?"

"I wanted to and then some," he started kissing me again. "There wasn't enough time to do all the things I wanted to do to you. I had to prioritize," he said between kisses on my neck. "I needed your blood. Now that I've got it, I'm all yours."

"Wait, what?" I asked, snapping out of his kissing trance. "Why was my blood a priority at all?"

"Trying to learn more about you. Inside and out."

The way he was looking at me sent a shiver up my spine, not the scared kind, but more like anticipation. He was in the mood and ready to figure me out.

"Priorities, huh? Well, no matter. You said you have wings, and that's a deal breaker. I can't see you anymore." He sat there, not saying a word, trying to determine if I was serious. "That's payback for your little prank on the island."

"That's the game you want to play? Just wait till next time. You'll get your payback."

"Don't you dare say it's time. We haven't been here longer than twenty minutes. How is it over already?"

"Time moves differently in a dream." He kissed me. "Until next time."

***

Tuesday was my favorite day of the week. Not usually a true statement for most people since it was still four days away from the weekend, but for me, I had no weekend. Every day was the same. Wake up at the same time, cook, run errands, do chores, rinse, and repeat, seven days a week. The one bright spot was on Tuesday, because Tuesday meant Maiz.

Maiz, my sister from another mister. The one person capable of picking me up high enough off the ground, that I could endure until the next meeting.

Every Tuesday afternoon, Maiz and I met for lunch at The Hotel Bar and Grill. I know, really original name, but they had the best cheeseburgers and caramelized pecans in the tri-state area. Not to mention, everything was half-price on Tuesdays. Back in the day, we used to meet up after Maiz was done working, and I would leave Lake home with Marc.

Soon enough, Marc said it was taking away from our "family" time, and I had to change our meeting time to afternoons, while Lake was in school and Marc at work. I didn't talk to him about my time with Maiz, and eventually, he stopped asking. I didn't bother letting Marc know that I still met up with Maiz. What he didn't know, wouldn't hurt him. Or me.

First things first, I started a pot of coffee brewing. After yesterday's scrambled egg fiasco, I opted for homemade Belgian waffles, topped with strawberries and blueberries, for breakfast. I even had a dollop of whipped cream ready for someone if they so desired. I added sausage links, hash browns, and whatever else I could think of to make this a good day. There was way more on my mind today than there had been yesterday, but I needed to keep it together until the boys were out of the house.

Lake drifted in, only giving me a stiff smile as he firmly fixed his nose in his sketchbook. He didn't even bother to look up when I placed a dish before him. He merely reached out for his fork and started eating. I assumed the tension from the last couple of days was getting to him. Before I could talk to him about it, Marc came down, taking his seat next to Lake.

"Hey, this is looking better than yesterday," he said sardonically. "Now let's see if she remembered the coffee."

I set down his plate and coffee mug in front of him. Before I could pull my hand away, he grabbed it and placed a kiss on my clenched fingers.

"Thank you, honey. I love you so much. You are too good to me."

It all felt fake. Faker than fake, but I didn't have a word for it. I knew I didn't like this "Marc". I didn't like him touching me, and I certainly didn't want him kissing me. If I was this bothered by him kissing my knuckles, how bad would it be if he tried to kiss me on the lips?

By this point, Marc was too busy shoving food into his mouth to notice me watching him. I'd never paid attention to how he ate with his mouth open. Trying to keep the disgust off my face, I listened to his loud, annoying *smack* every time he chewed. I secretly hoped he'd choke. *I did not just think that. Oh, but I did. I'm a terrible person.* Turning away from him, I started the cleanup process and washing the pans.

Marc finished his breakfast in record time—not surprising considering the way he was forking it in. Leaving his plate on the counter, he walked around the counter and wrapped his arms around me from behind.

"I should take the day off and spend some time with my beautiful wife," he said.

His body was pressed tightly against mine, trapping me against the counter. Unlike when Lucian touched me, my body didn't react. In fact, it was trying to rebel. I had to keep myself from lashing out to get him off me. There was a cross in a drawer somewhere; maybe if I held it out at him, he'd be forced to stay away.

Marc sniffed my hair loudly in my ear. "Mmm, you smell so good. If I didn't have so much work to do, you'd be all mine."

He gave me a final squeeze and let go. I wanted to give a loud sigh of relief, but I didn't think that would go over too well. While waiting for him to leave, I didn't dare move a muscle for fear of messing this up in some way, shape, or form. Somewhere behind me, I heard the door leading to the garage close without a reverberating slam.

I allowed myself to relax when I heard the garage door close and Marc's diesel truck accelerate down the street. Probably he was trying to be extra nice because he felt guilty about last night. I should be less on edge, but I was wound tighter than I'd ever been in my life. An unexpected punch to the face could do that to a person.

My eye. I had forgotten about what it might look like. I hadn't noticed much of the pain until now. No wonder Lake wouldn't look at me. My eye had to be four different shades of the rainbow. I turned to say something, but he was gone, his empty plate still sitting on the counter.

Upstairs, Lake's door was closed, no noise coming from inside. He was a very calm, quiet child, so that wasn't surprising. I tapped on his door. No answer. I leaned in close. Still no noise.

"Lake, honey, it's Mom. I just want to make sure you're okay."

There was some rustling, and the door popped open. Without a word, he wrapped me in a hug, the top of his head coming right up to the bottom of my nose. The scent of the Axe shampoo he used wafted up to me. My baby wasn't a baby anymore, but he was always going to be my baby. As suddenly as the affection started, it ended. That was all we needed from each other to know it was all going to be okay.

Once in my room, I took a few minutes to evaluate the severity of my eye. Honestly, I'd expected worse. There was some swelling, but my nose and cheekbone looked, for the most part, untouched. I ran my finger along the area where Marc's fist had made direct contact with the cheekbone. Nothing, not even pain. My face had hurt worse the day after he had slapped me. Some discoloration was the only indication that anything had happened.

My left eyelid was a shade of dark pink, while the skin beneath the eye was a deep shade of plum, fading to a light purple-green color at the top of my cheek. I would have to really work my makeup magic to try to hide this from Maiz. She would no doubt notice anyway and have lots of colorful words to say. If I could make it appear less serious, then hopefully it wouldn't be the main topic of our entire lunch.

Chapter 3

Maiz was already seated at our usual table at the back of the bar. We'd picked this spot years ago because it had the best vantage point for people-watching. You'd be amazed how many people were drunk or on their way to being drunk by noon. As the saying goes, "It's five o'clock somewhere."

She was idly tapping away at her phone when I first walked in. I knew the moment she saw me because her face turned from regular-day-blasé to it's-about-to-be-on. Hard to miss me with my big pink aviator sunglasses still on in the low lighting of the room.

After attempting to cover the darkest part of the bruise with some foundation, then swiping on a couple pounds of eyeshadow, I picked the biggest pair of sunglasses I had. My fashion faux pas had attracted the attention of some of the other patrons in the bar, too. It was as if I were wearing a neon sign saying, *look at me*. I picked up my pace and ducked into the booth opposite Maiz.

"What the fuck is this?" she asked, her face still crinkled with disgust.

"Thought I'd try out a new look. You like?"

I did some model poses with my hands poised around my face, trying to make light of the situation. I wasn't in the mood for causing a scene, and that's what Maiz specialized in.

"It's stupid," she said, snatching the glasses off my face. "Yep. I knew it. I knew you were trying to hide something from me. Should I kill him now or wait till you get some additional life insurance put on him? I'm sure I can come up with something really painful just for him, starting with his balls."

Typical Maiz overreaction. She automatically assumed that Marc had done something. He had, but she didn't know that. *Yet.*

Of course, our waitress chose that moment to take our drink orders. We always had a waitress named Sandi, but this was a new girl who looked to be fresh out of high school. Having just heard a possible plan for premeditated murder, she stood there wide-eyed, looking back and forth between the two of us.

"She's kidding!" I laughed, trying to put the girl at ease. "Also, we should be ready to order."

The girl gave us a hesitant smile and nodded. She nodded all through our order and walked away without saying one word when we'd finished.

"Can you keep your voice down? You know how word spreads around here. It will be a miracle if this doesn't make it to Marc by the time we're finished here."

"And I'm supposed to be worried about that dumbass? I don't give two shits about him. He didn't seem to care about the consequences when he did this to you." She was pointing her finger, circling it around my entire face.

"Damn woman, what's wrong with my face? I thought it was just my eye that was f'd up."

"Your whole face is messed up cuz you have seven layers of foundation and stripper eyeshadow on. What the hell were you thinking? It would have been less noticeable had you left it alone. You're lucky I love you so much, otherwise, I'd walk out."

"Wow. Thanks a lot," I said dryly.

"Seriously, dickface knows you go out to lunch with me, so he has to know I'd be pissed."

"Well actually, not."

Marc and Maiz had never really gotten along. For a short time, when Marc and I first started dating, Maiz tried to be nice, but that just wasn't her style. She couldn't hold back her true feelings for him. It had gotten to a point where they couldn't be in the same room together. Marc told me that Maiz was a bad influence, and I shouldn't be hanging around the likes of someone like her. To avoid any unnecessary arguments, I'd stopped telling him about our lunches.

"Marc doesn't know that we still go out for lunch. I told him I would stop because I didn't want to fight about it anymore. And I knew I wouldn't be able to hide this from you, not for long anyway. It's just that, you have a tendency to, how do I put this nicely? Go over the top?"

Maiz had her own version of my crazy face. Her eyes took on a ridiculously wide, deranged look, while her neck elongated, and her jaw went all crooked as she gritted her teeth. Our young waitress nearly threw our drinks at us before high-tailing it off to disappear somewhere in the back. I looked longingly after the dust trail she left, wishing I could go with her.

"*Seriously?*" Maiz said in a high, shrieking voice. So much for not drawing attention. "How are you *not* overreacting?" she continued in a more hushed tone. "This man swore before your God to love and cherish you. In what world does that mean to mar that beautiful face of yours? And for what? What did you do? Forget to dust a shelf? Put a cup upside down instead of right side up? It's always something with that man. He's an asshole, and you need to get the hell away from him. You are strong, gorgeous, and talented, and you can get anything you want in life if you just give it a try. I want better for you. No, I want the best for you. I want to see you happy, not living your life walking on eggshells. You deserve happiness. You don't need him, and you don't need Lake looking up to him. To be super real, I'm less worried about Lake than I am about you. Sad? I think so."

Her words brought tears to my eyes. That was the sweetest thing she'd ever said to me, pretty much ever. She didn't understand, though. She wasn't married. Sometimes you had to make sacrifices. In my mind, I was sacrificing my own happiness for my husband and child. I was doing what I had to in order to hold my family together.

"I get what you're saying, but I'm pretty sure it's not going to happen again." I didn't bother to mention what he'd done the night before. "Marc was really sweet to me this morning." I also thought it best not to say how turned off I was by his sleezy kindness. "He knows he screwed up and he has to feel terrible. The way he talks to me will probably never change, but so what? What damage can that do?"

"Fuck, Rose, enough has got to be enough. When is it gonna be enough? When it's too late for me to save you?"

Marc would never take it to the point where I couldn't be saved. He wouldn't take me from Lake. And what did she mean by "save me?" She was being more dramatic than usual. Taking a sip of my Coke to buy some time so I wouldn't say anything I couldn't take back, I reminded myself how she was saying all of this out of love, not to be malicious.

Maiz was my best friend. My only friend. I didn't want to say something to upset her or push her away. My stepmom had always told me if I couldn't say anything nice, to not say anything at all. She'd picked it up from a movie, but it was a good motto to live by.

Sandi, our usual waitress, arrived with our food. Saved by the dinner bell.

"Hey y'all." Her southern accent sounded thicker than usual. "What's happening over here? You two scared the bejeezus out of poor Sara. She went running out the back door," she said, placing the plates on the table. "Oh honey." She looked at my eye. "You poor thing."

Sandi was older and as sweet as can be. I loved listening to her drawl her words. Usually. I wasn't loving the attention my eye was getting.

"Ain't no man should treat a woman like that. You better give him the how do or kick him to the curb." She put her hand on my arm and gave a gentle squeeze. "Lunch is on the house today, hon." Sandi gave me a sympathetic smile and turned to Maiz. "Yours isn't. I expected you to raise this girl better than that. And I best be getting a good tip after you scared off that lil gal earlier."

"Why is it my fault?" Maiz sputtered.

"I'm old, not blind."

I laughed. Sandi was one tough cookie. She probably didn't take shit from anyone, especially not her husband. Through our weekly visits to this bar, I'd learned that Sandi had been married for thirty years, with seven grown children. From the way she talked, she was still happily married and planned on staying that way. I highly doubted her husband would talk to her the way Marc talked to me, but I wondered if other women's husbands ever spoke to them that way.

"Thanks, Sandi. I really don't want to talk about it anymore," I said, directed at Maiz.

"Sure, hon. Let me know if there is anything else I can help you ladies with."

Sandi turned back to the kitchen.

"There is one last thing I want to say," Maiz began. "I'm worried about you." She grabbed my hands and held them tightly, driving home her point. "This is becoming serious. You may not want to believe it, but I believe he will do it again. That's just the kind of dickface he is. Next time might not be as bad, or it could be way worse." She leaned over the table. "I promise you, if he hurts you again, I will kill him in the most painful way imaginable."

Leave it to Maiz not to hold anything back. I reminded myself of her earlier words and, more importantly, to tamp down my anger and not say anything rash.

"I love you, too, Maiz. Now that that's all out on the table, there is something else I want to talk to you about."

Before coming to lunch, I'd practiced how I might explain the crazy dreams I'd been having, but no matter how I said it, I sounded like a lunatic.

So, I met a four-thousand-year-old Greek god who looks like a demon but is totally delicious, and he's making me believe he's real. He told me he's a dream walker, and he bit me because he needs my blood. Oh, I have the marks to prove it. Or, I could go with something a little simpler. *I've been dreaming of this totally hot guy, I want him so bad, and now I'm questioning the world around me.*

Any way I told it, I saw Maiz laughing in my face, then questioning if I'd stopped taking my meds. It only took thirty seconds for her to upend my sunglasses idea, let's see how quickly she could set me straight on this predicament. She might be exactly what I needed to get a hold on all this dream nonsense.

"I met someone," I said.

"Hell yes. You should have led with this. Is he hot?"

"He's in my dreams."

Her face went from stoked to stumped. I would have laughed if I didn't have so much to say with so little time. I concluded the best course of action would be to tell her all of it, almost. I kept the lusty, more intimate parts to myself if they weren't pertinent to the ending. A rush of sentences later, I finished my story. I waited for her to fall off the bench seat in roaring laughter, but she remained oddly quiet, putting another fry in her mouth.

"What do you think? Crazy, right?" I asked.

"Did he tell you what he needed the blood for?"

"To learn about me. Like, what can he learn from my blood? My health history? My blood type?"

"Are you sure he took blood? Are you sure he wasn't just playing with you?"

"That's what I thought, till I found the marks."

Maiz's face stayed relatively collected except for some twitching in a jaw muscle.

"I don't know how you're not laughing in my face right now. This is where you would say something like, 'What the fuck, Rose?'" I said, doing my worst impersonation possible. "This shit is stupid. It's a fuckin dream, and you need to get your life straight."

"Right. It's only a dream. The Oneiroi only create a dream space. They're harmless."

I hadn't said anything about Oneiroi, mostly because I couldn't remember the word. Lucian had used a lot of words that I couldn't pronounce, let alone remember.

I tilted my head. "I didn't know you knew about Greek mythology."

"I took a class," Maiz said, not looking me in the face. "I have to go. I'll call you later. Oh, and leave that asshole."

She threw out a hundred-dollar bill and scooted out of the booth. Oh yeah, Sandi was getting a good tip. I sat there staring at the bill, rethinking our conversation. My summary of my dream world hadn't elicited the reaction I'd been expecting.

Maiz had only succeeded in making me more confused than ever. She'd stirred up emotions of anger and sadness regarding Marc and hadn't helped at all where Lucian was concerned. It was time I was honest with myself and accepted that it was only a dream. Pure and simple. No matter how real every touch, every emotion, and every smell were, it was all a dream.

That bitter pill was hard to swallow, and I felt like crying. Of all things, my heart was breaking over the illusion of Lucian. That he could be a real being. That we might actually be able to have something. That I could be something more. But no. Back to being plain old boring Rose again. Now I felt like an idiot for thinking anything different, for saying anything to Maiz about it.

"Hey, hon," Sandi said, "you need a box?"

"No," I replied as the tears I was trying to hold back spilled down my cheeks.

"Oh, darlin'." She bent to wrap an arm around my shoulders. "I know you ain't got no momma, just Maiz, so if you need anything, you can call me, ok darlin?"

She wrote her number on a napkin, folded it, and stuck it in the palm of my hand, closing my fingers around it.

"I don't care nothing about what time it is," she said. "You need me, I'll be there."

All I could do was nod at her. No words would have expressed how touched I was that she offered to be there when I felt so alone. Sucking up the last little bit of my pride, I pulled myself together, grabbed my purse, and walked out.

The rest of the day went by in a blur. Back at home, I stayed busy roaming the house—dusting, cleaning, and oiling everything that resembled wood in the slightest. All the windows within reach got a spot-free wipe down. The bathrooms were swabbed from top to bottom. Lake came in off the bus at a quarter after three. I took a short break to sit and read with him. Or I tried.

I read the same page over and over, trying to understand the words, but Lucian was stuck in my thoughts. My dreams were playing on repeat, keeping any words from making sense. I told myself there was a silver lining. I could still see him in my future dreams. *Hopefully.*

When we were done, he ran off to his room to watch TV, sketch, or do whatever kids his age did before supper. Marc was due home in less than two hours. I stowed my cleaning supplies, cleaned myself up, then moved to the kitchen to start cleaning potatoes to go with the steaks. I scrubbed and scrubbed, and then scrubbed some more.

"Mom? I think they're clean. You scrubbed all the skin off."

"What? Oh. I guess they are."

"Do you want some help?"

The offer tugged at my heartstrings. I wanted to throw the potatoes in the air, grab his adorable face, and kiss away his worry. At nine, he wasn't supposed to worry about his mom. Not till I was a senile old lady, and he was wondering if I'd do best with home health or a live-in facility. Maiz was right, again, even if she wouldn't hear it from me.

"No, honey, these were just really dirty. I'll have to pick better next time I'm at the store."

I finished washing the potatoes, spread on some melted butter, then topped them with a little sea salt. Once they were in the oven, I went out to get the grill ready for steaks. Grilling was the man's job, according to Marc, but it was up to me to make sure it was clean beforehand.

For mid-October, the weather was unusually nice. Today, the sun was bright and warm, the birds were chirping, and the gentle breeze carried the smell of chocolate from the nearby factory. Enjoying every second of peace I could before Marc got home, I relaxed on one of the deck chairs I hadn't packed away yet. Outside our wrought-iron fence, a deer grazed in the meadow. How nice to be so carefree, where survival was only based on eating and breeding. No other cares in the world.

Marc arrived home shortly after seven, much later than his usual 5:40p.m. homecoming. Much later than our six o'clock dinner bell, too. Instead of the planned juicy steak dinner, Lake and I ate ham sandwiches with chips. These late nights usually put Marc in a foul mood, either from missing supper, a long workday, or drama with coworkers. Tonight, was a different story. The jovial mood he'd been in this morning had carried through the day, but it felt more genuine this time.

"Sorry I was late, honey," Marc said. "I got busy crunching some numbers and lost all track of time. I'll make it up to you this weekend. We'll go out for dinner, have a couple drinks, or whatever you want to do. I've already arranged a babysitter. What do you think?"

He pulled me up next to him, kicking in my fight-or-flight mode, both of which were broken. I knew damn well I couldn't do either. At least my skin wasn't crawling at his touch.

"Yes, that sounds nice."

I had known, even when at my angriest tonight, that I wasn't going to start anything with him once he was home. I could tell myself until I was blue in the face that I was going to speak up, but it never happened. Now that he was home and being so sweet, all my animosity melted away. A date night seemed like exactly what I needed. What *we* needed.

The next couple of hours were uneventful. It was a nice change of pace. Strange, but nice. My old-lady-inner-self told me I was too tired to function shortly after nine, and I headed off to bed. I wondered if I'd see Lucian tonight. There would be no delusion as to whether he was real or not. It was all crystal clear now that it had all been a dream. My mind had been playing tricks on me from all the emotional distress. The dreams were a coping mechanism. All the mythology that I mysteriously knew about was from watching movies that I didn't remember.

I was already asleep when my head hit the pillow, but there were no dreams. No dreams equaled no Lucian. No Lucian made Rose a dull girl. I was more than a little disappointed. Any hope of him being real may have been squashed, but I'd still looked forward to having dreams featuring him. He was my Dream Man, both literally and figuratively.

Lucian had come to be because of the emotional upheaval caused by the life-altering altercation with Marc. Following that logic, he would be back if and when Marc got back to being "himself." It was only a matter of time. The prospect of that happening brought up both good and bad feelings. I didn't want to go back to worrying every minute of every day, but it would bring back Lucian. I really wanted to see Lucian.

My alarm was ringing. I had to put my disappointment on the back burner and get started with the day. It was a weekday, so Lake had school, Marc had work, and I had chores to do. I pulled myself together and trudged out of the bed. The show must go on.

For the next couple months, life went smoothly. Marc's change for the better never went back to the worse. For lack of a better word, he was delightful. More so than he'd been in years. He was positive, as in no more complaints regarding my food. Helpful, as in he'd pick up the slack with cleaning up around the house. And loving, as in plenty of kisses to go around.

He would come home after work and help finish dinner, set the table, then pitch in washing the dishes. It took me a good couple weeks to really believe that this wasn't some sort of ruse before I could really embrace the changes. My skin stopped crawling with each touch after I was able to fully forgive him. Life was good again.

The good ol' days carried into weeks, then months. My everyday routine stayed the same. I just didn't have the depression dogs nipping at my heels. Well, almost the same. Saturdays were now a date night, consisting of dinner, sometimes a movie, or bowling, or a play, or anything we felt like, before we went home to make love. There was a renewed sense of marital bliss. I hadn't realized how unhappy I was until the happiness came back. I was in love with my husband again. All his past acts toward me had been pardoned. I was sure he would never hurt me again.

Lake's changes were more subtle. His babysitter for date night, Kate, was a super sweet girl. Lake was mature enough he didn't need a babysitter, but as a habitual overthinker, I worried he would burn down the house trying to cook himself supper. He and Kate shared an interest in art. They would sit and draw for hours while Marc and I were out.

Her influence had lightened his drawings as well. His more recent sketches were of beautiful men and women decked out in elaborate clothing, dancing on clouds, or sitting in castles. Another theme was a large group of regular people celebrating, dancing, or doing both in a field of flowers. It was obvious that they were happy. The last sketch I'd glimpsed was a beach scene with two empty chairs under an oversized umbrella. If he'd done anything other than black and grey, I'd think it was Lucian's beach, but that was absurd.

Lucian was a faraway memory. He still crossed my mind from time to time, but it wasn't an obsessive misery that my dream prince wouldn't come to my rescue. It was more of a fond memory of the time when I'd temporarily lost my mind and thought dreams could come true.

I didn't miss him. I did, however, miss Maiz. The day I'd told her about Lucian was the last time we'd had a full conversation. The next week, she called me on Monday to let me know she would be out of town. The week after that, all I got was a text saying we needed to reschedule. Since then, I'd gotten nothing but silence and voicemail.

It was hard to determine how to feel about her sudden departure from my life. We'd been attached at the hip for years. Maiz was a grown woman, and I knew she could take care of herself, but that didn't keep me from worrying about her. I considered calling the cops, but my end of the conversation would have gone a little something like this:

Hi, my single and independent friend, who travels the world as an interior designer, isn't answering my calls. What happened the last time I talked to her? She told me to leave my husband, but I won't. No, I haven't talked to her family. Yes, I suppose it's possible she's in some part of the world that doesn't get good cell service. Yes, I am an idiot. Thanks for pointing that out. Have a nice day.

I wondered if it was something I'd said at lunch. Was it because I wouldn't leave Marc? Did I take my impersonation too far? Or had she realized that one too many birds flew over the cuckoo's nest when I believed I was talking to a real-life Greek god? Regardless of what I might have done, she should have talked to me. She would have, therefore it had to be something else. Then I circled back to worrying about her well-being. It was a vicious cycle.

***

On a Friday afternoon in early December, while waiting for Lake to get out of school, I went to his room to do some cleaning. Keeping his room clean was part of his chores, and he did a good job, but I still went in once a month to do a once-over. As I vacuumed, I accidentally knocked his sketchbook off the dresser, and it fell open on the floor. The picture caught my attention. It was one of his pre-Kate drawings. The last time I'd seen it, the morning after my first dream with Lucian, Lake had been in the early stages of his creativity.

Back then, there had only been the beginnings of a dragon wrapped around a streetlight. Now, an entire scene unfolded on the page. The dragon's body was still wrapped around the pole, its tail winding down to disappear beneath the snow that covered the landscape. Its head, made up of horns and sharp edges, towered above the top of the light. Lake had drawn little billows of smoke coming from the nostrils, possibly to intensify the anger that showed in the dragon's eyes. It was so beautiful and chilling at the same time. But what really drew my attention was the scene he'd added behind the dragon.

I didn't recognize the street or any of the surroundings, but the man, dressed all in black, wearing a hat with wisps of hair poking out, I did. The only bit of color he added to the entire picture were the man's two blood-red eyes. If the dragon looked angry, the man was furious. How Lake was able to convey such emotion in a drawing was unfathomable to me.

If Lake had Lucian in one of his drawings, that must have meant he'd dreamt of him, too. The only way that would be possible was if Lucian had been telling the truth. Right? Or maybe dreaming of the same person was hereditary. Same imagination, same dreams or something like that. More likely, we'd watched some show that had a character resembling Lucian, and we both had dreams of the same character. Of course, that's what it was. I was being silly again.

The sketch showed Lucian in his demon form. I was curious if there were any other sketches of him, possibly in human form. My heart raced at the prospect of seeing him, even if it was only a picture. Flipping the page, the next sketch had a small group of four black wolves. They looked blurry, like Lake had carelessly scribbled them on the page. The charcoal pencil lines were smudged enough to hide most of their features, except for their oddly slanted blood-red eyes, giving them an air of malicious intent. Behind the small pack stood demon-Lucian, the group of them staring right at me. The fear factor of it sent a chill down my spine.

I quickly turned the page. There he was. Lucian. It was as if someone had taken a candid photo of him when he wasn't looking. He was focusing on something off to the side, giving me a profile view of that handsome face I hadn't known I missed. Lake had drawn him with all his manly perfection, from the hard jawline to the dark stubble that speckled his face. He wore a fitted black t-shirt that showed off his muscled upper body. His hands were shoved into his pockets, like he was casually waiting for a coffee or something trivial.

My phone alarm was ringing from the kitchen downstairs. Time to pick Lake up from school. Since Marc had become a more relaxed version of himself, I'd sacrificed some of my cleaning time to take Lake to and from school instead of having him take the bus. It was nice having a little bit of extra time with him, and today I would have the opportunity to ask him about the sketches.

I replaced the book on his dresser then rushed down the stairs to shut off the phone. The deafening silence raised the hair on the back of my neck, giving me the feeling I was being watched by some unseen force. Thank goodness it was Friday, and I wouldn't have to be alone for the next couple days. I rushed out the door. Not because I was scared. *I'm not a child anymore, dammit.* I was rushing because I was now thirty seconds behind schedule.

Outside the school, I stood by the fourth graders' door, waiting for the last couple of minutes to tick down before the release bell chimed. On the open playground, there was no tree cover, and even the slightest wind could chill the bones. In my rush out the door, I had forgotten to grab my coat. The combination of wind and just slightly above-freezing temperatures were starting to hit me hard.

My shivering progressed from a slight muscle twitch to near seizure mode. Parents who were smart enough to plan for this cold December day gave me a wide berth, as if I were going to go down at any second, and they were afraid I'd take them with me.

Probably I should have stayed in the car, but I liked to be there for Lake to see me when he came out. The bell finally rang, and kids started flooding out each of the many doors. Looking through eyes that were now frozen wide open, I searched the faces for Lake. He came out somewhere in the middle, walking with his friend, Aiden.

Aiden was the same age as Lake, a head shorter, and cute as a button, with dark shaggy hair that hung in his eyes.

"Mom," Lake said, "can I sleep over at Aiden's tonight?"

It dawned on me then that Lake must have been avoiding going to friend's houses or having friends over to our house because of all the drama between Marc and me. Of course I wanted him to spend time with his friend, but that would mean I would have to go back home. *Alone.*

"Honey, I haven't talked to his mom. I can't send you over without permission first."

Aiden's mom picked that moment to appear with a big smile. Anna was the spitting image of her son, or vice versa. She was a head shorter than me, with short, dark hair that hung in her eyes, and cute as a button.

"Rose, it's been a long time," she said. "Aiden asked me last night if Lake could spend the night. I'm sorry I didn't text you earlier. I've been so busy with the little one."

"That's right, how is the baby? She's what, three months now?" I said through clenched teeth.

Lake either noticed I was freezing my ass off or he was trying to butter me up because he came over to wrap his small frame around me. My money was on the buttering up—he didn't offer public displays lightly. Whatever it was, I savored the love and the warmth that were offered.

"Allie is almost fourteen weeks now," Anna continued, beaming. "We still haven't gotten her on a good sleep schedule, so I'm usually sleeping during the day. If I'm not sleeping, then Allie isn't either, and she's screaming, and, well, that's why I forgot to text you."

"Are you sure it's okay for Lake to stay over?"

"AJ will be home this weekend, and my mom is in town to help. We will be fine. I plan to order a pizza for supper, and you can run over some clothes later if you want, or he can borrow some of Aiden's."

Did she not realize that there was a whole size difference between the two boys?

"Yeah okay, if you're fine with it, so am I. I'll run over some clothes later, after I get some errands done. I'll call in the morning, or you can call me to let me know when to come pick him up?"

Lake gave me a questioning look. He knew I was usually done with my errands before he got out of school, so there must be something up. I tried to give him a reassuring smile, but I was half-frozen, so I wasn't sure how reassuring it was.

"Well, boys, are you ready? Aiden, dad is at home with Allie, and I'm sure he needs help by now. Rose, it was good to see you.

Text me when you're on the way over. I'll send Aiden out to grab the clothes. You won't even need to get out of the car."

Collectively, we turned to make our way out of the school area. Lake pulled on my arm, forcing me down to his level.

"Don't worry, Mom. Dad won't let anything happen to you," he whispered.

I faltered at his words. The intuition of this boy was amazing. He must have sensed my hesitation about being alone. Maybe he had felt it too, knowing that with me or his dad around, nothing would happen. That we would protect him, and now he was passing that wisdom on to me.

"I know, sweet boy," I said. "We need to find some time to talk tomorrow, just you and me."

"I know," he said matter-of-factly.

Anna turned left outside the playground gate, and I went right. We said our goodbyes, and I hobbled my frozen legs as quickly as they would go to my car. Once inside, I wasn't sure what to do next. I knew for sure that I didn't want to go home. Marc wouldn't be off work for at least another two hours, and that could change if something came up.

Starting the car, I turned the heat to full blast, then waited for the parking lot to clear and my fingers to thaw. While I waited, I made a plan to drive to Harrisburg, where the nearest Target was located. It would take about twenty minutes to drive there, or about forty minutes round-trip. I could easily waste an hour tinkering around the store. On my way home, I would swing past Maiz's house to see if she was around, avoiding me, or if there was evidence of bodily harm that I could use to get the police involved. Her house was only about a five-minute drive from mine. That should eat up the remaining time before Marc got home, and if he was late, I'd stay in the car.

An hour into my two-hour wasting time block, I was aimlessly walking around Target. I'd stopped at the boys' section to find some new clothes for Lake when a tall, dark figure moved into my peripheral vision. When I turned to look, no one was there. With Christmas only a few weeks away, the store was rather busy. It was possible someone had been there seconds before, only to rush off to parts unknown. I continued shuffling through clothes, throwing a couple in the cart.

I was close enough to the book section that I thought I could run out the last remaining minutes on the time clock while perusing the new arrivals. Turning the cart, I caught sight of a tall man dressed in dark clothing, turning down an aisle. I only caught a fleeting glance, but he looked an awful lot like Lucian with his dark hair, hard jaw, and muscular build.

Like any normal crazy person, I raced my cart down the path to get a better look at the stranger. He wasn't there. He wasn't in the next aisle, or the next, or the next. I must have been seeing things. Must be time to make an eye appointment, and if that was good, then it might be time to see a head doctor. Shrink and neuro.

Maybe there was a toxic gas leak causing me to see things that weren't really there. For my safety, I moved towards the checkout. My time was about up anyway, and I'd take my time on the drive to Maiz's. Smart idea if I was seeing things. Wouldn't want to cause an accident.

All the checkout lanes were open due to the holiday rush. I was quickly out the door with my goodies and on my way to the car when I had that same creeping feeling I was being watched. Picking up the pace, I popped the trunk halfway to my car. I gathered my bags in one fell swoop to toss them in the back before slamming the trunk shut.

I loathed when people left their carts randomly sitting in the lot instead of putting them in one of the numerous cart returns, but I was making an exception today. I ran around to the driver's side, fumbled with the door handle, felt my heart skip a beat, then threw myself inside when I was finally able to get it open. I pulled the door shut and hit the lock about five times before I could relax.

I backed out of my spot, and before pulling ahead, I gave my rearview mirror one last look. There, by the building, stood a tall man dressed in dark clothing, looking my way. I turned for a better look, but he was gone. Customers bustled all around, going in, coming out. None of them matching the shadowy figure.

The entire ride back to town, I felt like a felon on the lookout for the cops. I was suspicious of every car around me. Checking, then double checking, for the dark figure. By the time I reached the sparsely travelled back road that led me to Maiz's, my knuckles were sore from gripping the steering wheel so tightly. At least on this road, it would be much easier to spot anything out of the ordinary.

The hills and winding roads could make it easy for someone to follow while staying at a safe distance. As a precaution, I took a couple extra turns to lose anyone that might be tailing me. After pulling into Maiz's driveway, I sat for an extra minute as my final precaution, watching to see if anyone drove by slowly. When I was certain the street was quiet and I was alone, I exited the car.

Maiz's house was bigger than mine by over a thousand square feet, a testament to how successful she was in her business. Examining the large house, it didn't appear that she was home. All the blinds and drapes were drawn except for a large transom window above the front entrance. I walked to the door and rang the bell. Inside, I could hear the sound echoing through the house, but there was no movement. I knocked in case the loud bell wasn't enough. Still nothing. I typed the code into the keypad for her keyless entry and listened as the lock slid open.

I stepped inside, calling out my presence, but there was no answer. The house was quiet. A little too quiet. Walking through the short hallway to the dining area, the house looked unlived-in. A little too unlived-in. Everything looked perfect. Way too perfect. On closer inspection, there was a fine film of dust on the glass-top table. Was that enough evidence to involve the police? It could be a double homicide, first the cleaning lady, then Maiz. I should check the rest of the house before making such assumptions.

I walked through the butler's pantry to the dining room. From there, I was able to get to the sitting room, then around to the stairs by the front door. At the top of the stairs, the large master bedroom was to my left. The bed was neatly made, and not an item was out of place. Moving through the room to the master bath, I still found nothing.

The size of her bathroom and closet were the same as my living room, so it took me a good minute to examine everything for signs of blood. In the closet, it didn't appear right away that any clothes were missing, but Maiz was an avid shopper, and the closet was overflowing with clothes and shoes, all neatly placed on their appropriate racks. When I was done with my investigation, I wanted to yell "all clear" like the cops do, giving myself a promotion from felon to detective. I thought better of it, when I decided I'd have to jump from the catwalk if someone answered me back.

Leaving the master bedroom, I travelled down the hall to the next bedroom that Maiz used as a home office. Like everything else I'd seen so far, it was in neat order. Neither paper, nor folder, nor scrap of fabric was out of place. I moved on.

Across the hall from the office was a guest room. Nothing amiss. At the end of the hall was a guest bathroom, all done up in coral colors with beach decor. Still nothing. I looked over the catwalk and down into the open living room. All perfect. I was both happy and disappointed that I hadn't found anything.

If something had happened, it apparently hadn't happened here. I still had the spooky unfinished basement to check, but I assumed I'd find more of the same. Now that I think about it, if I were some psycho killer, that would be the most attractive place in the house to kill someone.

Back on the main level of the house, I stood holding the knob to the basement. My heart hammering in my chest, unsure what might be waiting in the dark, I cautiously opened the door. No smell of decaying bodies. Good. I switched on the light. No bloody footprints or pools of blood in sight. Also, good. I went halfway down the stairs, just enough that I could see the entire room. Nothing. I turned, taking the stairs two at a time back up, flipping the light off and slamming the door at the same time, nearly catching my fingers in the process.

The triple stall garage was the only place left. There, I found all three of her cars—a sleek two-door Mercedes, a fancy four-door BMW, and a brand-new GMC Yukon Denali. The Denali was black with darkly tinted windows and looked like something the government would use. *That's it, Maiz works for the government.* It all made perfect sense.

Right now, she could be out of the country, working on a top-secret mission. She couldn't call or answer her phone because that would give away her location, compromising the mission. Government employees of that kind made megabucks—way more than an interior designer. The interior design business was just a facade to hide her true profession. Look at me, figuring it out all on my own.

Now that I knew she was safe on her secret mission and her house was clear, it was time to take my leave. Checking my phone, I realized it was well past the time Marc should be home. Leaving the same way I came in, I locked the door behind me and went to my car. I thought about running back in to leave a note, letting Maiz know I had been leaving fingerprints in her dust piles, but I could just as easily send her a text.

With no obvious threat on the street, I took the direct route home, arriving five minutes later. Marc's truck was already in the garage when I pulled up. Inside the house, I found Marc sitting on the couch, typing something on his laptop with the TV tuned to the evening news.

"Hey. Where were you?" he asked.

For a hot second, there was a tone reminiscent of the old Marc. Before leaving the school, I'd made sure to text him, letting him know my plan for the next couple of hours. I didn't tell him why, although that was just me being childish, and I'd rather keep that to myself. I'd suggested pizza and a movie night, which he'd agreed to, leaving no reason for him to be upset. I was just stressed from the weird day I'd had, and now I was trying to make mountains out of mole hills.

"You would not believe how crazy Target was with all the Christmas shoppers," I said, setting my bags in the kitchen. "And then, when I went to check on Maiz, she wasn't home, but I thought I should make sure she wasn't incapacitated somewhere, waiting to be rescued."

"She's a grown woman, Rose. She can take care of herself. Not sure why you're so concerned."

That time, there was a definite tone. Irritation. New Marc agreed with old Marc when it came to Maiz. He couldn't understand how I could be friends with a vile, foulmouthed woman like her. His words, not mine. I changed the subject.

"What kind of pizza should we order?" I asked.

"You pick. I have to finish this."

"Oh, okay. I'll order from that place down the road and pick it up on my way back from dropping off clothes for Lake."

He stopped typing as if to think about his reply.

"Alright," he said, tapping on the keyboard again.

I called the little mom-and-pop pizza shop on my way to Lake's room. Grabbing one of the ten unused backpacks out of his closet, I threw in a set of PJs and some clean clothes for tomorrow. His sketchbook sat right where I'd left it on the dresser. Anyone who may have been in the house, watching me, must not have been after the book.

Still, it might be safer in Lake's possession, so I stuffed it in the bag. I certainly was not doing this because I felt something evil might be summoned if I turned my back on it. That should be everything he needed for one night.

I sent a quick "on the way" text to Anna and let Marc know I'd be back soon. He made a peculiar grunting noise instead of genuinely acknowledging me. I didn't want to waste time pondering the meaning, especially if Aiden was out in the cold waiting for me.

Aiden lived in the same development as we did, and it only took me a few minutes to get there. Both Lake and Aiden were waiting for me in the driveway, giving me the opportunity to blow Lake a goodbye kiss. When Aiden wasn't looking, of course. After dropping off the bag, I picked up the pizza and was back home well within thirty minutes.

Plates in one hand and Cokes in the other, I placed one set on the coffee table in front of Marc. He closed his laptop with a loud snap and recklessly dropped it on the side table. He picked up his plate, then dropped his feet where the plate had been moments before, not saying a word. In fact, he hadn't said anything since I'd gotten home with the food. I tried not to overthink it. If I did, I might revert to the scared little girl I was not so long ago.

"What movie should we watch?" I asked.

"I told you to pick tonight," he snapped.

Whoa, I hadn't been expecting that. I hadn't done anything to warrant such a reply. The last couple months had been so happy. Peaceful. Calm. That gave me enough courage to speak up.

"Please don't talk to me like that. Did I do something wrong?"

"Nope."

The look he gave me, so full of fury, made me shrink back into myself. I hoped that this was just a tiny setback, not a full implosion of the new Marc. Trying to get back on his good side, I chose an action movie that he'd talked about wanting to see when it was still in the theaters.

The rest of the evening went about as well as it had started. With very few words exchanged. We watched the action movie, but I couldn't follow what was happening. The characters all blended together. I couldn't figure out who was good and who was bad. My mind wandered from Marc's mood to the shadowy figure following me around Target, then to Lake's sketches, and finally, to Lucian.

In the movie, one guy was rolling around on the floor, shooting at another guy, while people ran screaming from the room. Typical guy film. I quit focusing on the action and went back to devising my plan to get Lucian in a dream tonight. I had questions. He might only be part of my subconscious, concocted by my cortex, or a buried alter ego, but Lucian was the one capable of providing the answers I needed about the drawings in Lake's sketchbook. Tonight, I'd talk to Lucian, and Lake tomorrow.

The movie ended the way all these action flicks did. The good guy stood in a sea of wreckage after he'd defeated the bad guy, holding on to his lady and kissing her like there was no tomorrow. The camera panned out as the screen faded to black. I'm all for the guy getting the girl, but damn, can't the movie people switch it up a little?

We silently made our way up to the bedroom, doing our usual bedtime routine. I was already tucked in bed when Marc crawled in.

"Night," he said, his back turned to me.

"Good night. I love you."

No response. Not exactly the way I'd expected our kid-free night to go. I guess he was saving the good stuff for date night. Granted, if Marc was sullen like this tomorrow, I'd rather call in sick. A good night's rest could do a body good. Hopefully it would extend to his mood, as well. Whatever was going on with him this time around would eventually come to a head or go away. I was hoping for the latter.

Time for my master plan to get Lucian out of hiding. During the entirety of the almost three-hour movie, the only thing I'd come up with was to think really hard. My previous dreams had been brought on by a mix of circumstances and emotions. The dreams had been dark because of the state of mind I'd been in beforehand. Closing my eyes, I silently chanted, *Lucian, I need you.* I said this over and over, for who knows how long, continuing until I couldn't string words together anymore.

Chapter 4

Sand sifted between my toes as I walked along the stunning white-sand beach. The sapphire ocean twinkled like stars in the sky, just as I remembered it. Lifting my head, I let the bright sun warm my soul. I wanted to jump for joy. It had worked. I'd made it. Thank goodness I'd started on the sand instead of in the water this time around—I didn't want to push my luck on being saved again. I'd heard that if you died in a dream, you died in real life. That wasn't a theory I wanted to test.

Movement from the stagnant jungle drew my attention. Dreams that involved Lucian had all been borderline nightmares, so I half-expected an animal, or even some sort of monster, to come bounding out of the foliage. Instead, out stepped Lucian, tall and tan, his hair slicked back like he was fresh from the water. He wore only a pair of black and white board shorts that sat low on his hips. I took a long drink of that six-pack he was showing off.

He stopped right outside the jungle, making no further movement toward me. It wasn't gonna work for me to yell from twenty feet across the beach, so I started toward him. I had to fight the urge to run and jump in his arms. Judging by the solemn look on his face, he wasn't feeling the same urge. He didn't even look happy to see me. I stopped just short of our skin touching, looking up at those icy blue eyes.

"Why are you here?" he asked, sounding a lot like Marc.

"I found something strange in my son's room, and I need some answers."

"I have none."

There was no emotion, no hesitation. He didn't hide the fact that he couldn't care less about what I wanted to know.

"You don't even know what I'm going to ask."

I sounded more indignant than I'd intended.

"Don't need to."

"Why, because you're doing that little mind-reading trick again? I need to talk to you."

"No."

"Why are you acting like this? You sound like my husband. You almost had me fooled into thinking you were different, that there might be something better."

"I'm a dream, Rose. You interpret me the way you want. Sounds like you were wrong, though. I do that with everyone, giving them exactly what they want."

He sounded appalled, even a little offended, that I'd misconstrued our previous time together. Like Marc, he was turning things around on me, making it my fault.

"You need to go," he said.

Turning his back on me, he walked back into the sea of green leaves. What the hell had just happened? Lucian was right about one thing—this was a dream. I wasn't going to be treated this way in my own damn dream. I deserved respect and the answers I came for.

"Lucian, get your ass back here and talk to me!" I yelled. "Lucian! Lucian!"

My throat started to close up on me. I couldn't speak, I couldn't yell for help, and no matter how hard I tried, I couldn't breathe. Suddenly, I was a fish out of water, gasping for the tiniest bit of oxygen. Maybe this was Lucian's doing to get me off the island.

I fell to my hands and knees as the world went black. Tears stung my eyes as pain burned my lungs. My brain was reeling with the possibility that I could die. For realsies.

I tried to yell for Lucian once more, but there was no air left to exhale for sound. Darkness enveloped me. I struggled, kicking and punching, trying to break free. The pillow that covered my face was pulled away. I choked on the sudden intake of air filling my lungs. Marc sat on top of me, outrage contorting his face into someone I barely recognized.

"You bitch, I knew there was someone else," he screamed at me.

"What? What are you talking about?"

"I'm talking about Lucian. You were screaming his name just now."

"I don't know a Lucian, Marc. It was a dream."

There was a crazed look on his face. The new Marc from the last couple months was gone. This wasn't even the old Marc. The man perched over me was someone I'd never seen before, and he was dangerous. I was trying to be stronger than I'd ever been in my life. Which was quite difficult when a psychopath traipsing around in Marc's skin was hovering over the top of me.

"You're *mine*, and only *mine*."

Leaning over enough to reach his nightstand, but not enough that I could wriggle free, he pulled a piece of rope from the drawer. He tightly bound my wrists together, then tied them above me to the headboard of the bed. The rope bit into my skin, cutting off blood flow to my fingers.

Once he was certain I wouldn't be able to break free, he reached into the drawer again, this time pulling out a paring knife. It might be small, but the sharpness of the blade was mighty. Paring knife or butcher knife, both could do massive damage if wielded correctly. He examined it, smiling wide at his choice.

"Marc, please, why are you doing this? I love you."

My words brought his focus from the knife to my face. I could see in the light of the lamp on the nightstand that his pupils were the size of saucers. Had he taken something? Was he acting like this because he was high? As far as I knew, he had never done a drug in his life. He barely even drank.

"What's wrong? Talk to me," I said, trying to keep his focus on talking and not slicing and dicing. "Tell me what I can do to help."

"Rose?"

He looked confused as he examined my tied-up hands and the knife gripped tightly in his fingers. His pupils began to shrink.

"I don't know," he sounded genuinely confused. "I don't know what's wrong. I don't know what's happening."

"Then cut me loose and we can figure this out together. Ok, sweetie?"

His eyes widened and his mouth opened like he was about to say something, but nothing came out. Once again, his pupils dilated, and his demeanor changed.

"Sweetie? You trying to make it sound like you care about me?"

"I do care. I love you, Marc. I love our family."

"Then why would you be with someone else? You did this to yourself."

The blade was now resting on my cheek, digging into my skin. He didn't even hesitate before he pulled the blade from my cheekbone down to my jawline. The cold steel felt as if it were burning its way through my skin. Blood trickled down to mingle with tears that had already pooled in my ear. He copied the action on the other cheek.

"Let's see if he still loves you if you're scarred from head to toe."

"Marc, please think about Lake. You're gonna scar him too. He'll never be the same if you do this to me." That got his attention back to me. When I had his focus and his pupils were shrinking, I continued. "Lake said to me today that you would never hurt me. He believes in you."

A change in Marc's eyes meant a change in his state of mind. Enlarged pupils meant crazy Marc, while normal eyes meant normal Marc. I had to figure out how to keep him from going crazy. Or at the very least, keep him sane long enough to make my escape and let the cops deal with him.

"It's taking over, Rose," normal Marc said. "I can't stop it. It's like a parasite taking control. Ever since she touched me, I can feel it. It's getting stronger."

Maybe he was still crazy. Just a different kind because he wasn't making any sense.

"She who?"

"In my office. She touched me. Told me all these crazy things about you. Unbelievable things. About Lucian. She planted the parasite. It's going to kill you."

There was no time to analyze what he said. No time to plan my next step. The internal battle Marc was fighting was coming to a climax. His pupils began to grow then immediately shrink, back and forth, as he was frozen in place. I wasn't sure who was going to win. Only knew I needed to get out of here before the end.

I pulled at my restraints, hoping to find a weakness and break through. The pain of the rope biting into my skin was intense but not enough to make me stop for fear of what would happen if I stayed here. My fingers tingled with numbness, making untying the rope nearly impossible. I had taken my eyes off Marc to try and concentrate on freeing myself. A movement from him made me stop. The hand holding the knife was slowly being raised. This was it.

Death by paring knife seemed like it would be slow and painful as I bled to death. I squeezed my eyes shut as the blade swiped recklessly through the air, waiting for the inevitable. Instead, my hands came loose. Marc had cut through the rope, freeing me. Sort of. He still sat on top of me. At two hundred plus pounds, he was nearly double the size of me, effectively holding me in place.

I could tell by the tensing of his muscles and the dilation of his pupils when crazy Marc had taken hold. When he eased off, and normal Marc reappeared, I bucked as hard as I could, knocking him to the floor.

There was a lot of noise as he looked to be convulsing. I jumped from the bed, making sure not to get close enough that he could grab me.

"Run. Go. Hurry," he said, the knife outstretched in my direction.

Exhausted both physically and emotionally, I had to summon the last of my adrenaline to run as fast as my shaking legs would carry me. I was almost certain I was going to throw up, but there was no time for that now. The metaphorical clock was ticking. If I was going to get the hell out of dodge, now was the time.

Downstairs, I only stopped long enough to grab both of our vehicle keys off the hook. Marc wouldn't be able to catch up very easily if he couldn't start his truck. Pushing the button to open the large sliding garage door, I took a second to listen for running feet overhead. Hearing nothing, I slipped out the door, closing it quietly behind me, and ran the short distance to my car. The whole time, I expected Marc to grab me from behind, yelling "Surprise!"

Thankfully, I made it to the car without incident. I slammed the door shut, then pushed the lock button a few dozen times, for good measure. It helped to take my fight or flight response down a notch. I knew I wasn't free and clear just yet. Marc could easily come running out, smash the window, and yank me from the car. My betrayal of trying to leave would cause him to snap more than he already had tonight. That would be my end. No more me. I had to get out for Lake. I had to live for him.

Lake. I had to get Lake. I looked at the dash clock—it was almost 3:30a.m. Shoot. No use scaring the crap out of Anna in the middle of the night, or morning, if Lake would actually be safer there. Marc didn't know where Aiden lived. Even if he did, he didn't have a vehicle to go pick him up. Hopefully the cops would have him long before he left the house.

I reached over to the passenger seat to get my cell phone out of my purse. It wasn't there. In my rush to leave the house, I left it next to my coat and boots. My phone was still on the bedside table upstairs. With him.

There was no way in hell I was going back in. I could go to a neighbor and have them call the cops, but I didn't want to put them at risk. That would also require me to leave the car and Marc could come bursting out that door at any moment.

I could go to the hospital but that was a twenty-minute drive. My better option would be to drive to Maiz's house five minutes from here. She was probably one of the last people in the world to still have a landline, too. It felt like the logical choice for my scared brain.

With that decided, I started the car. I threw the shifter in reverse and jammed my foot down on the gas. My tires squealed loudly as my car struggled to get traction on the smooth garage floor. Suddenly, I was in the street and had to hit the brakes. I gave my house one last look, expecting Marc to be leaping through the air to stop me from leaving. He wasn't. I shifted into drive and hit the gas again. The car rushed forward, pushing me back into the seat.

The streets were deserted at this time of day. I didn't even bother slowing for the stop sign on the corner. It wasn't until my house was no longer in view, and I was sure Marc wasn't sprinting after me, that I finally felt out of harm's way. If he really wanted, Marc could run to Maiz's house, but I'd be safely locked inside.

Maiz's neighborhood was quiet, and her house looked the same as I had left it. There were no lights on inside, and no sign of life. I whipped my car into the driveway, leaving it running while I ran to the door. My fingers were shaking as I struggled to type in the code. Not just from the adrenaline rush, but from only wearing shorts and a tank top in the cold of the night. As soon as the deadbolt was free of its locked position, I pushed the door open and slammed it shut behind me, throwing the lock back into place.

In the instance that Marc gained super speed with his crazy, I thought it best to put my car in the garage. That way it would give the illusion that no one was here. To avoid being obvious, I left the lights off and groped my way into the kitchen. I was familiar enough with the house that I knew where everything was. She had some plug-in nightlights sporadically placed to give off a modicum of light that helped me along the way as well.

Between the kitchen and living area was a door that went out to the garage. There, I picked the BMW's keys off the hook, then went to the garage to move her car out and replace it with mine. Maiz would promptly kill me if she knew I was leaving her precious car in the elements, exposed to breezes, moonlight, and stardust. *Well too bad, Maiz, I just can't risk leaving my car in plain sight.*

I let myself back into the house, locking the door behind me even though I had closed the large garage door. Again, I didn't know what Marc was capable of anymore.

On a small desk next to the counter, was a cordless phone. The landline. My saving grace. I grabbed it to me like it was a precious baby. I pushed the power button and listened for a dial tone. There was only silence. Pushing the button again, I put the phone to my ear and listened. For anything. Once again, there was only silence. The buttons beeped at me when I pressed them, so there was power, but no service. She must have canceled it before going on her extended leave.

The feeling of helplessness overwhelmed me. I sank down the counter right there in the kitchen, landing in a pathetic heap on the floor, still holding the phone in case it miraculously decided to work. My adrenaline had worn off and I was utterly exhausted. Salty tears burned the open cuts on my cheeks, bringing more tears to my eyes in a never-ending cycle. I squeezed my eyes shut until I could get my emotions in check, letting sleep overtake me.

I woke with a start—I was still huddled against the counter. I wasn't sure how long I'd slept there—it could have been an hour, or it could have been five. Still, the only source of light was the little plug-ins, which were surprisingly bright, and the moonlight coming in through the little westward window over the sink. Most of the room was still cast in shadows. I carefully peeled my cheek off my arm, trying to avoid reopening the wounds. Probably I should go search for some butterfly bandages.

The hardwood floor had made my butt bones tingle, and my neck had a crick from the awkward position I had fallen asleep in. My head felt like Ricky Ricardo was using it as a bongo drum for one of his Cuban beats. I needed ibuprofen. Pronto.

Slowly but surely, using the counter for leverage, I hefted my heavy body off the floor. All twenty-four vertebrae popped loudly as they slid back into place when I straightened. Parts of me ached and smarted that I didn't know could ache and smart. After a short struggle with uncertain legs, I was upright. Taking a guarded step, my bare feet slipped on fresh blood, nearly taking me down. Crap, Maiz was gonna freak. First, I'd moved her car outside. Then, I was bleeding all over her expensive house.

I hobbled like a little old lady with bad hips over to the fridge, pulling the door open. The bright light left me temporarily blinded. Once my eyes adjusted, I found the shelves to be empty except for a few bottles of water. Maiz clearly planned ahead and rid the fridge of perishable items. Why wouldn't she have told me she was leaving? For payback, maybe I should leave my blood on her floor. There might even be some on her counter. That'd teach her. Or I'd drink my water with the fridge door hanging open, wasting electricity, and raising her bill. *Good one, Rose.*

A long drink of water later, and a fridge completely depleted of cold air, I let the door slowly swing closed. When I turned, two faces stared at me from the opposite side of the kitchen island. My fight or flight kicked for the second time in twenty-four hours. I screamed and threw my half empty water bottle at the shadows who easily dodged my projectile.

"We're gonna have to work on your aim," Maiz said.

"How the heck did you get in here?" I asked.

"This is my house, crazy lady."

"I know this is your house, but wouldn't I have heard you come in? I swear you weren't here a minute ago. Oh, I see. I'm dreaming. Because otherwise he wouldn't be here." I looked pointedly at Lucian. "You two appearing out of nowhere, is very dream-like. That's the only explanation for both of you being in the same room. Right? Although, I don't remember being in pain in any of the other dreams I've had."

Maiz was smiling at me. Lucian was not. As a matter of fact, he looked irritated.

"Oh crap, am I dead? I'm dead, aren't I? Did I crash on the way here? Did I even make it out of the house? *Lake*. Maiz, I need you to get Lake so Marc can't hurt him, too."

I grabbed at the counter to keep from collapsing.

"No darling, you are very much alive," Maiz said. "This is no dream, either. We're really here."

Lucian stood up from his seat, his smooth gait bringing him around the counter. I couldn't help but follow his every move, turning toward him as he stopped directly in front of me. He made no noise for such a big man. I wouldn't have known he was moving if I hadn't seen it with my own eyes. His summery scent comforted me. I wanted to hug him, but I was still mad at him.

"This never would have happened if you didn't leave me on the beach," I said. "He did this because of you."

I knew none of this was truly his fault. I just needed an outlet for my fear and anger.

"I'm sorry this happened to you," he said, looking me straight in the eyes. "I would do it differently if I could."

Red snaked through his irises until all the icy blue was completely red. He wrapped both arms around my shoulders and pulled me in for a hug that was too aggressive for my sore body. New pain rattled me. Tears stung my eyes once more. I tried to pull away, but the more I struggled against him, the more pain I felt.

Maiz was being unusually quiet. I wanted to yell at her to help me, but my lips wouldn't work. A whisper in my head told me to stop straining. The surprise of it shocked me into submission. I stopped fighting, letting Lucian hold me tight. Our bodies were so close, not even a sliver could come between us. His body grew hot. I mean, this man was damn fine to look at, but this was a different kind of hot.

Lake had battled the flu bug a few years back. On his worst days, his temp would spike to 104 degrees. His small body would be warm to the touch even as he was shaking in a cold sweat. I was no thermometer, but Lucian had to be at least ten degrees warmer than that, and still getting warmer. My pains were fading, melting from the heat of his body.

It only lasted a couple of minutes. Long enough to raise my body temp a couple degrees and bring a fine sheen of sweat to my skin. His arms dropped away from me, giving me my escape.

Okay, so I only backed up a couple steps. It was enough to see in the moonlight that Lucian was in one of his demon forms. His red eyes were sparkling like rubies and his hair looked like dripping blood. I suspected lava had flowed through his veins shortly before, bringing up his temperature to non-human heights. He dropped his head, taking a couple steadying breaths. I watched as black seeped from the roots of his hair, down to the ends, until all his hair was normal again.

I took another step back in case he hurled. Or fainted. A man of his size could easily take me down with him, and heck if I knew what was going on with him right now. I noticed then that nothing hurt anymore. Holding my wrists up, I could see that there were no more marks from the rope. I put a careful hand to my face. Nothing. My cuts had disappeared. The sticky blood from the lacerations was all that remained. I was completely healed.

"How did you do that?" I asked.

He raised his head. A face red with inflammation and cut from cheek to chin on each side looked back at me. His face was what mine had looked like before he'd taken away my pain. The only difference was that his cuts weren't bleeding. They were boiling.

Yes, boiling. Steaming hot blood bubbled out of the wounds, the bubbles growing larger until they popped, spraying tiny drops of blood on the floor. I could tell by his clenched fists that it wasn't just his face that mirrored mine. The cuts that I could see started healing, sealing themselves shut like little Ziploc bags.

My eye began to twitch as I watched the last of his wounds heal into perfect, unmarred skin. There was no way this was real life. In real life, mysterious men didn't absorb others' pain and make it their own. They didn't have magical healing blood. I was losing it. Nothing made sense. I was going down a path of emotional overload. I could hear my heart pounding in my ears as I started to hyperventilate.

"It's happening," Lucian said, looking at Maiz. "We have to go."

She nodded. I could see the worry written all over her face. That couldn't be good—Maiz was tough as nails, and if she was worried, I most definitely should be worried. Add that to the list of emotions I was feeling right now.

"Time for a nap," Lucian said.

Wait, what? That was a new one. Usually, he tells me wake up. This was some backwards shit.

Lucian closed the gap between us. Casually, he ran his hand from my forehead to my chin, letting a finger catch my lip. Was he really playing with me? At a time like this? Well, then, I would let him know exactly how I felt about that. Yep. I was gonna give him a piece of my mind. Any minute. Just that I was feeling so tired all of a sudden. My mind started to haze over. Any words I wanted to say slipped away like whispers in the wind.

A tingling numbness started in my toes, making its way up my legs. This had to be something to do with Lucian. I wanted to move away from him, but my legs were turning to mush. In fact, they were shaking from the effort it took just to hold me up. Seeing that I was fighting a losing battle, Lucian swept me off my feet, holding me close as the numbness reached my middle. My legs were now completely useless, and my arms were well on the way to Flopville. Since my face wasn't affected yet, I gave him the dirtiest look I could muster.

"Wha diddd you dooo ta meee?" I asked.

It came out sounding like I'd had one too many tequila shots. Since I hadn't had a single drink for the past ten years, that would have been a grand total of two to get me this wasted.

"She's sedated enough," he said ignoring my question and talking to Maiz instead. "We should be safe to leave."

He tightened his grip around me before moving towards the garage door.

My psyche took another tequila shot, spreading the worst case of pins and needles to my fingertips. My head felt like a giant bowling ball that I was losing the strength to hold up. I used what control I had left to lay my heavy head on his shoulder, tucking my forehead into his neck to keep it from rolling.

His heartbeat thumped a soothing lullaby under my ear. My eyes were fighting to stay open against my 3,000-pound lashes. The last thing I remembered was Maiz holding the door open, smiling at me, as Lucian stepped through. One last shot to the brain, then it was lights out.

***

Murmuring voices filtered into my subconscious, pulling me from the depths of slumber. At first, I thought my sleep-addled brain couldn't make out what they were saying, until it finally hit me that they were speaking in a different language. As someone who was barely fluent in English most days, I couldn't begin to make a guess at the language they were speaking now.

I was stowed in the second row of Maiz's government-issue Yukon. Drool had leaked from my open mouth, gluing my cheek to the leather seat. There was a ninety-nine percent chance I'd been snoring, too. Maiz had taken countless videos of my passed-out, wide-mouth snoring after a long night of drinking back in our college days. It was an obnoxious, loud exhale snore—not one of my more attractive qualities. If there had been any snoring, the two speaking in hushed tones in the front seat didn't seem to notice the sudden silence.

Sitting up, I wiped my cheek for any residual drool that might be lingering. I looked out the window, trying to get a sense of where we were going. There were lots of open fields, straight roads, and barely any trees. *Uh oh, we're definitely not in Pennsylvania anymore.* Although we could be in Kansas, I had my doubts. I tried to watch for signs to get a clue, but there weren't any. What the hell? Did the DOT just expect us to know where we were? I mean, really. What if a kidnap victim woke up in the back of a vehicle and needed to know their location for the authorities to rescue them? Hypothetically, of course.

Stay calm, no need to panic. Yet. Judging by the compass on the dash, we were headed west. The sun was rising behind us in the east. We couldn't have left Maiz's much before sunrise, so we could only have been on the road for a couple hours. That would be a relief, except that what I was calculating and what I was seeing weren't adding up. Pennsylvania roads were curving, winding, hilly little gems surrounded by trees and mountains. Complete opposite of what we were speeding by.

I might have lost a lot more time than I thought. If that were the case, we were a long way from home. And Lake. Lake was still there, with Marc. No, I couldn't leave him behind. Maiz should have known better. We had to turn around. We had to get my son.

"She's panicking," I heard Lucian say.

"Hey doll, I need you to stay calm, okay?" Maiz said, looking at me in the rearview mirror.

Lucian, who was riding shotgun, turned in his seat to face me. I had a momentary need to scold him for not wearing his seatbelt. He reached out a hand, running it down my face exactly the way he had at the house. Shit, I knew what that meant. The bastard was putting me back to sleep. And here I'd thought he was concerned about my wellbeing and wanted to get a better look at me. I had so much to say before I drifted off again. Starting with how much of a total dick Lucian was being.

The tingle was racing through my body this time. I could feel myself falling over as I lost the strength to hold my body up.

"Must. Get. Lake," I said. Each word was a struggle. "And you're a jerrrrrrkkk." My words were slurring as the sleepy-time juice reached my head.

"It's for your own good," Lucian said.

He placed a gentle hand on my cheek, guiding me back down to the seat. I tried to tell him to get his hand off me, but I only succeeded in sounding like Frankenstein's monster. I was killing the sexy thing today—no wonder Lucian couldn't keep his hands off me. On the bright side, I no longer looked like a monster. My eyes drifted closed as Lucian straightened the stray strands of hair that had fallen into my face.

The next time I came to, I was in an actual bed. The log cabin-style room was painted a rust color that complimented the wooden furniture. Pictures of buffalo, elk, and wolves hung on the walls around me. A stone fireplace was directly in front of the bed, the screen featured a black metal moose walking through the woods. The floor and ceiling were made of cedar, as were the dresser, night table, and bed frame. I lay on a bed stuffed with clouds and covered by a brown faux-fur comforter as soft as silk.

Flipping the cover away, I noticed that someone had changed my clothes to a pair of sweatpants and a tank top. No bra. I pulled out the waist of my pants enough to check down below. Fresh panties, too. Oh boy, I wonder who'd had the pleasure of getting me naked. Could have been anyone. The only thing I knew right now was my name was Rose. After everything that had happened, I could have been wrong about that, too.

The clock on the little bedside table read 9:05. It was dark outside the window to my left, so unless they had whisked me away to Alaska during their twenty-four hours of darkness, it only made sense that it was 9:05p.m. I had slept away an entire day. Thanks to Lucian's sleep-inducing hands, I was still groggy and disoriented.

I swung my feet out of the bed, slowly testing my ability to support my own weight. The chill in the air made me reconsider leaving the warm, fuzzy bed behind. Wrapping a brown and tan checked throw picturing a moose around my shoulders, I shuffled over to the window that overlooked a winter wonderland. Dang, maybe this really was Alaska. There was at least a foot of fresh, fluffy snow on the ground. A deer gracefully strolled through the deep snow, stopping only to look at me through the glass before turning to prance off through the trees surrounding the house.

In any city, it was hard to see the stars that weren't the biggest and brightest in the sky because of all the light pollution. Here, though, the only manmade light was the ambient glow coming from my window. The sky was crowded with thousands upon thousands of stars. The land that stretched out around me was illuminated by the full moon as it reflected off the snow, giving it an eerie yet peaceful glow.

In the corner of the room, between the window and the fireplace, stood a full-length mirror. I checked my appearance. Whoever had changed my clothes had also washed away any traces of blood from my face. Not a huge task but I couldn't believe I had slept through it all. Insomniacs all over the world would kill for Lucian's sleep-inducing hands.

Walking to the door, I put my ear against the wood to listen for any movement outside. The door was solid wood, too thick to hear anything other than the movement of my hair against the grain. Careful not to make a sound, I turned the knob, and pulled it open just enough to poke my head through. No armed guard at the door. The hall was empty except for some closed doors to my right.

Voices drifted to me from my left, both female. I recognized one as belonging to Maiz. The other was a voice from the past; their name was right on the tip of my tongue. I didn't have a lot of friends in general. This had to be someone I'd known before my time with Marc. That was a lifetime ago.

I followed the hall to a large sitting room with high, vaulted ceilings. It was filled with warm colors and similar decor to my bedroom. Light brown plaid couches circled a rustic coffee table, all of which sat before a wall of grey and brown stones with a large fireplace built into the middle.

Cedar bookshelves, filled with books and statues of wildlife, reached from the floor to the ceiling on either side of the fireplace. A large antler chandelier hung from the planked ceiling, lighting a large portion of the room. It was homey, inviting, and the kind of place I'd want to cuddle up on the couch with a good book.

The wall adjacent to the fireplace was floor-to-ceiling windows. Windows that overlooked a similar wonderland I could see from my room, except the trees were a little thinner out front, opening up more of a view. Or lack thereof. There were no other houses, no roads. No anything that I could make out at this time of night.

Behind the sitting area was a modern kitchen full of dark, stainless-steel appliances that looked fresh out of the box and much of the same warm colors and wildlife decor. Sitting alone at the cedar island was Maiz. No one else. I guess it was possible that I was a little bit mental and had only imagined multiple voices. Unless someone was hiding behind the counter, that was the only other explanation.

Maiz was smiling at me. The kind that needed deciphering. It could be a sad smile because I was crazy, or it could be sympathetic because of what I'd gone through with Marc. Maybe she was just happy to see me.

I took a seat next to her on one of the stools, my blanket still wrapped around me.

"I think I'm losing it," I said on a long sigh. "When Marc attacked me, he made it sound like he was being controlled by something inside him. He cut me, or I thought he did. I was magically healed after Lucian hugged me. And you. You were with Lucian. After you told me he wasn't real. Yet, you two spoke like you knew each other. Knew each other well. Well enough that you spoke the same, strange language. So, what the hell? Did you lie to me? Or am I going batshit crazy?"

"Whoa," Maiz said, grabbing my arms to stop the flailing. "Let's take a breath. You're not going batshit. There is a lot that's happened that's probably hard to comprehend. I'm not sure what happened with Marc. I tried to fix him for you."

"Fix him how? Because I'm pretty sure he still had his balls."

"I mean, if I had it my way, I'd have them hanging on a keychain."

"That's nasty."

"After I saw what he did to you, I sent a friend to have a word with him. Eros was supposed to make him more loving. It's not something that just wears off, so, I don't know why he snapped."

"Eros? The Greek cupid?" Maiz nodded. "He's your friend?" She nodded again.

That would explain his sudden change in demeanor. But then, that would mean Greek gods are real. In real life. My life.

"I can see the wheels turning and the crazy eye starting to pop. It'll all make sense soon."

Releasing her grip on my arms, she dropped back on her chair, defeated.

"I'm sorry I lied to you about Lucian," she said, looking down at her hands. "I didn't know him at the time. Not personally. When you brought him up, I wasn't sure how much I could tell you."

"Tell me? About what?" I was seriously confused.

"The truth about everything. Lucian started the ball rolling when he told you about himself. Which, by the way, was the truth. If I haven't said this already, he's real. And sooo hot, right? Sexiest damn four-thousand-year-old I've ever seen."

My emotions were in overdrive. There was a lovely dose of confusion, annoyance, frustration, and most of all, irritation, all mixed into one big bag of fun. I had to shove a palm to my eye twitching out of control.

"Everything? That's a very broad term. It can mean so much. You're gonna have to get more specific."

"Brace yourself," she said.

I took her words literally, grabbing the seat of my chair. There shouldn't have been much left that would shock me anymore, but with the turns my life had taken recently, who the hell knew.

"Like Lucian," she said, "I'm part of the Greek pantheon. I'm not nearly as old as that geezer, at only one thousand and some odd years, but I've been around the block a few times. I'm one of Nyx's daughters. I'm a death angel called a Ker. Most of the time, Keres are sent to war zones to, um, help move people along. In rare cases, we're used as bodyguards. Like for you."

If I wasn't holding on, I surely would be face-down on the floor. This had to be a joke. Maiz was my friend—I couldn't understand why she would say something like this.

"What the hell are you talking about? We grew up together."

My mind was screaming, *does not compute!* The puzzle pieces of information weren't fitting together.

"I was reborn and placed near you so we could grow up together," Maiz said, avoiding eye contact.

"So, what you're telling me is, all those years I thought you were my friend, you were actually just doing a job?"

I was having a hard time controlling the anger that was boiling up inside me.

"No, Rose, I was your friend. I *am* your friend. More than that, I'm your sister. I would be devastated if something happened to you."

"Sister?" I spat the word. "A sister wouldn't have lied to me my entire life."

Maiz was emphatically shaking her head. "It's not like that."

"No? If you didn't lie to me," I said, "then this is some sick game you're playing. Are you in cahoots with Marc? Are you two trying to get me locked up in a padded room so you don't have to get your hands dirty? Either way, our friendship." I made air quotes around the word *friendship*. "Was bullshit."

Probably I was overreacting. I felt like a volcano in the early stages of erupting. All my pent-up rage from years of abuse blew out in one big explosion. Maiz wasn't entirely to blame for the way I felt; she was more a victim of proximity. You get too close to a volcano, you're gonna get burned. Maiz was about to say something, so I cut her off.

"I'm done talking about it. The only thing I want to hear from you is where my son is. I need to see him."

"Lake isn't here, but he's safe."

"No, that's not good enough. Tell me where he is." I demanded.

"I'll have to get Lucian."

I gave a stiff shake of my head and crossed my arms over my chest like a stubborn child.

"I'm dealing with you. I'm not about to give him the chance to put me to sleep again."

"He's the only one who knows where Lake is. You know I would never force you to do anything, but if you want information, you'll have to talk to him."

"Yeah, great bodyguard you are," I muttered.

I was being childish, but dammit, everything was going to hell in a handbasket. I'd like to see anyone else handle it with more dignity.

"Fine. Go get him."

I said "fine," but I was really thinking, *screw this*. Time to get the hell out of here, and the hell away from these crazy people who were trying to bring me down with them. I would find someone, get a phone, and get the cops involved.

Maiz leaned forward, giving me another arm squeeze before she got up, heading towards the stairs at the side of the kitchen. What she needed was that handy dandy little trick Lucian had with the mind reading. Then she would know that I didn't plan to be here when they got back.

As soon as she was out of sight, I jumped off the stool, moving quickly to the door. A rack filled with different-sized coats stood by the door. Not wanting to run out into another winter night without some protection against the elements, I grabbed the nearest one to my hand, wrapping it around me. The sleeves stretched past my hands, and the hem was down to my knees. Boots were neatly lined on a mat on the other side of the door. Even the smallest pair I could find were too big, but it was better than losing my toes to frostbite. Slipping the boots on, I stealthily snuck out the door.

To my way of thinking, I had been kidnapped by psychopaths, and at some point, we were in a vehicle, so it had to be close by. I didn't have any keys, but I hoped since we were tucked away from other houses, they would still be dangling from the ignition. If not, there would be a road that we'd used to get here, where other cars would eventually travel. I could hitch a ride to the nearest town, getting the help I needed when I was safely away from these people. Yes, hitchhiking was dangerous. I figured it was the lesser of two evils. Multiple evils if Marc was added back to the equation.

Outside, I looked around. No car, of course. Maiz would shave her head before she would leave one of her car babies in the snow. Snowflake marks and all that. There was nothing but a bin of firewood, an axe, and tread tracks. Nothing of use to help with my quick getaway.

The tracks in the snow, too small to belong to a car, led away from the house. That was good enough for me—they had to lead somewhere. Anywhere was better than here. Good thing I had boots on.

The trees grew thicker the further I got from the house, blotting out the moon and plunging the tracks into darkness. I made it far enough that I could no longer see the house, but not far enough that I could see a road. Stopping to catch my breath, I reassessed my plan. It was colder than I'd expected, and I wasn't exactly dressed for a long hike through the snow-covered woods. The oversized coat gaped open at the bottom, sucking in the frigid winter air. Oh, shit, I was gonna freeze to death out here.

A shadowy figure appeared before me, stopping me cold in my snow tracks. Pun intended. Lucian. He looked angry, but not demon-eyed angry. Those icy blues looked like icicles reflecting the moonlight. It was eerie to see two floating blue orbs shining at me in the darkness. He was dressed in a pair of jeans that were tucked inside tall black boots, and a black double-breasted pea coat. Walking towards me with a purpose, he looked like a model from an article titled "How to Make Snow Look Good."

"Fancy meeting you here," I said when he stopped in front of me. "I don't need your help, though. So, thanks, bye."

I tried to step around him, running straight into the arm he put out. It was as good as hitting a brick wall.

"It's not safe out here."

"Oooo, is the big bad wolf going to get me?"

"Maybe," he said simply.

The drawing that Lake made in his sketchbook came to mind. The black wolves with angry red eyes standing before Lucian. A chill of a different nature ran up my spine. I hugged myself, as if that would protect me.

"I'm a big girl. I can handle myself. Now, if you'll move out of the way, I need to find my son."

"And how did you expect to do that?"

"None of your damn business."

As I tried to get past him, he pulled me against his body. His warmth felt so good. Being close to him again felt so good. I feigned trying to escape so that if he wasn't reading my mind, he wouldn't know I was enjoying this. He wrapped another arm around me. I wanted to laugh, like I had any chance of getting out of even just one arm.

"Lake's whereabouts *are* my business," he said, looking down at me. "I'm the only one who knows where he is."

"I bet the cops can find him."

"Don't bet your life savings."

"Joke's on you. I don't have any life savings to bet. I don't have any money at all. Now tell me where he is."

"Or you'll do what?"

His condescending tone made me want to scream. If I thought I had any chance at all, I'd kick him in the crown jewels to make him talk.

"You don't, and I wouldn't," he said, reading my thoughts. "Unless you want to make me angry."

"Stop reading my mind, you je-je-jerk!"

The cold was leaching into my bones, and my body was starting to convulse with shivers. Lucian unbuttoned his coat, and taking the larger coat off me, he wrapped me in his. All his heat was stored up in the threads of the coat, giving me that fresh-from-the-dryer feel, and I instantly felt warmer with it on. I felt a smidge bad about leaving him wearing only a short-sleeve shirt out here, but that passed quickly. He deserved it.

He plucked me into his arms as he started back to the house, the same way he had at Maiz's, except I was fully awake to enjoy it this time. My body was pressed against his, his arms holding me tight.

"I just want to know where Lake is."

"Lake is safe. You must trust me on this. I can't tell you where he is because that could put him in danger if someone else were to read you."

"Is there a second option?"

Lake and I had never been away from each other longer than a night. Of course, I still wanted to know where he was so I could be one hundred percent certain he was safe, but there was something deep inside telling me Lucian was trustworthy. That he would protect me, and Lake, with his life.

"There is a bigger situation going on here that needs to be addressed first. He's safer away from you right now. No more running, no more trying to get away. You need to stay here, or I will take measures to make you stay put. Understand?"

"Yes, El Capitan."

I was always sounding so childish around him. In comparison to a four-thousand-year-old Greek dream god, I was merely a child. The way he talked to me was very much like a parent scolding a child, too. Very Marc-like. How did I get so very lucky to be surrounded by assholes who did nothing but boss me around and try to control my life?

Hopelessness overwhelmed me. Tears spilled down my face. Trying to avoid drawing attention to my unattractive crying, I tucked my chin to my chest, squeezing my eyes shut as hard as I could. If I could shut them a little bit harder, maybe the tears would stop. Maybe if I wasn't a mental punching bag, the tears would stop. Instead, Lucian stopped, putting me back on the ground. I nearly had a panic attack thinking he was going to leave my blubbering ass in the wilderness. He cupped my chin, making me look up at him.

"I'm sorry," he said, wiping a tear from under my eye. "That came out wrong—it was not my intention to upset you. I want to protect you, and I cannot do that if you continue to run away from me."

"I don't know what's wrong with me."

"Nothing. You are perfect. You've been through a lot over the years. It's only natural to be a bit—"

"Emotional? Try a lot."

"It will be okay. You're not alone here."

Simple words. Sincere words that I'd always wanted to hear from Marc. I couldn't hold back the tears anymore. They left little trails down my cheeks, freezing as they went, down to my chin, where I was sure they froze into icicles.

Lucian nestled me close, putting his arms around me as he laid his cheek on my head. I felt warmer, inside and out, knowing he was there for me. When he let go of me, we were back in my little cabin room. Shocked, I looked up at him, our faces inches apart. Those inscrutable eyes held mine in their icy depths. Up close, the light blue was nearly washed out by white flecks.

It was getting harder and harder to deny that he was some sort of supernatural being.

"You mean, you simply could have blinked us back to the house to begin with?'

"Any use of power is risky. We never know who's watching."

After whisking me off my feet again, he placed me on the bed. No wonder he was so muscular—as often as he picked me up, he had to be getting quite the workout. Not to mention all the other women he was probably sweeping off their feet. Even the thought spurred my jealousy.

"There's no one else. Only you."

"Yeah, here and now. What about in dreams? You said you're there for them, in any capacity they want. I'm guessing that means women. All over the world. Am I right?"

"I quit working dreams years ago."

He leaned over me, hands pressing into the mattress on either side of me. Moments like these, I wished I could read him the way he read me. I wanted to know what all the turmoil on his beautiful face meant.

"You're beautiful, too," he said, reading my mind again.

He bent down and kissed me hard enough to make my toes curl. Any remnants of cold from my trek outdoors fled with the heat that rushed up from the south. I helped him slip the coat off me when he pulled at the sleeves. He pulled away from me, his coat hooked around his arm.

"Get some rest," he said. "We have a lot of work ahead of us."

"I can't sleep now." My voice came out sounding more desperate than I intended.

Something about Lucian lit my body on fire. No, not something; everything about him. A normal person probably wouldn't jump into bed with another man after everything that had happened, but I had this irrational feeling of wanting to be close to him. He was familiar. When he wasn't around, I missed him. I felt comfortable with him—like I was free to be myself. All of that, a cup of sugar, a tablespoon of vanilla, and a sexy Greek god. I couldn't control what my body wanted.

"I mean, I've slept an entire day away. I don't know anyone who would be able to go right back to sleep after that."

He leaned in for a slower kiss, distracting me so that when he pulled away, he could do the sleepy-hand maneuver.

"Damn you. Damn… you… all… to…"

Pulling at the covers, he tucked me in. He kissed my forehead, lingering a second longer than necessary, then switched off the lamp before turning to leave. I was out cold before the door even closed.

Chapter 5

Bright sun streamed through the window by the bed. We must have been closer to the sun here, as the rays were nearly blinding as they shone through. Taking some time to remind myself where I was, I thought through the events of the last couple nights. I was still trying to distinguish between what was real and what was not. Some of it must have been real if I was waking up in a strange bed. Either that, or this was the longest dream in history.

What was I supposed to do with my days here? At home, my day started with Lake, followed by cleaning and errands. I figured that wasn't what Lucian had meant by "a lot of work ahead." This house was spotless from what I could see. Without Lake here, I didn't feel the need to get out of bed, but there was nothing for me to do in this little room. No TV to watch. No books to read. No paper to write on. And with as much sleep as I'd gotten, I certainly couldn't do anymore of that. I was feeling more rested than I had in a long time.

A sharp pain twisted my stomach. Crap was I hungry. No, hungry was an understatement—I was starving. The last time I ate anything was pizza with Marc on Friday night, however long ago that was. The clock by the bed told me it was almost noon. An enticing aroma wafted from the kitchen, prompting my stomach to roar in anger.

I rolled out of bed to clean myself up before making my way to the kitchen. A note hung on the closet door caught my attention.

Rose,

I filled the chest of drawers and the closet with clothes. Hope you likey. If you don't, suck it. Or if it's really that bad, I guess I can exchange or return them. Also, filled the bathroom with some supplies you may need. Shampoo, conditioner, makeup, etc. Let me know if I've forgotten anything.

- Maiz

I pulled open the sliding doors of the closet to find it filled with new tank tops, t-shirts, long sleeves, and sweaters, all with tags still attached. Maiz knew me well enough to know my style. I chose a hoodie and moved to the dresser, where I found drawers full of bras, underwear, jeans, and sweatpants. Maiz and I were close friends, but if asked, I wouldn't know what size she wore. Maybe part of her guardian job was to know what size I would need for instances such as these.

My stomach clenched in pain, and I picked up my pace. I pulled out a bra, fresh undies, and a pair of jeans. I glanced at the price tag still attached and nearly fell over. One hundred and fifty dollars. Once Lake was born, I became a lot more money conscious, never wanting to spend extra on myself when I could put it toward him. After dressing, I checked myself in the mirror. A hundred fifty dollars' worth of curve-hugging denim looked good on me.

In the bathroom, I searched through the cupboards, establishing that Maiz had done a nice job supplying all the essentials, even remembering my much-needed hairdryer and straightener. There was no time to worry about that now—my stomach was threatening to eat my other organs if I didn't get moving. I washed my greasy face, brushed my grimy teeth, then detangled my matted hair, pulling it into a messy bun. I gave myself a final look in the mirror. Feeling satisfied, I stepped outside the bedroom.

Once in the hall, I heard multiple voices, most of them male. Hoping one of the voices was Lucian, I was sadly disappointed to find he wasn't among the group gathered in the kitchen and dining area. My sexy jeans were for nothing.

I wasn't disappointed for long, though. The kitchen was filled with hunky, muscular men, all gorgeous in their own way. Each one of them had a plate piled high with food. Four of them sat at the little dining table, and another three were at the kitchen island. My stomach whimpered loudly at the sight of food. A couple of the men who hadn't been engaged in conversation turned to look at me as if they could hear the rumbling.

Maiz was in the kitchen, flipping French toast on one large electric griddle and pancakes on another. Platters of food were arranged along the counter: biscuits and gravy, muffins, scrambled eggs, bacon, sausage, ham, and fresh fruit. You name it, it was there. Maiz's food skills put mine to shame.

"I didn't know you could cook," I said when I was close enough.

As every head turned to look at the newcomer, all conversation ceased. I felt my cheeks flush with the unwanted attention.

"Shit yes, I can cook. I just don't do it because I don't have to." She smiled. "But if I do say so myself, I'm pretty fuckin awesome at it."

All the men cheered "Hell, yeah" at the same time, making me jump.

Last night, I had said some harsh words. I still hadn't quite figured out how I felt about Maiz after her revelations. Any doubts I had about the status of our friendship were relieved when she came over and hugged me before returning to the stove. She turned to face the group between pancake flips.

"Guys, this is Rose. Fuck with her and I will destroy you. Rose," she continued, like she hadn't just threatened to squash seven giant men like bugs. "That's Kane, Zane, Cyrus, Stolly, Bram, Matt, and Adam."

Maiz pointed to each one as she called out their names. Each corresponding man nodded, then returned to whatever he'd been doing prior to the introduction.

The names were rattled off too quickly, leaving me blank as to who was who, except for Adam, the last guy at the island. The rhyming names, Zane and Kane, had to belong to the identical twins sitting at the table. They were identical in every sense. Same shade of blond hair pulled back into a tight ponytail, same shaggy beard, and the same crooked smile. The only distinguishing features were their eyes. One had a blue right eye with a brown left eye, the other a brown right eye and a blue left eye.

I wanted to ask for a repeat, but I knew better than to upset a room full of hungry men. Also, I didn't want to draw their attention again. It would be nice not to have all my actions scrutinized. If these guys were regulars around here, I'd catch on eventually.

"Shit Rose, you better grab a plate before your stomach gnaws its way out to get one itself. There's plenty here, so help yourself. If there's something you want that isn't here, you'll have to cook it yourself. I've had my fill of cooking for the day just trying to feed these ravenous beasts."

She gave me a hip check and pointed out the cupboard with the plates. I took out one of the larger plates, filling it with a little bit of everything, then grabbed a fork out of a flatware caddy sitting by the stove.

"Damn, that's a lot of food. I guess three days with no food will do that to ya."

"Yeah—wait. Three days?"

I stared at her blankly, trying to do the calculations in my head. Friday night to Saturday night to this morning, Sunday, was only a day and a half. I had lost a day somewhere. "Isn't it Sunday today?"

"No. Monday," she said, hesitating.

"Monday," I said a little too loudly, turning heads. "I slept through most of Saturday and Sunday? Maiz, I think you have more 'splainin to do."

"Oh, Rosey," she said in a nasal voice. "We'll talk later. Now, you feast like a queen."

It was comforting to be back on joking terms with her. What wasn't so comforting was that I had been away from Lake a lot longer than I thought. I was half tempted to go on a hunger strike until I got some assurance that he was alright. My stomach swore at me in the language of its people, and I knew I wasn't strong enough to do that. Besides, I'd be no good to him if I starved to death. I felt torn between eating and getting answers regarding where my son was.

"I promise he's fine," Maiz said.

She must have seen the worry on my face. No matter what, we had grown up together. I did trust her. Mostly.

She flipped a piece of French toast on top of my overflowing plate. My eyes had to be bigger than my stomach this morning, but with Lucian walking around with a loaded sleepy-hand, I never knew when I might need the extra calories.

The only open chair was at the kitchen island, next to the man named Adam. He smiled brightly at me when I sat next to him. It was an attractive smile, full of straight, white teeth, wrinkling the skin around his eyes.

His eyes were a captivating gold color that I'd never seen on any other person before. His short hair was spiked on top, then buzzed short and clean on the sides and back. It was a salt-and-pepper color, even though he didn't look older than twenty-five. Although Maiz and Lucian looked my age, we were all centuries apart. I considered what kind of special being Adam might be. The possibilities were endless.

"It's true what they say," he said, catching me mid-bite.

"Hmm?" I said, trying not to talk with my mouth full.

I may have sounded like a perpetual idiot with all my questions these days, but at least I could keep my manners.

"It's true what they say about beauty sleep. You look amazing this morning. I mean, I'm sure you look good all the time, but you look really good this morning."

His out-of-the-blue comment made me laugh. I had to cover my mouth with my free hand to keep food from spitting out. Even his flirting made him sound young. I hadn't heard a lame pick-up line like that in ages. Which instantly made me feel old. Maybe he wasn't like Maiz and Lucian. Maybe I'd found a normal person like me for once. That would be a breath of fresh air in a world full of the supernatural.

"I'm Adam, by the way. I'll be your chaperone today."

I swallowed. "My what?"

Damn, another stupid question.

"I'll be showing you around. I'll take you to town if you need anything, or we could lounge around your room if you beg me to. Or just ask me. Well, truthfully, you don't even need to ask. Just give me a wink. Or a nod. Or anything, really."

I was laughing again.

"You're a feisty one, aren't you?" I asked.

"I just like to see you smile. I know you've had a hard go of things, and you have a beautiful smile."

"Sorry to break your heart, but I'm going to pass on the bedroom. I just got out of bed. I'm in no rush to get back in it for anything."

Which was comical since just last night, I'd have used Adam's tactics to try to get Lucian in bed with me. Now, I had an extremely handsome man using all the tricks in his book, but I was too hooked on the one who was not interested. *Mental issues, party of one right here.* As Maiz would say, I needed to get my life straight. *Sound advice, if I do say so myself.* Not to mention, I had just gotten out of a marriage mere days ago.

He wagged his eyebrows at me. "It doesn't have to be a bed."

"Down boy," Maiz said from the other side of the kitchen.

I focused my attention back on my plate before I started thinking about Adam in my room. Where were all the old, unattractive guys? They must have been run off by all the hotties. Adam put a hand on mine.

"Did I go too far? I'm not trying to make you uncomfortable. Really. I'm just trying to have a little fun with you."

Oh yeah, I'd picked up on what kind of "fun" he was trying to have with me.

"If he oversteps," the man next to Adam added, "just punch him. Or let one of us know. We'll take care of him."

He gave Adam a stern look and punched him in the arm.

"Oh, no, I don't think I'll need to do that." I shuddered. "I've been on the receiving end, and I'd rather not do that to anyone else."

"Yeah, we heard," Adam said, giving the man next to him a withering look. "Lucian filled us in on your situation. I'm sorry for what you had to go through."

How dare Lucian tell other people about my business. It was not his place to give away that information. Add that to the mental list of things I had to be pissed about.

"How nice of him to fill everyone in on what's going on," I said through gritted teeth. "But I'm left completely in the dark. Where is Lucian, anyway?"

I was trying to keep a cool head, but I was failing miserably. No one appeared to notice except me. Or they did an excellent job of pretending.

"He's sleeping. He usually sleeps through the day."

Sleeps all day, up all night, yet I was the first to think he was a vampire. *What the hell ever.*

"You take your time. When you're finished, we'll head out. I've got some clothes for you to put on before we go."

I looked down at what I was wearing, silently asking what was wrong with what I already had on.

"No, you look great. I'd love to get you out of those clothes in a different sort of way, but if we're going out, you'll need something warmer."

Still not understanding why I would need warmer clothes to drive into town, I just nodded at him. Adam smiled, then excused himself, taking his empty plate. He took it to the sink, rinsed it off, and put it in the dishwasher. All without being told or asked to do so. Two women in the room, and he didn't expect Maiz or me to clean up after him. Before now, I hadn't known men could do that.

Adam reached an arm around Maiz, whispered something in her ear, then followed it up with a kiss on her cheek. On his way to the door, he gave me a devastating smile that almost made me second-guess my choice of not going to the bedroom. *Almost* being the keyword.

Only the twins were left at the table. They were huddled together in conversation. I had been so caught up with Adam, I hadn't even noticed any of the other guys leave. A whole pack of big, burly men had dispersed without raising a clatter. Marc, a regular-sized man, was noisy as hell wherever he went—stomping feet, slamming doors, banging cupboards. Not even Adam, as tall and built as he was, made a noise while I watched. They were like jaguars—stealthy, silent, and, if Lucian was trusting them to watch over me, deadly.

My plate was mostly empty, and my stomach had been tamed. I was feeling pleasantly plump. After so much food, I was tempted to lock myself in the bedroom alone and settle down with a good book. All those books by the fireplace, one of them had to be good. I didn't want to miss an opportunity to get more answers, though.

The twins approached me, standing side by side. I wondered if there was anyone within a fifty-mile radius who was shorter than six feet tall. The way they were standing, their brown eyes were on the same side.

"If anyone gives you any trouble," the one on the right said, "you let us know and we'll take care of 'em."

"Even Adam," the other said. "He can be a real shit bird. Every now and then he needs a good ass-whoopin'."

The serious look on their faces told me they'd done it before and would be happy to do it again.

"Thanks, uh, fellas."

They were intimidating, to say the least.

"Zane," the one on the right said.

"Kane," the other said.

"I'll try to remember that. You have any scars or piercings or anything that might help me remember who is who?"

They gave me a look that said I was an idiot for not being able to tell them apart.

"No," Zane said. "We're not able to have piercings with the change. I have a scar on my ass, though."

His face never changed. He wasn't being flirtatious or obscene. This was him seriously trying to help the dense lady who couldn't tell identical twins apart.

"Well, unless you want to whip out your ass cheek every time we meet, I don't think that will help."

"I can do that."

Alright, Zane was not modest. Judging by the looks of his stature, he didn't have a reason to be.

"No, no. That's okay. Maybe just consider a tattoo or something."

"You go ahead," Kane said. "I'll take care of your plate."

He grabbed my plate off the counter. Exactly like Adam, both men went to the sink, rinsed their plates, and added them to the dishwasher. Kane, or was it Zane, had even started the wash cycle. It was a beautiful sight to behold. They didn't stop there, either. Both men helped Maiz clean up the rest of the food, putting leftovers in storage containers, then in the fridge. They all worked together to wash what wouldn't fit in the dishwasher. *It's the damn twilight zone around here. Nothing is as it appears.* Who am I kidding? My life was the f-ing twilight zone.

As if on cue, Adam walked in with an armload of clothes. No, not clothes; snow gear.

"Maiz told me what size to get, so if they don't fit, blame her," Adam said, handing me a pair of snow pants.

Without question, I slipped them on right there by the kitchen island. Since I was still clothed, I didn't find it necessary to go to a different room to dress. Until I finished pulling them on and realized everyone was watching me. Adam was standing in front of me, a big smile on his face.

"I look forward to watching you take them off," he said.

In perfect gentleman fashion, he held open the coat for me to slip into. He put a hat on my head while I pulled on some gloves and, lastly, boots.

"You are one sexy lady, even in all those layers."

"He's right, Rose," Maiz said from behind me. "You can make anything look good. Try to have a good time today."

"Aren't you going with us?" I asked.

"Nope, just you and Adam."

I felt a twang of panic rise up. It was so strange that I was worried about being alone with someone like Adam, who didn't look like he would hurt a fly, but I was comfortable being alone with Lucian, a man of immeasurable power. Marc had really done a number on my mental stability. It must have shown on my face, too, because Maiz walked over to give me a hug.

"You'll be fine," she whispered in my ear. "He's a super sweet guy. Even so, he'll be dead before the tear hits the ground if he hurts you in any way. I know I haven't been truthful lately, but you can trust me on this one."

She pointed to the twins. I caught both Zane and Kane giving Adam a "be on your best behavior or you'll regret it" look. It even scared me a bit.

Outside, I looked for the car, but there wasn't one. Adam stopped next to a group of snowmobiles, then grabbed a helmet off the handlebar. Although I grew up in the Midwest, where wintertime snowmobiling was common, I'd never been on one myself. Not knowing what to do next, I stood there like an idiot, twiddling my thumbs. Adam plopped the helmet on his head. Turning toward me, he flipped the visor up, his face visible through the opening.

"What's up?" he asked.

"I don't know if you think I'm gonna drive one of those, cause I can't. I've never been on one. I've been told I can barely drive a car properly, so this might not be the best idea."

Images of me crashing and burning were running through my head. I couldn't help it.

"My day just got even better," he said, grabbing a helmet off another sled. "Put this on. You'll ride with me."

I took the helmet from him. Shoving it on my head, I immediately felt claustrophobic. My breath came in short, raspy gasps. I tried to concentrate on breathing slower in the tight space, which only made it worse. I flipped open the visor, taking deep, icy air into my lungs.

"You okay over there?" a voice boomed through my helmet.

"Who's there," I yelped, looking around.

"It's me, Adam. We have Bluetooth." He was sitting on the snowmobile, giving me a little wave when I looked his way. "You were huffing and puffing right into the mic."

"Oh, sorry. I never knew how small these things were. I'm suffocating in here."

"You get used to it. If you're more comfortable with the visor up, you can leave it, but your face might freeze. You still want to go?"

Nodding, I climbed on behind him. I wrapped my arms around his waist, and we started forward. He wasn't lying. We weren't moving more than five minutes when I couldn't feel my nose anymore. My eyeballs felt like they had been replaced with ice cubes. I closed the visor, trusting Adam that I would, hopefully, get used to it.

Surprisingly enough, I did trust him. What Maiz said before we left may have played a role in that. There was a goodness about him. He seemed honorable. Immature, but honorable. I felt safer than I had in a long time. Even if I was on the back of a death machine that could crash and burn me alive, or crush me like a bug, or cut me in two. Something told me he would pee to extinguish the fire, hulk it to pull the machine off me, or sew me back together if he had to.

We rode through the snowy landscape, trees flanking us, for several miles before we came to a road. Adam didn't follow any tracks, and he didn't use a map—he just knew the way. I'd still have been lost out there if Lucian hadn't found me.

Slowing down, Adam pointed out a herd of bison at the side of the road, standing near an iced-over river. I watched as one of the bison stuck his head in the snow and rutted around in search of food. Others of varying sizes mimicked his example. Some came up chewing their prize, and all came up covered in snow dust. Life was tough out here. I took back my previous statements about wanting to be an animal.

We cruised along a while longer. A smell, like rotten eggs, permeated my helmet. At first, I thought it had come from Adam, but then the smell got stronger and I knew that wasn't from anything living. So strong, my eyes began to water in the locked-in little housing of the helmet. I blinked rapidly, trying to blow the smell away with my lashes.

"What is that smell? I can taste it it's so bad," I said trying to breath as little as possible.

"Soda Butte," Adam said, pointing to a snow-covered mound. "The stink concentrates close to the ground this time of year. Don't worry, it'll pass once we get around the curve up here."

"What's a Soda Butte?"

"Fumarole. It's like an exhaust pipe."

I still was unsure what he was talking about, but I was relieved when it was far behind us. With any luck, that'd be the only stinky butte around. Adam pointed again, and I prepared to hold my breath. This time, it was a pack of wolves. Five that I could see, strolling next to the road. They were larger than I expected, kings of this snow-covered land. Fierce and powerful, deadly enough to take on a one-ton bison. Adam and I wouldn't stand a chance against them.

"What are you doing?" I asked as he pulled the sled to the side of the road. "Is this safe?"

We were parked twenty feet behind the pack—the closest I've ever been to a dangerous animal. I didn't plan on getting any closer. Adam had other ideas. Taking his helmet off, he climbed off the sled. I remained where I was. He smiled at me, inducing a relaxing effect on my tense body. Then he howled. *Yes, howled.* A beautiful cry from deep inside his throat that sounded more animal than human. It must have taken him years to perfect it.

The wolves turned to face us, eyeing us suspiciously at first, smelling the air. Having recognized that it was safe, they trotted over to us, tails wagging. My jaw nearly hit the seat of the sled when Adam crouched to bump heads with one of the wolves.

Larger than the others, its golden eyes stood in stark contrast to its fluffy, black fur coat. The rest of the pack made happy whining noises while they licked his face. It was adorable and terrifying all at the same time.

Adam extended his arm, motioning for me to join him. Now, as a child, I had a fascination with wolves. They were majestic, smart, and lethal. Why else would they be considered an apex predator? Cuddly to strangers, not so much. I shook my head to decline the offer. I'd much rather stay in one piece. He pushed to his feet.

He carefully removed my helmet and set it aside, freeing up both hands to yank me off the seat. He put an encouraging arm around my back, nudging me forward and keeping me from bolting until we stood in front of the pack. With his free hand, he grabbed my wrist, holding it out for the small posse of wolves to smell. I held my breath, waiting for one of them to bite my hand off at the wrist. When two of the wolves, smaller than the rest but nonetheless frightening, bared their teeth with hackles raised, I nearly jumped out of my skin.

A deep, menacing growl emanated from one of the pack. I tried to back away, but Adam's grip tightened around me. While I was worried for my own safety, I was just as concerned about Adam's life.

Thoughts of his demise at the hands of a group of angry men, Maiz, and a demonic Lucian flashed before my eyes.

I didn't want him to be ripped limb from limb, or flipped inside out, or whatever Lucian could do with his little dreamland magic. Since I hadn't learned the extent of Lucian's powers, I wasn't certain about the magnitude of his abilities. I'd only seen him do good thus far. Some of it *really* good.

Thoughts of Lucian made me smile, distracting me from the situation at hand. A hand that was still shoved right in the faces of growling beasts. Close enough that I could reach out and polish a tooth. I looked up at Adam. He was so handsome and sweet and funny, and growling. It wasn't any of the wolves growling, it was Adam.

Adam. A sinister sound that made the hair on my arms stand up.

The black wolf turned on the two smaller ones, fangs snapping, spittle flying. He must have been the alpha, and he was showing his dominance over his subordinates.

"That's Slade, the alpha. He's letting them know you're okay," Adam said. "Those two girls can be real bitches. See what I did there?"

I was too concerned about what was happening to laugh at his quip.

The two females were now down on the ground, licking at Slade, who stood over them with his mouth pulled back in a snarl. Side note: I definitely took back the thing about wanting to be an animal. Slade stepped away, allowing them to get to their feet, more subdued than they'd been minutes before. They backed away from the rest of the group. I didn't get the same accepting licks, whines, and tail wags from them, but they weren't ready to pounce. Or the wolf version of pounce.

Adam finally loosened his grip on me, bending to mingle with them. I bent down as well, reaching out a tentative hand to touch Slade. His coat was thick and luxurious. I had an absurd need to rub my cheek against it. That didn't seem wise, so I stuck to rubbing my fingers through it.

"I could use Slade as a body pillow. He's so soft," I said.

Slade made some wolfy noises, and I kid you not, he winked at me.

"Gross," Adam said. "I'm not going to tell her that."

He pulled his coat sleeve back, checking the large watch face.

"We should be getting back. I was told not to keep you after dark."

"Captain Lucian's orders, I'm sure," I said, though I didn't really need to ask this time.

I already knew who was running the show around here. Lucian had the gall to kidnap me, threaten me, and now control my every move.

I planted my hands on my hips. "I'm not ready to leave. We've been out for, what, two hours? Isn't there more we could see? Please Adam, pleeeeaase?"

"I'm. Not. So. Suuurrre," Adam said, but I was giving him my best puppy dog eyes. "Oh, alright."

Slade growled at him and gave him a little bark.

"I'm an adult." Adam said. "You need to let me make my own decisions. I'll deal with anything that comes down the line."

In answer, Slade growled more but it was softer this time. As if he got Adam's point and was trying to reason with the man.

"Pop, we're all out here. We can keep her safe. The girl deserves a little fun, doesn't she?"

This was getting weirder by the second. Adam was having a full conversation with a wolf. People personified their dogs all the time, but Slade appeared as though he understood what Adam was saying. And vice versa.

"Alright, my lovely lady, ever seen Old Faithful? Or we could go see Steamboat. A lot of people don't know that she's the largest geyser in the world. She just isn't as famous since she can go decades without erupting. Mammoth is closer, though." He stopped to think about what the best landmark might be to visit.

"Old Faithful. As in Yellowstone's Old Faithful? As in Yellowstone National Park in Wyoming?"

I can't believe I hadn't figured that out by now. Bison, wolves, and deer should have been a major hint.

"Uh, yeah, *that* Yellowstone. I thought you knew."

Of course not. Why would anyone tell me anything? I might freak out. I might protest. Easier to just make me go to sleep and take me across the country, far, far away from everything I'm familiar with. Oh, and let's not forget, let's take her son and hide him away and not tell her where he is, either. Yeah, I'm just supposed to assume he's okay. I'd like to believe that Maiz wouldn't let anything happen to him. She'd known him his entire life. She was as protective of him as she was of me.

"Nope, no one filled me in about where we were. Is there anything else I should know?"

Adam looked nervous. He glanced at his wolf friends. None of them made a sound. They all looked very serious. To be fair, wolves always looked serious. Not like some dogs that gave the appearance of smiling.

"Well," he said, turning to me. "I'm not sure what I should and shouldn't say."

"You mean what you *can* and *can't* say, according to Lucian. Come on, Adam, everyone is treating me like I'm made of glass. I'm not going to shatter if you say the wrong thing. I just want to know what the hell is happening."

"Well," he said, looking back at the wolves, "this is my pack."

My brain was trying to connect the dots. There was something I was supposed to see, but I either didn't want to know the truth, or I was too slow. I should have had more coffee. A normal morning consisted of four, five, or ten cups of coffee. Love me some coffee. Okay, I was getting off subject, and now I really wanted coffee.

"Okay. That's not exactly what I meant by tell me something. So, you're like a biologist? Are you one of those wolf tracker guys? I had an article pop up on my news feed once, about how badly Yellowstone suffered when the wolves were killed off."

"No, not a scientist." He hesitated. "I'm a wolf."

Dots were starting to connect. I just couldn't see the bigger picture.

"A wolf. Oh, you're like Mowgli. Abandoned as a baby, raised by wolves, and now you're a part of their pack?"

"Not that either. I'm a wolf of the 'were' persuasion. Thought you'd get that since you've dipped your toe in the world of supernaturals."

Dipped a toe? Someone had flung my entire body into the pool. Pool didn't do it justice. I'd been shoved into something bigger. Something with monsters. I was in Loch Ness, and Nessie was nipping at my toes.

"Rose," Adam interrupted my thoughts, "are you okay? Your eye is doing this weird, twitchy thing."

"Absolutely." My voice came out in a high screech. "Yes. I'm fine. Great. You're a werewolf. No biggie. Ya know what though, you're right, we should go back."

I wasn't sure why I was so freaked out by this new information. Lucian being a dream god, Maiz being a guardian angel of death. Those didn't scare me. Probably because I'd never known they existed. Werewolves, on the other hand, always get bad press. In movies, TV series, and books, they were always the bad guys. The full moon rises, and out comes the big bad wolf, ready to eat your face.

I stood to leave, but Adam grabbed my hand.

"Rose, I can sense your fear. I've had ample opportunity to hurt you if I wanted. You're surrounded by other werewolves, and you're just fine."

Of course, his pack is a pack of werewolves.

"I've been petting a person? That's not weird at all."

"Not just any person, Slade is my dad. By were law, a back scratch and an ear rub are equal to marriage. You're my new step-mommy!"

"What? No. I didn't. This can't be."

"I was kidding. Wanted to get your mind off the whole werewolf thing. I'd say I was successful judging by the way your fear level dropped and your 'oh shit, I messed that one up' level shot up. Seriously, I don't want you to be afraid. I'm still just lil ol' Adam, but if you're too uncomfortable with me now, I'll take you back to the house. I can even show you how to drive the sled, and you can leave me out here if that eases your soul. Just say the word."

As my guardian, Maiz would have known who and what Adam was. I might have been mad at her for a lifetime of lies, but I still felt I could trust her trust in Adam.

"No, I think I'm alright," I said, hesitantly sitting back down. "It's just gonna take a real hot minute to get used to the fact that there's more to this world than I've been led to believe."

I absently started to pet Slade. Who came to lay next to me. Oops. Joke or no joke, I didn't want to get myself into some sort of wolfie arrangement I didn't know about.

"Ever hear the story about how werewolves came to be?" Adam asked.

"I only know what I've seen in movies or read in fairy tales."

"This is the story my grandmother used to tell us at bedtime. A few centuries ago, there was a king named Lycaon. He was a cocky prick who wanted to test Zeus' omniscience by killing one of his own sons and feeding his flesh to the almighty king of the gods. Zeus, being Zeus, knew of Lycaon's treachery instantly, and he was pissed. The only thing more famous than Zeus is Zeus' anger. He planned to kill the evil king and all fifty of his sons, damning their souls to the worst parts of Tartarus, but Gaia stepped in. She had convinced the god-king to let them live out their lives as wolves. Lycaon and his sons owed their lives to Gaia, and they spent their time serving her any way she wished. As time went on, favor grew with the goddess, and she allowed the descendants of Lycaon to transform from wolf to human so that they could once again walk among man. To this day, we still worship the beautiful, incredible, amazing, and super cool Gaia for what she did for us."

"Oh wow, she must be really wonderful."

"She might be listening," he whispered to me, looking around. "My Grams was more eloquent in her storytelling," he continued in a normal voice. "She wouldn't have said cocky prick, but the meaning's the same."

I laughed. "Don't underestimate your magical storytelling powers. What I'm getting is that you all can change whenever you want. You're not cursed to change with the moon like most stories suggest. So, can I see it? The change?"

"One thing the movies got right, is that we're naked when in wolf form. I'm happy to show you, but I'll end up naked. You sure you want to see that?"

I was conflicted. On the one hand was the opportunity to see a real-life werewolf transformation. On the other hand, looking at a naked Adam didn't seem like a good idea. He was a cutie, but he wasn't the one I wanted to see naked. I shook my head in answer.

"If you change your mind, I would be more than happy to get naked for you. I mean, show you my wolf," he said with a lopsided grin. "Now, if we're still planning on playing hooky, then we should make it count. We'll head over to Old Faithful, making a stop at the Midway Basin. You've got to see the Grand Prismatic at sunset, it's unbelievable." He stuck his hand out to me. "C'mon, let's blow this popsicle stand."

Slade growled at Adam, baring his teeth again.

"It's fine. You know he can't kill me, only royally maim me. Good thing you have other sons to give you heirs." Slade growled louder. "I'm kidding. Mostly. Later Pops. Fellas. Star, Sky, I'll tell Zane and Kane you said hello, and let them know how accommodating you were to our guest."

I'm no expert in the field of wolfonese, but I'd bet my life all the growling and barking the two females were doing was their way of cursing Adam the F out.

***

After exploring the Midway geyser basin and watching Old Faithful's eruption, we were seated inside the Old Faithful Inn. A sign on the door said it was closed for the season, but evidently, that didn't apply to the year-round supernatural residents.

The inn was built from large pine logs, giving it a rustic charm. Taking off the bulky snow gear, we sat before a giant, four-sided stone fireplace that was the centerpiece of the lobby. A warm fire crackled behind the safety screen, slowly taking the frostbite out of my fingers. The sun had gone down an hour ago, taking the temperature with it. It had to be twenty below out there.

A short, pretty woman with strawberry blond hair, brought us some cups filled with coffee. Her eyes were a dazzling shade of turquoise, and her pupils were slit like a cat's. I'd think she was a werecat if there were such a thing. Then again, who knew what other magical creatures existed? The deep cut of her shirt told me she wasn't wearing a bra. I could have figured that out from the nipple in my face when she practically threw a cup at me.

She grabbed Adam's hand when he reached for his cup, bending close to whisper something in his ear and giving him a full-frontal view down her shirt. Releasing the cup to him, she gave me a mean girl cold shoulder, strutting away to the dining room behind us.

"She should have been more obvious," I said, nudging Adam with my elbow. I'm not sure you got the message."

"Ember has never been subtle in her advances. I gave up telling her no because she just gets more aggressive."

"Why aren't you interested? She's cute. She brings you stuff. She's got perky breasts."

"You saw that, huh?"

"Anyone in eyeshot could see those things when she bent down for you. What's the matter, she's not the same religion?"

"Something like that. She's a Caldera."

He said it very matter-of-factly, like I should know exactly what that meant.

"You're forgetting that I'm new here, and I have absolutely no idea what Caldera means."

"Right. A Caldera is a crater formed from a collapsed volcano. Ember is a type of demon that resides around volcanoes and calderas all over the world. That's how they got their name."

"So, we're near a volcano?"

"Babe, we're sitting on one. Yellowstone is a supervolcano. It's a big ol' cauldron of lava and primal power that draws from the core. It might not be the biggest one in the world, but there are more geothermal features here than anywhere else on the planet, all of which are just churning with power. The amount of power in the air is tangible to those of us who can sense it. That's why you were brought here. Anyone looking for you shouldn't be able to sense you over what's already in the air."

Adam was a cauldron of information that was boiling over. He had given me more info in the last few hours than Maiz and Lucian had in the last few days. Decades even. I was going to milk this for all I could get out of him. The hardest part would be deciding where to start. I didn't want him to shut down before I got real answers. Go big or go home.

"Why am I being hidden? From whom? And is that why Maiz has been guarding me for my whole life?"

"Shit."

I could tell by the way he took a sip of his coffee and desperately scanned the room that he was trying to figure out a way to avoid my questions.

"Please, Adam, I'm totally in the dark here. Please, please, please. I'll keep everything you tell me in confidence."

"When you give me that look, I understand why he's so in love with you."

"Who's in love with me?"

"Dammit, never mind that. I'm gonna get my ass reamed enough the way it is." He took another sip of his coffee. "I'm not very high on the totem pole. I don't know everything, but I'll tell you what I do know. You're some sort of supreme power, and there are some very bad people after you because of it."

"Supreme power? I couldn't even fight back against my husband when he almost killed me."

"It's locked up inside you. I can't tell you anything more about that or about who's after you, other than that they're close. We were told to keep you safe at all costs."

I slowly shook my head and took a sip of my coffee.

"You're handling this rather well," he said, one eye pinching shut as though he didn't believe what he was saying.

"Why not? I was kidnapped by a dream god. My best friend is an immortal guardian that was reborn for me. I'm sitting here, drinking coffee that was served to me by a demon, and talking to a werewolf. Why would it freak me out to discover that I'm hiding a superpower? I don't think anything will surprise me ever again. Looking on the bright side, if I were a normal person, I wouldn't have Maiz, or you, and there's no way in hell a guy like Lucian would be interested in someone like me."

"Don't sell yourself short." He took my hand and squeezed it gently. "You are remarkable, power or no power. I can see that even though I just met you."

"Thank you. You're too sweet. Let's talk about something else. Tell me more about demons. From the short time Ember was over here, she seemed okay, if maybe a little pushy. And they must be peaceful if you are all living here together."

"There are different kinds of demons belonging to different pantheons. I'm sure you've heard of the demons in Christianity that work for the devil. Same thing. They were created to do the dirty work. The Caldera demons were created to protect the primal power. For the most part, we all get along, but it wasn't always that way."

He told me about how, in the early 1900s, there was a war between the wolves and the Calderas. No one could agree on what had really started the war. The wolves said it was because the demons were eating their pups, while the demons said it was because the wolves were destroying the land of their goddess. For the next couple of decades, the two species fought until all the wolves that lived here were either killed or scared off.

It took almost seventy years for them to broker peace. Wolves started coming back, slowly. Testing the waters, so to speak. Now, twenty years later, they all lived together in harmony. Sort of. Some of the parties still felt a lot of contempt over the war, while others believed it all to be in the past.

"I was born here after the reintroduction, to purebred parents," he said. "My parents are the type who let bygones be bygones, but they think we need to keep within our species.

Others have a more lackadaisical approach, a kind of 'love the one you're with' attitude. So much so that they, how do I want to say this—" He stopped to think, then said, "Crossbreed?"

"Demons and wolves can mate and procreate? Are there babies from these unions?"

"Yes. Demon dog is the most common name. They have it really tough because they aren't full-blooded wolf, or a pure demon. Being called a dog when you're a wolf is a derogatory name. Some packs will cast out a wolf that gets involved with a demon, or they may keep the wolf but not allow the pups to be raised in the pack. The demons aren't as harsh, but the demon dogs can never move up in the clan. My pack is pretty lax about it. We take no issue with demons, or pups that come from the coupling. It's just that my parents don't allow me to couple with a demon."

"Because you're at the bottom of your pack?"

"Something like that," he said it sort of under his breath.

"What if a werewolf and a human have a baby? Is that even possible?"

"There's a fifty-fifty chance of having a normal child, or a full-blooded wolf."

"Why isn't it like that when a demon and a wolf get together?"

"I guess 'cause a were and a demon are both supernaturals. I don't really know. Do I look like a scientist to you?"

I laughed. "Sorry, this is all so interesting. There's so much to learn. I feel like a little kid with my curiosity. Thank you for answering my questions and spending the day with me."

He was still holding my hand. It felt so natural that I didn't even notice until he picked it up off the armrest and placed a tender kiss on my knuckles.

"We should get you back."

We finished our coffees, and Adam took the empty cups to toss in a nearby trash can. I stood to don my snow gear, and a flash of strawberry blond caught my eye. Ember had cornered Adam by the trash. She was standing on tiptoe, arms wrapped around his neck, and her body pressed as close to his as she could possibly get. Her slim figure melded with his.

I thought she was whispering in his ear again until Adam tried to push her away, but his earlobe was caught between her teeth. Once she released him from her grip, he trotted back to our seats. I was completely dressed and ready to go.

"Let's get out of here," he said, scooping up his clothes.

Clearly eager to be on his way, he hopped and bounced into his gear all the way to the door. It was quite comical to see someone like Adam, so confident, so flirtatious, running from a tiny little thing like Ember. I jogged along behind him, snickering all the way back to the sled. Then the laughter died. The downside of not being near a big city with all its light pollution was that even with the light of the moon, it was darker than pitch out here.

Adam drove in silence. I figure he was using his wolfie senses to watch for anything that might bound out in front of us. It was a long ride back to the cabin, leaving me too much time to think.

Breaking the rules just to irritate Lucian had seemed like a good idea at the time, but now I was worried about what the consequences might be. Yeah, sure, I'd only ever seen him do good things with his god power, but that didn't mean he couldn't do harm. He wasn't a doctor. He hadn't taken an oath to do no harm. I'd seen the beginning stages of his anger, and that was scary enough. I might have been safe because of my supreme gift, but Adam wouldn't be so lucky.

Lucian was waiting on the porch when Adam parked the sled. My heart dropped to my feet when I saw him. I wasn't sure if it was from how hot-looking he was in his jeans and dark-colored cardigan, unbuttoned at the top to show off a bit of chest, or if it was from how hot-physically he was. The temperature had to be below zero, yet I could see steam rising from him. He was steaming mad, alright, *literally*. Aside from the steam, he stood frozen solid.

"Let me talk," Adam said into the headset before pulling off his helmet.

I gave a nod before removing mine.

While Lucian stood watching us in silence, Adam dismounted and held out a hand to help me. I wanted him to hold my hand as we approached our fate, but he dropped it as soon as I was free of the sled. The crunching of the snow under my feet sounded like firecrackers going off with each step. We stopped just in front of Lucian, and fury sparked in his red eyes. Rivulets of lava flowed down his face.

Oh crap, his demon was showing.

"You had specific orders to be back before dark." His voice had taken on a lower pitch, dripping with malevolence. "Do you want to live long enough to have pups?"

Obviously, a rhetorical question, but I could tell Adam was gearing up to say some smart-ass comment. I would never forgive myself if something happened to Adam on account of my childish whims to rebel.

"It was my fault." I said before Adam could get his last words out.

Lucian turned his devil eyes on me. I felt like one of the females Slade had turned on. If I were a wolf, I'd be on the ground right now, whining for mercy.

"I can handle this, Rose," Adam said.

The carefree, frisky wolf was gone. The man before me was on edge, ready to attack. Adam was an ant compared to Lucian. I couldn't let him get squished. Turning towards Adam, I tugged on him to face me and grabbed his hands for extra effect.

"Please don't do anything stupid," I said, my eyes pleading with him. "Please. For me."

He straightened, notching his head up, holding on to his honor and dignity. Dropping one of my hands, he turned back to

Lucian, casting his eyes to the ground. I held my breath, waiting for what would come out of his mouth.

"I'm sorry, Lucian. You did give me orders, and I went against them. I will take whatever punishment you deem appropriate. But you should know, you also told me to do what she wanted, and so I did."

The lava on Lucian's face flared. Adam had him on a technicality, and there wasn't anything he could do about it. A rumble came from deep in Lucian's chest. He looked in disgust at our still clasped hands.

"You may go, wolf. Your pack is waiting for you."

Thank goodness, the worst was over. Adam would be okay, and I came out the other side a little smarter.

Adam leaned down to kiss my forehead.

"Good luck," he whispered in my ear.

He went into the cabin without another word, or glance, at Lucian. Okay, so maybe the worst was not behind me.

I kept my head bent. "Thank you for not punishing him."

"I may have let him go, but don't think he'll get away so easily with his pack."

My head snapped up. "But it wasn't his fault. Slade let us go earlier."

"Slade is hoping his son will make good choices. Adam went against orders. He isn't high enough in the ranks to make those kinds of decisions. When you go against the alpha, you get your ass chewed. Enough about that dumb dog. What were you thinking? I know you don't understand how dangerous it is for you right now, but you cannot be running around at all hours of the night."

"If you would treat me like an equal and explain what the hell is going on, then maybe I would show some better judgment."

Lucian raised an eyebrow. I knew what he was thinking. He was thinking I used to put up with Marc telling me what I could and couldn't do without saying a word against him. I'd just bowed to his every whim. Now I was feeling bold enough to step up against a Greek god. He was probably wondering what had happened during our outing that had emboldened me so much.

The lava dried up, reabsorbing into his skin, while icy blue snakes slithered through the red in his eyes, turning them back to their mesmerizing shade.

"What's going on between you and the wolf?"

"Nothing. He was a friend to me today. Why does it matter to you, anyway? You've made it perfectly clear that you're not interested in me. You keep me asleep instead of spending time with me or talking to me. You push me away every chance you get."

Lucian hauled me against him, his body radiating heat, melting away any indignation I had left. He kissed me deeply. Passionately.

"Lucian," I said breathlessly, pushing him away. "You can't just kiss me and expect me to forget everything. If you're only doing this to keep me from going to Adam, or anyone else for that matter, then you can just stop. It isn't fair to me when you run hot and cold."

Hard as it was, I stepped away from him. I wanted to be close to him, to be with him so stinking bad it hurt. My body was screaming in outrage, but I had to respect my feelings. *Myself.*

He shoved his hands in his pockets, making him look almost human. "I can't help but have feelings for you after so much time together. But when men and women get involved, it makes them weak. Vulnerable. You're a distraction. A gorgeous, wonderful distraction. If I'm distracted, you can be hurt by the forces that are after you." He closed the small distance I had put between us, touching his forehead against mine. "I—care for you."

Care didn't feel like the word he was going for, but it seemed as though he was too scared to say anything stronger than that. I wondered if Lucian was who Adam had referred to with the *love* comment.

"I think the wol—Adam, talks too much," he said in answer to my musings.

He lifted his head, reverting to the proud Greek god who wouldn't be taken down by some measly little feelings. That was the end of the conversation. I had no say in the matter. I made him weak and therefore he needed to keep his distance. Too bad I didn't see it that way.

Placing my hands on each side of his cheeks, I pulled him down to kiss me again.

"I care about you, too," I said, still holding him close. "If you would just let me in, we could work together. You know where to find me if you change your mind."

I stepped past him and let myself into the house. He made no move to follow me, only stood there looking up to the heavens. I couldn't even begin to guess what he might be thinking.

In the kitchen, Maiz was flipping burgers. Wow, twice in one day—where was a camera when I needed it? One of the men I had been introduced to earlier in the day was standing in front of the sink. By the looks of the stack of plates he was rinsing and loading into the dishwasher, I had just missed a full house.

They must have been in a hurry to rush out since they hadn't rinsed their plates. Was that because Adam had shown up and they had to inflict their punishment on him? I didn't want to think about that. It was because of me that he was in this mess. Even though I was aware that Adam had ultimately made his own decision, I vowed to never again risk someone else's punishment as a result of my actions.

Maiz turned toward me, waving the spatula in greeting. "Fresh bison burgers," she said. "They are fuckin' awesome. Make yourself cozy by the fire. Cyrus will bring a plate over."

I made myself comfortable on the side of the couch closest to the crackling fire. It didn't hit me how hungry I was until Cyrus stood beside me, holding a plate piled high with fries and a giant burger. Taking the plate, I thanked him, and he gave me a warm smile. Like everyone else, Cyrus was tall and muscular, but he looked older than the rest. His hair was varying shades of grey and white, and there were fine lines around his eyes and mouth. Though seasoned, he wasn't any less handsome than the younger men.

From behind me, Maiz wrapped a blanket around my shoulders. She jumped over the couch to flop down beside me. Always a kid, just like me.

"How did it go today?" she asked. "How was Adam?"

Back in the kitchen, I could see Cyrus had paused, waiting to hear my answer. He must have been part of the pack, or at the very least, a wolf. I'd better watch what I said. I didn't want to inadvertently add fuel to the fire.

"He was great. Took me around the park. Showed me some of the sights. I didn't want to come back right away, and he humored me. It was fun."

"That's it?"

I jerked my head toward the kitchen, indicating we had a third party in this conversation.

"Hey Cyrus," Maiz called to him. He straightened from leaning on the counter. "I'm not gonna need anything else tonight. You're free to change."

I waited until Cyrus was out of the room before I asked, "Change?"

I had a pretty good idea what she meant, thanks to Adam, but there was a chance she meant to change clothes. Like a human would do.

"Slade told us that Adam filled you in on the werewolves of the park."

I nodded.

"Sorry, I didn't tell you. I was a little worried you'd lock yourself in that thing they call a bedroom. I thought some fresh air and freedom would be good for you."

"I think Adam was the right one to break it to me. It helped to meet the pack, and he was so sweet and understanding of my hesitation. So, Slade is the alpha of all the wolves?"

"One of them. There are a few different packs in the park. He is the shit, though, and so freaking hot. Shit, they're all eye candy. Must be that high-protein diet. Does a body good." She stopped. Lost in thoughts of bodies, probably. "Tell me more about your day with Adam. Isn't he yummy?"

"I wasn't kidding when I said he's great. A little flirty, but not pushy about it."

"That's not what I asked. I asked, 'Isn't he yummy.' Wouldn't you love to just run your hands down that body? I've seen him after a change. They're naked, ya know. All I have to say is he will make some woman very happy."

She made some gestures with her hands, showing length and girth. I choked on a fry. *Yowza.*

"Jeez Maiz, leave a little to be discovered." I laughed. How I'd missed laughing with my bestie.

"Oh, so you plan to do some exploring. Get it, girl!"

"No, no, no, that's not what I meant. I should have said imagination."

"Mmhmm."

We both laughed. This felt like the old us.

"Maiz," I said seriously. "I'm sorry about what I said. Everything is changing and everyone is being so cryptic."

"You have nothing to apologize for. I would have told you sooner if I could have. You need to know that our friendship was not a lie. I'm closer to you than any of my other sisters."

"You have sisters?"

"A lot of them. And brothers. My family is huge."

When we were younger, Maiz had been raised as an only child by a single mother. There'd never been any mention of grandparents, uncles, aunts, or cousins. Maiz had told me once in grade school that her dad had run off with another woman while her mom was still pregnant. My parents said it would be rude to bring it up if Maiz didn't want to talk about it, so I never brought it up again. Neither did she. Maiz's mother, Sheri, still lived in the same house, only a couple blocks from my own childhood home in South Dakota. Did Sheri know the truth? Or was she living a secret life like Maiz?

"You've met one of them," Maiz said before I could ask about her mom.

"I have? How? When? Who is it?"

"It's Vex."

"Vex? My sister's best friend, Vex? The annoying girl my annoying sister hung out with that drove us crazy?" Maiz was nodding at me. "What the hell? I never would have put that together. Was it hard to keep it a secret when you were both at the house at the same time? Did you know you were sisters then? And if she's your sister, does that mean she's a guardian like you? Is she guarding Rae? Oh crap, is Rae in danger?"

"Whoa girl, slow your roll. You don't need to worry about Rae. She's safe. Although that boyfriend of hers is kind of a high-class dickwad. He reminds me of Marc. The way he talks to her."

That was quite worrisome to me. It wasn't written in stone that her boyfriend would follow the same path as Marc, but if something happened to her, I might have to kill someone.

"I've already told Vex what happened to you. She's keeping a close eye on douche Dan."

"You girls aren't very good at guarding us against dickwads."

"We aren't supposed to interfere unless it involves your safety. Even then, we need to get clearance to act. Hierarchy and all that bullshit. I brought it to the higher ups multiple times to let me do something about Marc, but it was never bad enough. Then when I saw your eye, I thought that would be it. That's why I left after I saw you that day. I needed the all clear to kill him. If I had it my way, he would've been long dead before that night he lost it.

Other than that, I can only encourage you. I tried to tell you at the beginning that I didn't like Marc. He was an arrogant prick."

"Oh sure, turn it back around on me."

In my heart, I knew she was right. I had ignored her warnings about Marc. Worse yet, I'd ignored my own instincts. I was like a frog in hot water. By the time it started to boil, I didn't even notice.

"Look around you now, you're surrounded by fine ass men that I very much approve of. Go get one. Or two. Take on the whole pack if you want."

"Maiz. I'm not that kind of girl."

"I'm just letting you know I advocate for all of these fine men. You don't want to get your freak on, then fine, go with one. I know Adam is way into you if he's willing to go against Lucian and his alpha to keep you out past curfew. If you're not into it, I'm in the room right next to you. You holler and I'll be right there to rip the pelt right off his furry ass."

That wasn't an image I wanted in my head. Adam was very attractive, and I was sure he'd be lots of fun in bed, but I felt protective of him, not sexual toward him.

"What about you?" I changed the subject. "Is there any of them you'd want to, you know?"

"Do the bump and grind with? Oh, girl, heck yes."

That opened a can of worms. I finished eating while she talked, and boy did she talk. She started by telling me about some of the other guys she had seen after "the change" and how impressive they were. It didn't matter if they were younger, older, tall, short, blond, or brown-haired, she was happy with anything.

It had obviously been too damn long since she'd had any D in the V. Her words, not mine. I knew that was a lie, she'd go on like this even if she'd had a roll in the hay yesterday. Maiz was the friskiest person I'd ever met.

Then she asked if I wanted to talk about that last night with Marc. I did, of course, because Maiz was my best friend, and I was used to telling her everything. I needed to get it off my chest. I'd always heard it was better to talk through things. Unburden yourself. Keeping it inside would only cause it to fester, pulling my mind to a dark place.

I'd been there, and it was a hard place to escape from. I'd only had myself to talk to for so long. I'd become an expert at being negative and making excuses. Something I needed to work on.

I told her everything. How his eyes dilated when he seemingly switched personalities. I told her what he'd said about feeling something taking over after a woman in his office touched him. That he looked like he was fighting with himself on whether to kill me or save me.

Maiz didn't make any other comments. She just listened, holding my hand for strength and nodding to let me know she was paying attention. When I finished, she hugged me.

"I'm so sorry I wasn't there for you," she said. "I got held up on Olympus trying to figure out what Lucian wanted with your blood. Time moves slower there. I will do everything I can to keep you safe now. Even if that means my life for yours. I love you, sister."

"I don't know what's going on, but I really hope it doesn't come to that. I need my sister for the rest of my life, however long that is. Before I drown us with tears, I need to shower. I can feel my feet again, and holy crap, do they feel disgusting. You might need to burn this blanket; it could be considered a biohazard. There's so much grease in my hair, I might spontaneously combust."

"Damn woman, I get it. Get the hell out of here."

"Even though you're a total fraud, I love you, too."

She smacked my butt as I walked past her. Typical Maiz.

Chapter 6

After a long, scalding hot shower, I felt like I had washed away all the remnants of that terrible night. Twirling my hair in a towel, I wrapped another around my body before leaving the attached bathroom. In my room, I was surprised to find Lucian lounging on my bed. I looked at the bedroom door that was still locked. Of course that wouldn't stop a dream God.

He was a vision with his tight, black t-shirt and jeans displaying his shipshape body. He smiled at me, and I felt inexplicably self-conscious. It would be pretty damn easy for him to give the loose cloth a yank, leaving me standing there in all my naked glory.

That's what I wanted, wasn't it? To have him. In my bed. Naked. Naked on top of me. *Crap*. The possibility left me suddenly lightheaded. He was too sexy, way too sexy for me. I was too broken. So not good enough for him.

I clung tighter to my cotton barrier.

"You're not broken," he said.

Getting off the bed, he pulled his shirt over his head, dropping it to the floor as he crossed to where I stood.

"Would you believe that you're too sexy for me?" he asked, pulling the towel from my hair. "I can prove it to you, if you'll let me."

Standing right in front of me, I tipped back my head and stared into his hungry eyes. *Be brave, Rose.*

"If you weren't brave, you wouldn't have made it this far," he said. "I may have healed your skin, but I can't heal your mind. That can be worse than any physical hurt. You're strong because you're still here. You're still functioning. You're still smiling."

His hands were running the length of my arms, stopping at my fists, which were still clenched in a bear hug around my chest. He loosened my grip with ease, and the towel fell to the floor. So much for making him work for it.

"I'm the weak one. I can't stay away from you. No matter how hard I try."

He walked around me, making me squirm at his inspection of my naked body.

"You are even more beautiful than I remember," he said.

I watched as he ran a finger along a stretch mark that ran from the middle of my side to the top of my hip bone. Then another line that ran from my belly button down to the top of my panty line, causing my stomach to flutter. Those marks had always embarrassed me. They were large, discolored, and ugly. Lucian used his finger to make me look back up at him, his pure black eyes looking back.

"You have nothing to be ashamed of. You brought a beautiful life into the world. Wear them proudly."

I reached out my hands and tentatively touched his chest, his defined muscles twitching beneath my questing fingers. Looking away long enough to unbutton his jeans, which were now a little tighter with the bulge that pushed against them, I found that he had not six but eight distinct abs. I ran my fingers along each one, making him shiver with my touch. Moving lower, I found him at full attention. It was impressive.

The touch to his most sensitive area sent him into overdrive. He easily lifted me into his arms. Wrapping myself around him, I kissed his neck. He gently placed me on the bed, straightening up long enough to snap his fingers, making the last of his clothes disappear.

"That's a handy party trick," I said.

He climbed onto the bed, positioning himself over me. My thoughts went back to the last time a man was over me like this.

"Your heart is racing," Lucian said.

"Just having a moment of déjà vu. Nothing to worry about," I said, the uncertainty coming through my words.

"I'll just have to prove to you that I plan to only treat your body as a temple."

He moved down the bed only to kiss his way back, starting at the tip of my right foot. Kisses that were delicate and caring. I wouldn't have been sure he was there if I hadn't felt the heat of his breath on my skin. He stopped only when he reached the top of my leg, to place an extra-special kiss at my pleasure center, before moving back to repeat the process on my other leg.

This time, when he reached the top, he spent more time playing with me. His tongue delved in and out, making me want to scream in ecstasy. He teased and played until I hit my peak. Stars flashed in front of my eyes. I knew he was a talented kisser, but damn.

I was still coming down from my euphoric high when he started kissing his way up my stomach. He stopped at each breast, showing each one his special appreciation before moving on. His tender kisses were making their way up my neck, over my chin, to land my lips as he pressed his body to mine. His large manhood teased my center, still tingling with pleasure from the orgasm minutes before.

He pulled away, and I looked into black eyes that were pools of darkness, but I saw no evil behind them. Wrapping my arms around him, I tugged him back to me, letting go of all my hesitation. Our bodies touched, but it wasn't good enough. I wanted to be closer. Reaching between us, I guided him into me.

In one smooth thrust, I had taken all of him. Holy goodness, the sheer size of him stole my breath, making me dizzy.

His movements were slow and calculated, tormenting me into wanting more. I felt him smile against my lips when I moaned in yearning. He pushed himself up, giving himself better leverage, and better access to my pleasure points. Each thrust was a little faster, a little harder, sending shockwaves of pleasure to my core. It didn't take long before I was rocked by an earth-shattering, 10.0-magnitude orgasm. I wasn't sure if I'd ever recover.

Lucian wrapped his arms around me, rolling us over on the bed until he lay on his back. I wedged myself between his arm and his sweet, sweet body.

"That was—I don't even have the words."

"That's a good thing, right?" he asked.

"Oh yes, baby, it's definitely a good thing," I said, idly running a finger up and down his chest.

"Funny, you calling me baby when I'm four thousand years your senior."

"It's a term of endearment, like darling, honey, sugar, cupcake. Know what I mean?"

"Oh, I know what you mean, Butter." I laughed at the term he chose for me. "I never understood why humans would call each other types of food."

"Why Butter?"

"You're silky smooth, creamy, and you melt when I warm you up."

"That's—"

Suddenly, I was hit with the most terrible pain in my head. A sharp, staking pain right at the front of my brain, as if I had just swallowed a gallon of ice cream and was now experiencing the most intense brain freeze of my life. All I could do was curl up in the fetal position and hold on to my head for dear life. As if that would help. It didn't. I didn't know what would help calm this pain, short of cutting the damn thing off.

"What's wrong?" Lucian demanded, his voice a mixture of alarm and panic.

But I couldn't answer. I couldn't move or open my eyes. I couldn't feel anything other than my brain cells splitting open. Images flashed through my mind. Years of memories that I had forgotten. No, Lucian had *made* me forget. They were all coming back to me. Cramming themselves back into remembrance. They came at me so quickly, I could only pick out bits and pieces.

The first time I'd met him in my dreams had been eleven years before the train. I was a nineteen-year-old college student, footloose and fancy-free. That was long before Marc had sucked the life out of me. I still knew how to have fun back then. Glimpses of some memories showed me I'd had my fair share of fun with the handsome man in my dreams. The exact same man who lay in bed with me in the present.

Back then, my dreams were filled with sunny and warm places, full of color and passion. Lucian and I were happy. Loving. I loved him. I loved him, and he loved me.

More images filtered in. Darker. Colder. The kind of dream I'd gotten used to in recent years. They spanned the years after I had married Marc. I never talked, and I never smiled. The feeling of hopelessness was nearly overwhelming. The only one helping me keep it together was Lucian. He was always with me in those dark days. Holding me. Comforting me.

As quickly as it came on, the pain stopped. Years of emotions that I suddenly remembered made me want to laugh and cry all at the same time. I hesitantly peeked through my lashes in case it wasn't really over. During the onslaught of images, Lucian had scooped me up to cradle me in his arms. I looked up into glowing eyes that appeared more than a little concerned. I suppose he'd tried to heal whatever was causing me to hurt, but when he was unable to stop the pain, he'd prepared to rush me from the room.

"I know you," I said.

"Of course you do. What do you need? Should I call in a doctor?"

"Not sure a doctor will do much good. I think I'm having a severe case of déjà rêvé from slurping an Icee the size of eleven years."

His face changed with understanding.

"I should tell you something," he said.

"No shit, Sherlock. There is a lot of something you need to tell me. Let's start with the fact that we've known each other a lot longer than you've led me to believe. Oh, and let's not forget the fact that this is not our first intimate encounter. Not even close."

"It is if you don't count the dream-state relations," he said.

"Lucian. Be real with me, or I'll figure it out myself."

Resigned, he started. "It was pure luck that I chose your stone from Morpheus' basket that night. The girl I met was so intriguing, so full of life, and had such a beautiful soul. A hard thing to come by in the dream state. I wanted you all to myself. I wanted to visit you as much as I could. Instead of returning your stone as I should have, I kept it." He stopped, looking as if he were going through his own images of memory. "Then you met Marc."

I had hurt him. It was written all over his face. I flipped through the memories to right before I was married. There I found my last happy dream. Lucian and I lay entwined in silky soft sheets in a bright room on an ornately carved wooden four-poster bed. The sheer canopy that hung from the bed billowed in the breeze that blew in through the open French doors. The room felt familiar, but I didn't recognize it.

Lucian was confessing his love for me, looking more vulnerable than I'd ever seen him. I was shaking my head decisively as I told him I couldn't dream of him anymore. That I had met someone else and needed to let him go. Otherwise, it wouldn't be fair to either of them. That was when I told him about the baby I was carrying.

The last image I saw was of Lucian's despair-filled eyes. Like an old movie, the reel ran out, and the image flickered away. Tears filled my eyes.

"Lucian. I'm so sorry," I said, sorrow choking me.

"Don't be. You were happy, and that's all I wanted for you," he said. "You deserved a life beyond me. I thought it would be easier if I erased myself from your mind. Being the selfish prick that I am, I couldn't bring myself to give up your stone. Every so often, I would visit, but I wouldn't allow you to remember."

"Selfish? You gave up your own happiness for mine. That is the farthest thing from selfishness that I can think of. Who would have known it would end up the way it did."

"I saw the change in your dreams, but you didn't tell me what was wrong. You didn't ask for help. You didn't ask for me. All I could do was be there for you and then let you go."

What he wasn't saying, was that he feared being hurt again.

"Not until the night your stone turned black. The only time that happens is when a mortal dies, or a deity is in distress. I came to you as soon as I could."

"That's when you showed up in your demon form. On the train. Why didn't you say something then?"

"I couldn't. Your stone was black. As a human, you should have been dead. Clearly, you weren't."

"That meant I was a deity in distress."

He nodded. "That's why I needed your blood. I needed to figure out who, or rather, *what* you are."

More and more pieces were coming together on this puzzle called my life. It was after I started seeing Lucian, again, that things started to change.

"Why didn't you erase my memory, like all the other times?" I asked.

"Something changed. You had released the tiniest bit of your contained power. Enough that I could still read your mind, not change it. Each visit we had, I could feel your power had grown. I should have given your stone to your mother, but I was being selfish again. I had you back in my life. You wanted to see me again." He hesitated. "It's because of me that Marc attacked you."

"What? What do you mean?"

I struggled out of his arms, then flopped out of the bed, grabbing his shirt off the floor. Scrambling to cover my nakedness as quickly as possible, I had twisted the opening and was now lost in the fabric. My head was lodged in an armhole when Lucian straightened it and tugged it into the correct position.

"Let me show you."

He placed a hand on each of my temples, starting a type of flashback behind my eyes. My viewpoint of the room, an office, was from an upper corner. I was looking down on a woman, standing by a closed door. She had shoulder-length hair with the ultra-popular ombre look. Black at the roots, gradually fading to platinum blond. Her skin was pale and flawless. From this height, it was hard to tell if her eyes were brown or black, but I could see the wicked a mile away.

She walked around the desk that was in the center of the room, the camera following her every sultry step. On the other side of the desk, she ran a hand provocatively up Marc's arm. Were my eyes deceiving me? Nope, that was Marc alright. This was taking place in his private office at the bank. The woman leaned down behind him, the camera pointed at the back of their heads, as I heard her whisper "she betrayed you" in his ear. He spun the chair to face her, and I could see that he had the same wild eyes he'd had the night he attacked me.

"She's been keeping secrets," the woman said, no longer whispering. "Sneaking around behind your back, and now she's fucking another man."

She was smiling with a giant helping of malice.

"No," Marc crossed his arms over his chest as he shook his head. "I don't believe it. We've been so good."

"Oh, believe it," she said.

She straddled him in a way that wouldn't have been possible if the chair had arms. The heels of her stilettos looked more like a weapon than the back end of a shoe. Marc looked a little shocked at the brash woman, but he started to smile when she ran a hand down his chest to grab between his legs. I didn't want to watch anymore but I couldn't turn it off.

"Are you listening to me?"

Her long tongue flicked at his earlobe as she spoke to him. Marc's eyes glazed over. He let his head fall back on the chair, enjoying his afternoon delight.

"Yes, what do you want me to do?" he asked.

"She betrayed you with a man named Lucian. A sin like that deserves death. You must kill her."

"Why wouldn't I kill him?"

"You can't. It must be Rose. Understand? Kill Rose," she said.

The camera went black.

"That must be the woman Marc told me about. Who is she?"

"Lyssa, the goddess of mad rage. Her touch sends men into a frenzy. She used me to turn Marc against you," Lucian said. "It was because I brought your blood to Olympus that they knew my association with you."

I felt like a pawn in a game that I didn't understand. A pawn that was being played with, manipulated, and tossed around. I didn't know all the players in the game, or even how many there were. Most importantly, I didn't know who I could trust.

"I need you to do something."

"I'd do anything for you."

"I need you to take me to Lake," I said, Lucian immediately shaking his head. "I need to know he's alright. My son is the most important thing in my life. Please."

Lucian held out his hands like he was about to plead with me to trust him.

"I can't tell you where he is, and you won't be able to speak to him."

He spread his hands like he was opening a book and an image appeared in his palms. Lake lay in an oversized bed, his focus on the sketchbook and his current work of art. I couldn't make out what it was from our vantage point. His head bobbed to music I couldn't hear but he looked to be enjoying it. Someone in an area of the room I couldn't see must have said something, prompting Lake to raise his head to acknowledge them. My heart nearly burst when he smiled, reminding me just how adorable he was.

Lucian closed his hands, disconnecting whatever line he had to Lake. I could feel the sob welling in my throat. It was a big lump of emotion that had built up over the last few days. I covered my mouth with both hands, trying to lock it down. And I was doing a good job until Lucian asked if I was ok.

The flood gates burst open, releasing all the tears that had pooled behind my eyes. No matter how hard I tried, I couldn't stop. Lucian pulled me against him, holding me, silently letting know it was going to be ok.

"I wish I could stay but I need to go," he said. "Do you want me to get Maiz?"

Feeling like I could pull myself together, I stepped back and gave him the best smile I could muster. Using my shirt—his shirt—I wiped away the tears that I had left behind on his chest. He smiled at me and placed a kiss on my forehead. Without another word, he strolled out of the room completely naked, looking completely natural. Like it was trivial to be roaming the house, full of guests, I might add, butt naked.

He had nothing to be modest about, his form was stunning to behold. And according to my new-old memories, I had behold-ed it many a time. I really needed to rummage through those and learn about my past with him.

The room felt empty without him in it—he took up a lot of space. This empty, though, was a different kind of empty. One that reached my soul. I was disappointed that he had left. I crawled back into bed, only to be bombarded by Lucian's delectable scent all over the sheets. Damn him for being so irresistible.

After a mental slap, I felt clear-headed enough to work my way through more of my regained memories. They took place in varying locations. Some I recognized, others I didn't. One such place that I had been to more often than others was Lucian's island, Oneiropolos.

That's right, I knew the name of the island. Took a few dreams, but I got it. I hadn't just walked on his beach; I'd swum in the ocean. An ocean that was alive with waves and current. I'd been in his house. No. *Our house.* We'd called it ours. And the room with the big, ornate bed was our room. Back then, the island was alive—breathing, singing, chirping—it had a heart.

In our time together, we'd done various activities, ranging from surfing to snowboarding, mountain climbing to horseback riding. I was more active in my dream life than in real life. One of the more popular choices was spending time in the bed, tangled in sheets, while naked. When we weren't preoccupied with other activities, we would talk.

We had lengthy conversations about him and his family. I knew that he worked his dream god job with his brothers, sisters, cousins, uncles, and his dad. His dad, I had already learned, was Morpheus, and his mom was the powerful Gaia, goddess of the earth. Some people came from large families, but Lucian's was one hundred times worse and that much harder to follow. His uncle Hypnos had a thousand sons alone. The Greek gods were promiscuous, to say the least, and reproduced like bunnies. I couldn't even grasp a family get-together.

Back then, Lucian was playful and unguarded. I knew him. The real him. It was very apparent that Lucian was caring, sincere, devoted to his family, and most of all, devoted to me. He was enchanted with the person that I was. He didn't have any plans to change me to someone who suited him better. That was more than I could say for Marc. He'd been a dick from the very beginning, and for some damn reason, I'd chosen to stay oblivious to it.

I shut down the memories. They had shown me what I needed to know—that Lucian was more than trustworthy. He had already proven himself but now I was one hundred and ten percent sure of it. The Greek gods may not have been known for their compassion, but for him, the apple had fallen far from the Greek tree.

Switching off the lamp, I put my worries to rest. The ones about Lucian, anyway. I was exhausted after such an informative day.

***

I walked down a deserted gravel road that stretched endlessly in front of me. Each side was guarded by large, dead trees, their mangled limbs twisting up and over, encircling the road in a morbid tunnel. My only source of light sifted through the branches from the full blood moon perched high above me. A light fog hung just above the ground, blanketing the dark land for slumber. Someone had forgotten to tell the crickets and frogs, though—they sang a tune that was near deafening.

"Lucian?" I called out in the darkness, waiting for him to appear from behind a tree. He knew how to make an entrance. "Are you here?"

"Sorry to disappoint you, darling, it's just me."

My blood ran cold. The grounds grew quiet, the crickets and frogs feeling the same dread I did. Marc had that effect.

The sound of shifting gravel had me whirling on my heel. Marc stood there, though I barely recognized him. He looked— well, he looked dead. The clothes he wore hung on his frame. They were soiled beyond recognition. His once-brown eyes were milky and bulging. His ashen skin drooped from his bones. A section of his cheek had been ripped off. The jagged edges were black with necrosis, and maggots dripped out of the open wound. An ear had also been ripped off, and snakes poked in and out of the exposed orifice, one of them slithering from the ear to disappear in the gaping cheek hole.

"Darling," Marc said, his teeth clicking while he talked. "You left before we had a chance to finish our fun the other night. There's so much more I have planned for us."

He reached out a hand, the skin completely gone except for bits of muscle that flapped with his movement. The bones were still red from the blood that had once circulated there.

Twirling on my heel, I fled through the woods, running as fast as the adrenaline would carry my trembling legs. I stumbled over a fallen branch. I bumped into trees. I was whipped in the face with foliage. When finally, I came to a clearing in the woods. An old, dilapidated barn stood in front of me. The entire building leaned precariously to one side, and the roof had succumbed to old age in the middle.

I ran through a barn door that barely clung to its rusty hinges. Inside, the smell of moldy hay and death assaulted my senses. A large swath of ground was lit by the moonlight pouring through the gaping roof. Blood soaked the dirt beneath my shoes, and bits of bone, skin, and brain matter were strewn about.

A flicker towards the back of the barn caught my eye. As much as I didn't want to, my legs moved me forward. The smell of death grew stronger, causing me to gag. I pulled at some loose hay, uncovering the horror hidden below. Lucian lay mangled in a heap, a faint glow coming from his unseeing eyes. They stared blankly at me, his bruised and bloodied face forever frozen in a look of horror. His silky black hair was caked in blood, and a large chunk of skull and brain were missing. The rest of him was twisted like the trees that enclosed the road, with bones protruding out of his skin.

My hands covered my mouth to hold back the scream that would surely reveal my location. I dropped to my knees, sobbing silently in the dark over the only man who had ever truly loved me. Reaching out, I closed his eyes. Then I staggered to my feet, stumbling over to the nearest bale of hay, reaching it just before my legs gave out.

"Mommy," a voice choked from behind me.

Lake lay spread out in the dirt, blood oozing from a cut on his neck that spanned from ear to ear. I scrambled off the bale, bending beside him on the bloodied floor. Pulling my shirt off, I used it to apply pressure to stop the bleeding.

"It's okay, Mom." He stopped to cough up blood. "Dad won't let anything happen to you."

"Oh, honey, I don't think Dad is here to help us. Something is wrong with him."

Lake tried to shake his head, and blood seeped through my fingers.

"Don't move, sweetie, we have to stop the bleeding. You're going to be okay."

I never understood why they always said that in the movies, when I, the viewer, knew the person had absolutely no chance of surviving. Now I understood. I used it to comfort him, keep him calm. Panic would cause his heart to race, forcing what little blood he had left out of the large cut.

I also said it for me. I needed the tiniest bit of hope that my only child would make it through this. He was strong. Stronger than me. I needed him to survive.

"You are strong, Mom. You can kill him. You have to. Or we all die." Blood now flowed freely from his mouth. "I love you."

If there was anything else, he didn't say. He couldn't. His eyes, like Lucian's, were blank and empty.

There was no holding back the scream this time. I picked up my lifeless son, holding his limp body tight to mine as I sobbed. Clutching him in my arms, I rocked him, just as I had done countless times when he was a baby. He was still my baby. Forever my baby. I placed a hand on his chest, his unbeating heart ripping my own heart to shreds. We rocked and rocked and rocked.

We rocked until I sat straight up in bed, drenched in sweat. I patted the bed in search of Lake, but he wasn't there. I groped at my shirt for blood, there was none. It was a dream. More accurately, a nightmare of hellish proportions. If someone had constructed such a dream to scare me, they had succeeded.

What they failed to realize was that it had not only scared me, but it had also emboldened me. I didn't know who Marc had gotten involved with, but never again would I let him hurt me or anyone I loved. That included Lucian.

Even though I had no idea where Lake was, according to Lucian, he was safe. There was no other choice but to believe that Marc couldn't get to him. I could, however, check to make sure that Lucian was still whole.

Leaving the room, I moved quickly down the hall to the sitting area. I stopped next to one of the couches when I heard the seriousness in Maiz's voice. She was pacing the kitchen, highly agitated. A man, one I had been introduced to at lunch, was standing just inside the front door, and something he said had obviously upset her.

"Shit. Shit. Shit. How bad is it?" Maiz asked him.

"Looks like it was a search party," he said. "The issue's been handled, but we lost a few of our own. They knew to go after the Lycaons."

Maiz stopped pacing to look at him. Lycaon was a name I recognized. It was the king from Adam's story. He'd failed to mention there were any of the king's family left, or why they would be targeted.

"Who?" Maiz asked.

She sounded as out of the loop as I did.

"Slade, Lucy, Matt, Oliver, Knox, Roxy, and—" The man stumbled over his words. "And Mia."

"Shit, Stolly, I'm sorry. She was a kickass fighter, and I'm sure she didn't go down easy."

He wiped his eye as he flashed a fanged smile. "She took seven of those bastards out before they got her."

"Where's Lucian?" I asked.

Stolly jumped around to face me in a crouch, ready to pounce at any sign that I might be a threat. Most definitely a werewolf.

"Heel boy, it's just Rose," Maiz said.

"Lucian is gone," Stolly said.

My legs faltered when I tried to move toward the kitchen, and I could feel the blood drain from my face.

"Why don't you retire for the night," Maiz said to Stolly. "You've been through enough. Those clothes are gonna need to be burned. Toss them in the bathroom, and I'll gather them all when everyone is back."

Stolly bowed to both of us before he moved toward the stairs. It was then I noticed he had spatters of both green and red on his clothes, like he was decorated for some macabre Christmas party. The smell of metallic rotten eggs that followed in his wake made my eyes burn. I blinked rapidly, trying to wipe the acidic air from the surface. It was hard to determine if the tears that filled my eyes were from the stink, or from the thought that I may have already lost Lucian. If he'd been taken out already, then it was possible Lake could be in danger, too.

"I can see you're freaking out," Maiz said.

"You think?"

"Stolly told us there was an attack. Lucian just stepped out to help the injured. He's fine."

I had mixed emotions about that. I was happy that Lucian was okay, but others were not. From what I'd heard, Slade, Adam's dad, hadn't made it, and neither had Matt, another one of the guys I had met earlier in the day. I really didn't know them, but it was sad that now, I never would. It was still a loss of life. Lives that were possibly lost because of me. My vision blurred and the lightheadedness made me feel unstable. I had to grab my knees for support.

"What's going on?" Maiz asked.

"I had a nightmare. In it, Marc killed Lucian and Lake. It was horrible. And when Stolly said Lucian was gone, I thought—"

Maiz flashed a look I couldn't decipher. Before I could ask about it, the front door slammed open. Lucian stepped through the doorway carrying the body of a man that I didn't recognize. Not at first. The man made no sound, even though his face was twisted in agony. Blood dripped from his ears, eyes, and nose. His naked form had been shredded by something, leaving his skin looking like tattered threads hanging from his body. Sharp teeth had punctured holes in his neck. Blood was steadily dripping from his entire body. Even his salt and pepper hair.

Adam.

Men and women were filing in the door behind them, but I couldn't take my eyes off Adam. He was seriously hurt. The words *mortally wounded* came to mind. I ran to where Lucian stood.

"Adam?" I whispered.

He opened his eyes, which had been clamped shut, to look at me. Any part of the eye that should have been white was bright red with blood. He looked as if he were crying blood as it poured from the corners of his eyes. I gasped at the horror of it all. Without thinking about what it might do to him, I reached out a hand to wipe some hair from his forehead. He spasmed from the pain as my fingers made contact. Still, he made no noise. He gritted his teeth instead, giving me a clear view of a mouth full of blood.

"Vis got him," Lucian said. "He's lucky his insides aren't on the outside."

"She got his neck," Maiz said somberly.

Lucian turned to hand Adam off to Zane and Kane. "Take him to his room. It won't be long now."

The group followed the two men as they carried him up the stairs, disappearing into a room.

"No," I said. "You can't let him die. I know you can save him, just like you saved me."

"They found us. They found you. I need to keep my strength so I can protect you."

"Protect me? I've been told that I'm strong and powerful. Adam is the one that needs protection now." I pleaded with Lucian. "You said you would do anything for me. If you ever loved me like you said you did, then you will save him."

"Rose—" Maiz started to object, but Lucian held up a hand to silence her.

"No," he said with devastating finality. "He's not worth it."

"I can't believe this. You're not who I thought you were."

I didn't wait for him to say anything else. I didn't want to hear it. Turning away, I went back to my room, securely closing myself in before I let the tears go. After my last cry session, I didn't think there would be anything left. Years of built-up grief flowed from me now. Grief for the loss of my family and friends, new and old, and for the love that I thought I had rekindled.

I considered going to be with Adam, to be there for him in his final moments. In my current state of mind, I didn't think I could bear to see him suffer. I wanted to remember him for the good time we'd had only hours ago. Also, I didn't know if the people around him blamed me for what happened. It gave me comfort knowing he was surrounded by people who loved him. I climbed into bed, pulling the covers high over my head.

Sleep eluded me for a long time. I couldn't make my brain shut off, and images of my life kept flashing through my thoughts. Everything made me cry, too. The happy times. The sad times. Even the thought of just sitting in my house and reading a book made me cry. Instead of trying to hold it in, I let it go. When my head was pounding from the lack of hydration and could no longer sustain a thought, I was able to doze off at last.

Vanden Bosch

153

Chapter 7

Voices drifted through the door, waking me from a dreamless sleep. Probably mourners here to celebrate the lives that were lost in last night's battle. I wanted to stay in bed, but I, too, should pay my respects. I was totally exhausted and totally unprepared to face such a dismal day. The sun may have been shining outside, but I felt dark. Adam had most likely succumbed to his injuries by now.

There was a very real possibility that more people would die. I wasn't sure if I could handle anymore. And then there was Lucian. How could I face him? I understood he was playing it safe by not healing Adam, but there were others who could have protected me while his skin healed.

I grabbed some fresh clothes to swap out with Lucian's shirt from the night before. A pair of black jeans with a black sweater seemed appropriate for the occasion. I pulled my hair into a ponytail and gave myself a pep talk before leaving the room.

A wide variety of people spilled from the sitting room into the kitchen and up the stairs. Tall, short, old, and young. Some I knew to be wolves, some I assumed to be demons from their catlike eyes and pointed teeth. Almost everyone had a scratch, scrape, bruise, limp, or a little bit of everything. The only ones who were exempt were the very old or the very young.

Food in containers, pots, and pans littered every inch of counter space. A line of people made their way through the kitchen, everyone filling paper plates full of the donated goods. The room hummed with soft conversation. That was, until I came fully into view. Then, all conversation ceased.

I held my breath as I waited for their reaction to my presence. Somewhere in the room, someone started clapping. Then another. Then another. The ones holding plates of food smiled wide at me. This was completely unexpected. All I could do was stand there, dumbfounded.

Maiz made her way through the crowd, stopping to wrap an arm around me.

"What is this?" I asked.

"They heard you saved their king. Adam's alive. Lucian saved him because of you."

"What do you mean, their king? Adam is a king? Where is he? Where's Lucian?" I asked, standing on my tippy toes to search the room.

Dammit, why were there so many tall people?

"It's not good, Rose," Maiz said quietly. "The effort weakened Lucian. He may not survive."

I snapped back to face my friend.

"Where is he?"

"In his quarters upstairs. The large one at the end of the hall."

I pushed my way through the crowd, getting praise and pats on the back as I passed. By the time I reached the stairs, people must have noticed I was in no mood for celebrating. They moved out of my way, allowing me to take the stairs two at a time. I hit the landing at a run. Following the hall to a set of double doors, my stocking feet slid to a stop a hair away from slamming into the frame. Without a knock or an invitation, I softly pushed open the door to slip inside, closing it just as quietly as I came in.

The curtains had been tightly closed, but since they weren't blackouts, enough light filtered in for me to see the room. It was the same cabin-style room as mine, except on a grandiose scale. Adam sat in a chair by a king-size bed made of the same logs as the cabin.

Other than looking like he hadn't slept last night, he was fine. No slashes in his skin. No bite on his neck. All his blood was staying inside his body. His arms were resting on his legs, his head bent over them. He was speaking to his folded hands in a language I couldn't understand. From his tone, I presumed he was praying to his gods.

Lucian slumped against the headboard. I couldn't tell if he was alive or dead. My feet refused to move me any closer to find out. Adam must have sensed my hesitation. He finished his mantra, stood to whisper something in Lucian's ear, and came to stand in front of me.

"I don't know what you said, but he really shouldn't have saved me," he said.

"Adam—Your highness. I don't even know what to call you."

"Just Adam, please."

"How in hell are you a king, and why didn't you tell me?"

"My name is Adam Lycaon. With the death of my family, I am the last descendant of King Lycaon. I know, right?" he said in answer to my look of shock.

"I'm sorry about your family."

"Not my first experience with loss. Won't be the last."

I looked past Adam's shoulder to the bed. When I first came in, Lucian's eyes were closed. Now, his dull eyes looked in our direction.

"He's still fighting," Adam said. "I think his chances are better if you stay with him."

"Wouldn't want to be anywhere else," I replied, pulling my gaze from the bed. "You have a room of loyal subjects waiting for you downstairs anyway."

He offered a sad smile in return.

I hugged him before he could walk past me to the door. He left then, and the click of the latch seemed to echo in the quiet room.

My heart started to race, and I had to steady myself as I closed the distance to the bed. I was hesitant to sit on the bed for fear of jostling him and causing more pain, so I took a seat in the chair Adam had vacated.

Lucian gingerly turned his head to face me. For a man who'd been consistently sun-kissed throughout the years, his pallid appearance was a shock to the system. A sob choked my throat. His hand lay flat on the sheet, flipped over, slowly inching toward mine on the bed. I rested my hand in his, finding it to be cold and dry. His eyes watched me, a silvery, viscous liquid dripping from the corners.

"Butter," Lucian said in a hoarse whisper.

His term of endearment immediately brought tears to my eyes.

"What can I do?"

"Stay," he said, closing his eyes again.

He moved tentatively into a laying position so that he was facing me. Not once did he grimace, or show any signs of pain, but his hesitant movements told me the truth. The bed was large enough to fit three people comfortably. Lucian lay in the middle. Moving his arm out of the way, I climbed in next to him, being extra careful not to bump any part of him. As fragile as he was, I could probably break him with the tiniest bit of pressure. I cuddled up close, pressing my nose against his.

This close to him, I could hear his shallow breaths and almost inaudible wheezes. I curled my hand inside his, using my other hand to wrap his fingers around mine.

We lay that way for many hours, Lucian sleeping for most of the duration. I remained vigilant. I was too worried that if I slept, I would lose him, and never get the chance to tell him goodbye.

The door clicked behind an entering figure. I carefully lifted my head from the pillow. A gorgeous woman, who looked to be around the same age as me, walked lightly toward the bed. Her gown, brown with juniper accents, flowed behind her. Long, tan legs peeked out of the slits in the skirt with each shoeless step. She was well over six feet tall, and her flowing brown hair shone in perfect spirals all the way down to her hips. I thought she was staring at Lucian in his vulnerable state, but as she stepped closer, I could see she was staring at me. Glowing emerald eyes blazed a hole in my forehead.

"I hear this is your doing," she said with a regal tone. She softened when her gaze shifted to Lucian. "You may go now."

When a tall, intimidating woman whose dress continues to flutter in a windless room tells you to do something, it's better for your life to do it. Just a guess. Lucian's grip tightened on my hand when he felt me leave his side, forcing me to peel his fingers from mine.

Under the woman's harsh stare, I placed a gentle kiss on his lips before taking my leave. Once the door was closed, I could hear her murmuring voice from inside. I couldn't understand the words, but I knew she wasn't happy with him.

Downstairs, the crowd had cleared. The house no longer buzzed with activity. In the sitting room, Maiz, Adam, Stolly, and another man all sat in the chairs around the crackling fire. I waved at Maiz when I reached the bottom of the stairs and headed to the kitchen, where the food was still spread out. My stepmom would have been appalled that all this food had been left out all day, and I still planned on eating it. I wasn't repulsed—I was famished.

I pulled a paper plate from the stack near the food and threw on a slice of ham, topping it with mashed potatoes, gravy, and finishing it all off with corn. Needing a little space to get my mind right, I sat at the counter to eat. I was so lost in thought that I didn't even hear the others' conversations.

When I was finished, I dropped the plate in the overflowing garbage and poured myself a cup of coffee before joining them in the sitting room. Maiz sat on the couch, on the side farthest from the fire, with Adam next to her in the middle. I sat next to him on the side closest to the fire. The two of them were huddled close, discussing reinforcements that were en route to Yellowstone and where they were all going to stay.

"I met you the other morning. I've forgotten your name, though," I said to the man sitting in the chair opposite me.

He looked lost in thought, but I couldn't just sit here. I'd go crazy.

"Bram," he said.

His voice was deeper than I expected. He was more muscular than any of the other men I'd met, very tan, and his brown hair was pulled back in a tight man bun. His eyes were a beautiful shade of reddish brown, and he had a little cleft in his chin.

"Bram is part of my pack," Adam said, answering my silent question.

"If you don't mind my asking, how did you come to be named after the man who wrote *Dracula* when you're a werewolf?"

Everyone laughed but Bram, who glowered at Adam.

"My parents were saved by a man named Zac Odin, who is—" Bram started.

"Who is a big fan of Dracula and anything vampire-related," Adam said, cutting him off.

"Yes, that," Bram said. "When my parents asked what they could do to repay him, he only asked that they name their firstborn Bram. Thanks to that dick, I get asked why a werewolf is named after a vampire novelist on the daily."

"I'm sorry. I didn't mean to offend you," I said. "Could be worse. He could have asked that you be named Dracula."

"Don't apologize. It was rude of me to snap at you."

"Are you sure this Zac guy knew he was saving werewolves? Maybe he was just trying to draw attention to his favorite author."

"Oh, he knew what he was doing," Bram said, his pouty expression incongruent with his size. "If you've ever watched one of his movies, then you know he's full of shit. He thinks because he's famous, he can do whatever he wants. He did this to poke fun at us."

"This Zac guy, is he like you?"

The room was silent as they exchanged glances, not knowing how to answer my question. They were saved from answering when the woman from Lucian's room floated down the stairs. No joke, her feet never touched the ground. She looked royally pissed as she came towards us. I was ashamed to admit it, but I pulled my legs up on the couch, trying to hide behind my mug. It was an awful disguise. One she saw through immediately. The men all stood in her presence.

"He would like for you to rejoin him," she said to me. To Adam, she said, "I'm sorry, little one, for your great loss. I've increased the protection for you. Let me know if there is anything else I can do."

"Thank you, goddess. You have always been very accommodating, and we are grateful to you."

She tipped her head regally at him.

"Maiz," she said. "Get to work on that sister of yours." She looked me up and down. "And get this over with. If anything else happens to my son, you'll be the first one I come looking for."

Ah, so this was Gaia.

"Yes, goddess," Maiz said, tipping her head to Gaia.

A light wind whirled around us, and she disappeared. The room was silent. I think we were all waiting to see if she came back. After a long pause, the men sat back down.

"That's Lucian's mom, eh?" I said when I figured the coast was clear.

"Yep," Adam answered. "She's really not that bad when you get to know her."

I laughed. That sounded like such a typical answer someone would give for a royal bitch.

"She's just stressed out about her son being caught up in the war."

"Someone is going to have to explain that to me one of these days," I said.

The three men looked at Maiz.

"What the shit?" Maiz said. "I'm just the guardian. I thought Lucian would have told her by now."

"And you." I pointed at Maiz. "Why did she look at me when she said, 'work on that sister?'"

"I told you we were sisters," Maiz said, her tone matter-of-fact.

"I thought you meant that figuratively."

"That was my way of putting it out there," Maiz said. "Trying to ease you into everything instead of dropping bombs at every step. Like the fact that we have the same mother. My dad is Erebus, though. Yours is Chaos."

"Are you kidding me?" I jumped out of my seat. "You mean to tell me my parents were not my parents?"

"Yes and no. They were your parents because they were the mom and dad who raised you, just not the ones who created you."

"I can't believe this," I said pacing, trying to wrap my head around yet another curveball. "I was birthed by a human mother, so if I have gods for parents, how is that possible?"

"Well, when a man and a woman love each other very much," she began.

"Maiz, stop, this is serious."

"You were a meeting of the minds, a combining of spirits, a tethering of powers," Maiz said, making it sound magical. "There was no touching of sexy bits. They put you together parthenogenetically. It's a common practice up there."

"I'm a sort of test-tube baby?"

"Something like that. Once they had your embryo, they put you in the womb of a human, thinking you'd be safe there. They didn't expect that even with your power locked away, you were still too much."

Maiz abruptly stopped.

"Too much what?" I asked.

"Too much for your human mother to birth on her own."

"I killed her?" I asked, falling back onto the couch. "What am I?"

The men's heads went back and forth from Maiz to me and back. It would have been funny if I hadn't just found out I'd killed my dad's first wife.

"You're a sort of secret weapon of mass destruction."

Everyone stared at me, waiting for my overreaction.

"Breathe, people," I said. "I'm fine, thanks to Adam, the one person who actually talks to me," Adam winked at me. "So, what was I created for?"

"I'd tell you more," he said, "but I'm not high enough on the totem pole. Oh, right, I guess I kind of am now." He stopped to think. "No, I still better not. I'm not going to get my ass kicked by pissed-off deities. That shit stings."

No one else said anything.

"If none of you are going to enlighten me about my destructive tendencies, then I need to check on Lucian. This has been—maddening. You know, you can be honest. I'm not gonna break, guys."

I stood from the couch, and for good measure, pointed a finger at Maiz so she knew I meant business. She went to say something, thought better of it, and huffed. It was so uncharacteristic of the Maiz I knew, who always had her proverbial shit together, that I had to laugh.

The laughing was cut short when I reached Lucian's door. It was quiet inside, and I wasn't sure what I was going to find. Poking my head in the door, I saw Lucian lying right where I'd left him. He looked exactly the same: pale and weak. One positive improvement: he smiled at me when I came in.

"You're looking better," I said, standing next to the bed. "Looks like all you needed was a visit from your mom. What the heck am I doing here?"

I was joking, but he clutched my hand to keep me from leaving. His grip wasn't yet strong enough to hold me, but it was the thought that counted.

"She fed me," he said.

His voice was still low and raspy.

"Ummmm. Unless that has some other meaning that I don't want to know about, you could have asked. There is a ton of food down there. I would have brought something up for you."

"No. Nectar and ambrosia."

I knew that from my past dreams. We had talked about how he didn't eat "normal" food. It had to be nectar and ambrosia. I also remembered him saying he could feed on others' life forces, but it wasn't something that would sustain his hunger for long. It would help in a pinch to bring his strength up. The similarities to a vampire were never-ending.

"If you need to." I patted my neck. "You can. If it will help."

"I won't."

"Maybe you should consider it."

I ran my fingers through his disheveled hair, trying to comb the pieces back into place. His eyes were no longer dripping the silver fluid, but streaks still stained his face. I excused myself and stepped into his attached bathroom.

The space was larger than the room I slept in downstairs. A memory came to mind. I'd been here, in this room, in the large jacuzzi. Lucian and I had used it many times. In fact, I'd been to this house, and in his bedroom, many times. This was *his* house.

Because I was so familiar with this room, I knew exactly where to find the washcloths. I grabbed one out of the middle drawer of the vanity. Turning the sink on, I held the cloth under the water until it was warm and soaked all the way through. Wringing it out, I walked back to the bedside. Lucian hadn't moved while I was gone, other than to close his eyes. A crinkle between his eyebrows told me he was feeling some pain but trying not to draw attention to it.

I sat on the chair, gently wiping away the streaks. First from his eyes, then his nose, mouth, and ears. The large bite mark on his neck, which had been hidden from view when he'd turned his head earlier, looked black with infection. He sucked in his breath sharply when I tried to clean the area around it. Any other claw marks that he may have absorbed from Adam were gone, with no trace of ever having been there. The bite, however, was keeping him down.

"Can you tell me what this is?" I asked.

"Demon bite. Toxic venom." It was obvious that even talking was painful. "Melts inside."

That explained the blood running from all the openings. As if on cue, silvery fluid dripped out of his mouth just from talking. His insides were liquifying and pouring out. Adam was a supernatural being, but he wasn't immortal. It wouldn't have taken long for the venom to make quick work of his mortal organs.

"Okay. Adam would have died, but you won't, right?" Lucian just looked at me with sad eyes. "What aren't you telling me?"

"Egypt demon," he said.

"Okay. A demon from a different pantheon, but you're going to be okay, right?"

"Fifteen. Maybe twenty."

"Percent? Only fifteen or twenty percent chance of dying?" He didn't answer. He didn't have to. The defeated look on his face said it all. "No!"

I jumped up from the chair so quickly that it clattered to the floor. Outside the door, feet pounded up the stairs. Maiz was the first to run through the door, followed by Adam, Bram, and Stolly.

"What's happened?" Maiz asked, breathless, looking from me to Lucian and back again.

"Why didn't you tell me?" I demanded, unable to hide the anguish in my voice. "Why didn't anyone stop me?"

"I tried," Maiz said. "He didn't want me to." She was looking at Lucian. I remembered Maiz trying to say something the night before when Lucian held up his hand to stop her. "He wanted to do this for you."

"Not. Your. Fault," Lucian said. "Mine."

Maiz was hustling the boys back out of the room. I bent next to the bed so he wouldn't have to strain to be heard.

"The one time you choose to listen to me is the time when you can actually die? Why would you do that, you stupid, stupid man?"

"Always listening. If you want to be with the wolf. Adam. Then I would fix him, so you would be happy. You care for him."

The effort of giving such a speech seemed to wear him out. He closed his eyes, the crinkle returning to crease his brow.

"If that's what you heard, you heard wrong. I do care for Adam. But I love you. I've loved you for the last ten years. I loved you even when I couldn't remember you. I named my son Laken because I couldn't remember the name Lucian to name him that. You can't leave me now that I have you back."

A tear slipped from his sealed eyes. I could tell these were actual tears because they were not silver in color. All the pain he was in, and he was getting emotional from my words. The sight of it shattered me into a million pieces.

"I'm strong."

Except his voice came out only as a whisper, his eyes still shut tight.

"I know you are, honey." I grabbed both of his hands in mine. "Please, let me help you."

"Not yet."

I almost dropped the issue. Almost. For too many years, I let Marc tell me when and what I could do. Now was no time for that. There was no way I was going to sit here, watching him suffer, if I could help him. Even just a little.

"Now," I said. That got him to open his eyes and look at me. "I'm stronger than you right now, I can force you. Shoot, I'll hook up an IV if I have to."

He smiled at me.

"Now," he said.

"What do I do? Will you take it from the same place as the dream? Or my wrist? Do I need to cut it for you?"

"Kiss me."

I would never deny the love of my life something as simple as a kiss. Sitting on the bed, I leaned over him to lightly touch my lips to his. With a hand at the back of my head, he pulled me in for a much deeper kiss. Something pricked my tongue, causing me to flinch away from him. Two elongated teeth became visible between his parted lips. His black eyes watched me. Waiting to see if I lost my nerve. And I nearly did before I reminded myself how much he needed this.

The hand at the back of my head pulled me back down. This time, though, he ducked his head to push my chin up with his, exposing my neck. My body tensed in anticipation of the pain of the bite. There wasn't any. He was only kissing the exposed skin, causing my face to tingle. The only indication that he bit me was a little pinch, and then he was sucking. I felt like a teenager again, getting my first hickey. But while hickies were ugly and pointless, this would hopefully save his life. Totally worth the lightheaded feeling it was causing.

A part of me knew that he'd never put me at risk. He'd never take enough from me to save himself if he thought I might come to harm.

"I can't heal you," he said when he released me.

I touched my neck. The small punctures were almost completely scabbed over. Only a drop of blood was left, which I wiped away with my finger. Lucian reached for it before I could wipe it on my shirt, sucking it clean.

"Come. Sleep," he said.

"No sleepy tricks. I want to be able to wake if you need anything."

"No sleepy tricks left."

His eyes were already closed, and his breathing began to steady.

I pulled off my sweater and tucked myself in next to him, being careful not to pull away the covers, or shake his liquifying form. I didn't know any man who would be so calm and considerate in the same position. Marc was cranky and demanding any time he had a sore throat. Anything worse, and he was unbearable. I'd be stuck waiting on him hand and foot. Even as he demanded I get all my errands done for the week.

For a long while, I listened to the soft wheezing whistle that came from beside me. The room was dark now. Sleep was creeping up on me. Maybe a nap, a short power nap, would help. Allowing my eyes to close, I drifted off.

****

I was back in the barn. The same damn barn where I'd found Lucian murdered and watched as my son bled out between my fingers. This time, there were no bodies. No blood. No evidence that anything terrible had ever transpired here. There must be some hidden horrors somewhere, just waiting for me to stumble upon them. That wouldn't work on me this time. I knew this was only a dream, and I wasn't scared of Marc. When that ass-wipe showed up this time, I was going to punch him right in his decaying face.

I threw open the barn door, the rotten hinges gave way and the door slammed to the ground. I waited, but there was no sign of Marc.

"Come out, come out wherever you are," I called to the dark tree line. "I'm calling you out, Marc. I'm ready for you."

"But are you ready for me?" a voice hissed, coming from all around me.

A pair of bright, red eyes opened in the darkness of the woods. To the left of the red eyes, a pair of yellow eyes opened. Followed by another pair of yellow eyes. Then another. Until the woods around me were dotted with yellow orbs, all watching me from obscurity.

A creature as white as a ghost and as big as a tiger crawled out of the woods. Down on all fours, it crept toward me as a tiger would. The closer the thing got, the uglier it got. Its hairless body looked like it had been wrapped in a leather bodysuit with only a hole cut out for the mouth. There were no visible eyes, nose, or ears. Just a mouth full of razor-sharp, jagged teeth that dripped long, slimy strands of saliva.

My heart thumped wildly as the thing moved close enough that I could hear its gurgling growl deep in its throat. I wanted to run, but fear froze me to the ground. My legs finally decided to work as the creature leapt at me. I moved a millisecond before I would have been face-to-face with it.

I stepped to the side, out of the thing's direct path. The creature hit the ground hard, sliding on its side to stop only feet from me. Others like it were stepping out of the woods, taking slow, calculated steps toward me. They were circling—stalking me.

Dream or no dream, I did not want to be eaten by a group of scary condoms with mouths. I moved faster than I've ever moved in my life, not daring to look behind me. I'd watched enough movies to know that if I even peeked, I'd trip, run into a tree, fall down a hole, or have one bite me right in the ass. So I just ran, not knowing what sinister thing would come next.

The trees thinned, eventually giving way to an open field with a lone house in the middle. I would be completely vulnerable without the cover of trees, but with no other choice, I urged my tired legs forward. Faster. The grass seemed to rattle, growing louder with each pounding step until the whole field vibrated from it. Rattlesnakes lay coiled in the grass everywhere I looked. If I worried about the snakes, I would slow down, giving the creatures the chance to catch up. If I didn't slow down, I ran the risk of being bitten. *Damned if I do, damned if I don't.*

The house was within reach now. I could hear the creatures gaining ground behind me, and with a final push, I managed to run up the small stoop. There was a split second of panic when I realized it could be locked, but when I turned the knob, the door slid open. I swiftly dodged inside, slamming the door closed and turning the lock. One of the creatures smashed into it, sending a reverberating thud through the quiet house. Something scraped the length of the door, sounding like nails screaming down a chalkboard.

I ran up the entryway stairs, turning the corner at the top, and entered a living room that I recognized. Having spent eighteen years in this house, I would never forget this room. I recalled all the good times my family and I had together. A fake family, but I loved them nonetheless. This was my childhood home, but there was something off about it. As if it were a bad imitation. The exterior of the house wasn't even right. And of course, it wasn't located in a field right outside a dense forest. It was in a busy city, on a busy street, surrounded by other houses.

Walking into the kitchen, I could see that a door at the end of the little hallway was ajar. I should have been apprehensive. I should have taken my chances with the monsters outside. But curiosity got the better of me. Cautiously, I followed the little hall past the bathroom on the left, past my parents' room on the right, to the door at the end. Raven's bedroom. I pushed open the door and screamed.

Sprawled on the bed lay the body of a woman. Her sleek, black hair was spread out around her head like a headdress.

Ligature marks marred the skin around her ankles, wrists, and throat. Her neck was at an odd angle, obviously broken.

Raven.

I ran to the side of the bed, laying my head on her chest. There was no heartbeat; she was dead.

"Sissy, I'm so sorry this happened to you. This wasn't your fight. I should have protected you."

I knew this was only a dream. I came into it, planning on controlling the outcome, but it had all gone horribly wrong. There was a player here that I hadn't met yet, and he came to play dirty.

Lost in feelings of grief and failure, I didn't hear the figure creep up behind me. Sharp claws sank into my shoulders, boring holes into the skin. I screamed as red-hot pain shot down my arms. Whatever had grabbed me yanked me upright by the muscles between his fingers, using them as handles. I was sure they would rip right off the bone, but they held tight, just like the thing that had me. It pulled me against his body, his hands still fastened around my raw, bleeding shoulders. A cold, scaly face pressed against my cheek, its forked tongue flicking at my face.

"I'm coming for you. Are you ready? Are you ready to watch everyone you love die? They will. Jusssst as you will," he said.

His tongue flicked at my ear, giving me the willies.

There was a horrible cracking sound as bones broke and splintered, but they weren't mine. They were Raven's. She lay crumpled, much like Lucian in the barn, with bones jutting out of the skin. Lucian sprawled in a corner of the room, Lake at my feet, and Maiz at the end of the bed, all in similar condition as Raven. Their terrified faces were forever frozen, while their dead eyes begged me for help.

Screaming at the horrific sight, I closed my eyes, trying to block out the atrocities of my loved ones, but their faces were engraved on the backs of my eyelids. I screamed louder. I couldn't stop. I couldn't stop seeing them.

"Rose. Wake up, Rose."

His voice was not harsh or cruel. I opened my eyes at the soothing tone. A blurry face hovered above mine. *Lucian.* He looked worried as he wiped sweat and tears from my face.

The door to the room flew open, slamming against the wall with a loud bang. A naked Adam ran in, holding out a shoe in a defensive position, ready to strike with the heel of it if need be.

"Who is it? What happened?" Adam asked.

"Rose had a nightmare," Lucian said.

Only then did I notice his voice had less rasp to it. He didn't sound as if he was straining, or in pain with every word.

"A shoe, wolf?" Lucian asked incredulously.

"I just grabbed the nearest thing. I wanted to get over here to save my lady."

Adam winked at me.

"And who is going to save you when I break your ass in two?" Lucian asked with a quirk of his eyebrow.

Adam turned, pointing to his backside, and said, "My ass is already in two, and besides, I could crush you like a flea in your current state."

"Okay boys, put your dicks away," Maiz said, coming in behind Adam. "Literally."

She looked down at Adam's package, then over at Lucian. The covers had slipped down during my nightmare, leaving a naked Lucian exposed. Maiz raised her eyebrows at me and smiled. Adam put the shoe over his sizable manhood, while Lucian made no attempt to cover himself.

I flipped the covers over his waist.

"Your nightmare, was it the same as the other?" Maiz asked.

"No, it started with me being chased through the woods by these monsters to my family's home. It wasn't where it was supposed to be, and it didn't feel right. Not like the zombie dream I had with you," I said to Lucian. "Inside, I found Rae." I turned to Maiz. "She was dead. She'd been tortured. Something grabbed me from behind. Whatever it was, it was cold, scaly, and had a forked tongue."

Everyone exchanged glances.

"Apep," Maiz said. "He must have gotten her nightmare stone. He's trying to scare her away."

"Who's Apep?" I asked.

Nobody answered.

"Even if they have her stone, they'd still need a screamer to help construct the dream," Lucian said. "My cousins may deal in nightmares, but I doubt they would side with him."

Maiz shook her head. "I would never have thought my own sister would side with him, but she did."

"Which sister?" I asked. "It's not Vex, is it?"

Still no answer.

"Sorry Lucian, but most walkers ain't got shit to lose," Maiz said.

"Where did Apep grab you, Rose?" Adam asked, his eyes dipping below my chin line.

"You better pull your eyes up, boy," Lucian growled.

"Get over yourself," Adam said. "I'm looking at the skin around her clavicles. I think she's bleeding."

Lucian touched my shoulder, making me cringe at the sting I felt there.

"It's dried blood," Lucian said. "The rest is bruise."

"I'll be fine," I said, giving him a reassuring smile. I rotated my shoulders a few times, testing them out. "Doesn't feel like anything is broken."

"Did he bite you, too?" Adam asked.

The room was still fairly dark since the sun hadn't come up yet. Adam was using his wolf sight, allowing him to notice the marks Lucian had left on my neck. I hoped he couldn't see my blush. Avoiding his eyes, I appealed to Maiz.

"You moron, if you weren't so busy waving your dick around, you might have noticed that Lucian is sitting up on his own. You could have put two and two together."

"Right. Sorry. I didn't mean to step in your business. I was just worried about you," Adam said to me.

I nodded at him.

"Maiz, I need you to do me a favor," I said, trying to get the attention off my neck. "Can you please check on Rae? I need to know she's okay." I turned to Lucian. "I need you to check on Lake. I haven't had the chance to tell you about my first nightmare because of all the chaos, but I've seen him dead twice now."

"If something happened, I would have heard about it," he said.

"Please, Lucian. Call it mother's intuition, call me a worrywart, whatever you want. I need to know that he's okay."

Lucian grabbed a cell phone out of a drawer in the little bedside table. He hit a button, then held the phone to his ear. I couldn't hear the phone ringing on the other end or the voice that answered.

All I heard was Lucian say, "It's me." His face never changed during the silence. A long minute later, he said, "Thanks, Gideon," and hung up.

He looked at Maiz before telling me Lake was fine. I wondered if there was some code between the two that I was unaware of.

"Are you sure?" I asked.

"He's managing well," he said. "I'm sure Raven is fine, too. You said the house was wrong. That tells me Apep doesn't really know where it is. He's only pulling images stored in the stone he stole."

"I'll still go call Vex and have her check on Rae," Maiz said. "Give you some peace of mind."

"And I'm going back to bed since I'm not needed," Adam declared.

He tossed the shoe over his shoulder as he walked out the door. Maiz playfully slapped his tushy as he walked by. He did a little hop, then stuck out his tongue at her. Hard to believe that guy was a king. You'd never know it by looking at him.

Alone now, I flipped the lamp on to take a better look at Lucian. Maiz had pointed out that he was sitting up on his own, and I was ashamed to say Adam wasn't the only one who hadn't noticed. Hard to focus when there were multiple naked men in the room. Add that to the disturbing nightmare, and I had a pretty good excuse for being distracted.

The lamp's light wasn't very bright, but it was enough to show me a man who had improved considerably. His color wasn't his usual beach bum tan, but he was no longer the same ashen color as the walking condoms. There was no crease in his brow and no wheezing breaths. His eyes still didn't glow, which I supposed had something to do with the destruction the venom had caused on the inside.

"You look—" I started.

"Positively beddable," he finished for me. "Show me how much you think so."

He positioned himself on top of me, pulling my tank top over my head.

"You need to save your strength," I protested.

He was nuzzling my neck. My mouth was saying no, but my body was saying *yes, please.* The bulge pressing at my jeans told me his was, too. My brain and my lady parts were at odds. He'd made great strides in his healing, and I didn't want any setbacks. Making love could bolster his spirits and help him along as well, though.

"Alright then. I'll save my strength." He rolled over to his back, pulling me with him. "You can be on top."

I climbed out of the bed so that I could teasingly strip off the rest of my clothes. Lucian lay with his hands behind his head, appearing relaxed. His taut muscles indicated he was feeling anything but relaxed. I stepped out of my panties, my last piece of clothing, before climbing back into the bed. Lucian's scrutinizing gaze took in every inch of my body as I climbed on top of him, his eyes instantly turning black.

I started with kisses on his lips, moving lower to his neck, chest, and stomach. Moving lower still, I teased the tip of him with my mouth, getting him all kinds of worked up. When the time was right, I released him from my mouth and helped guide him inside me. That was always my favorite part. The first thrust inside, our bodies connecting, becoming one in love and passion. The pleasure of it was enough to make me cry out.

I started to move on top of him while his hands explored my body. The feel of his warm hands on my skin enhanced the pleasure. All fear of what lay in the future, and the horrors I'd experienced in my dreams were temporarily forgotten. I rocked on top of him, my muscles clenching until I couldn't take anymore. When I threw my head back during the peak of my climax, Lucian sat up to sink his teeth into my neck. It was the very epitome of pleasure.

The room exploded in vivid colors all around me, lighting the room in a sort of pleasure-induced synesthesia. Every object in the room was a different color that vibrated and blended into the next thing. Lucian was the brightest of all. His vivid, bright white light radiated off him like a star. Everything around me started to spin like a crazy rainbow tornado, and the only thing keeping me from being swept away was Lucian. I wrapped my arms around him, anchoring myself, holding on for dear life. I had to close my eyes against the seizure-inducing flashes.

"Breathe, Rose. It will pass."

Something ruptured deep inside me, sending a bolt of lightning through my whole body. All my nerves were suddenly on fire. On edge. Hyper-sensitive. I could feel everything. Even the air itself. I could feel my heart pumping, all four chambers contracting, pushing blood through my body. I could feel my cells transforming. My muscles spasmed painfully and combined with the worst case of vertigo in the history of the world. I was sure I'd hurl.

As quick as the pain started, it subsided. I opened my eyes. It was over. There was no more spinning, no more colors, no more feeling of my insides.

"What the hell was that?" I asked, still clinging to him.

"Your power releasing."

"Damn, I'm glad that's over."

"That was only part of it."

"You mean there's more? No way," I said, sitting back to look at him. I vehemently shook my head. "Nope. I don't want to do that again."

"I promise, you will get through it. You are the strongest being out there."

I detected apprehension in his words. *I fear that once you have served the purpose for which you were created, you will be destroyed.* His lips didn't move, so I knew I had picked that up directly from his mind.

"What do you mean, destroyed?" I asked. "Why? What was I created for?"

Lucian's eyes widened at my questions. He knew I was able to read him the same way he read me.

"No more avoiding this. I need answers."

"You're right," he said. "I should have told you sooner. What do you know about Egyptian history? Specifically, their gods."

"Even less than the Greek stuff. I learned some names from a computer game I played when I was younger. There were four of them, but I only remember Ra and Osiris."

"That's—something. Ra is the king of the Egyptian pantheon. Every day, he and his mortal enemy, Apep, did battle. Every day, Ra won. No matter what Ra did, he was never able to destroy Apep, only defeat him. Apep was always able to heal and come back for more. Even when Ra merged with the god Amun to become even more powerful as Amun Ra, he still wasn't able to kill Apep."

More pieces of the puzzle were being laid out in front of me. I still wasn't exactly sure where they fit.

"How did the Greeks get involved?" I asked.

"Patience, love, I'm getting to it," Lucian said. "One day, Apep didn't show up. This was very unusual for him, but Amun Ra thought he had finally succeeded in killing the bastard. Then there were sightings. Now, Apep is the embodiment of chaos and evil. He causes nothing but pain and sorrow. He's not widely worshipped except by a rare few. Legend says that once upon a time in history, Apep was king, but he was so lousy, he was dethroned by Osiris."

"I thought you said Ra was king?"

"That's a different story for another day. Their history is as complicated as ours," he said.

I was getting impatient with the history lesson. But at least Lucian was talking, giving me the answers I'd been desperately wanting for days. Years, really.

"Deities that aren't widely worshipped or liked are weaker than the rest. The more adoration a god or goddess receives, the stronger they are. Primordials, like my mother and yours, draw power from the earth's core. Very few can do that. Unless you're a primordial that can take from the core, you're stuck needing to be worshipped."

"Can you?"

"Not directly. Gaia allows me to draw from her. When I worked dreams, I'd get most of my power from the mortals I visited."

That spurred some jealousy knowing he was so good at his job, he was able to draw power from the people he was with. I knew firsthand how good he was. Hopefully I'd be the only one he was drawing power from, from now on.

"The Greeks have become masters of getting power in unconventional ways, pushing us to the top of the heap," he said.

That didn't sound good. I could recall some of the stories Lucian had told me about the Greeks, and I knew they could be absolutely despicable. They could be holding people hostage, forcing them to give worship. Would that even work?

"No," Lucian said, picking up the question in my head. "It has to be given through free will. We're not forcing anyone; we're getting adoration through odd jobs. Painting, acting, singing, modeling, pro-sports, things of that nature."

That's not at all what I'd expected. I didn't watch much TV anymore, so I wasn't sure who was who in Hollywood. Growing up, though, I'd idolized some of the women on TV. They were so beautiful, so talented, and so lucky to have such a fun job. The men, some of them were just so damn hot. I'd watch every movie I could with my favorite actors, jealous of the women who got to share a romantic scene with them. It didn't even matter if the movie or show looked good, so long as that person was in it.

I didn't listen to much music these days, either. As a teenager, I'd gone fangirl crazy over a particular boy band. Maiz and I both had. We had posters of them hanging all over our walls. We'd sit and fantasize about being their wives someday. Traveling the world with them. We were only two of millions of girls all over the world with the same fantasy. When we were older, we went to countless rock concerts where we screamed ourselves hoarse and head-banged ourselves into a stupor late into the night.

I might not do much idolizing anymore, but I was only one person. Professional sports alone drew billions of fans.

In all my years, I'd never noticed anyone who didn't age. That had to be a hard thing to hide. Even with the advancement of cosmetic surgery, mere mortals were unable to stop the aging process.

"The whole time I've known you, you don't look like you've aged a day. If a deity is in the public eye, wouldn't that draw unwanted attention?"

"We can look like we age. And once we get old in human years, we can appear to die. Then we reinvent ourselves as someone new."

Maiz had to have done something of that nature to grow up with me, but she wasn't my main concern right now. We had gone off on a whole different tangent, and I had to get Lucian back on topic.

"Okay, so the Greek gods are getting very powerful, and Apep is missing. Then what?"

"He's not really missing. He's hiding. Building an army of misfit gods. Minor deities are joining his cause, giving him the worship he needs to become more powerful."

"Why is he doing this?"

"A source on the inside told us Apep is tired of being spit on, and he's tired of getting the shit kicked out of him. He plans to take from the most powerful and use it to destroy the world. He would then recreate it in his image, with him as the supreme being. There's only one who can stop him."

Oh shit. It wasn't just my life at stake or the lives of the gods. Nearly eight billion people were relying on me, even if they didn't know it. The weight of the world was literally on my shoulders. *No pressure.*

Chapter 8

It was too much. It was all too much. The room started to close in on me, making me claustrophobic as all get-out. I needed to get out of here before I suffocated to death. Then I'd be no good to anyone. Except Apep. I was the only one standing in his way of overtaking the world.

Leaving the bed, I pulled on my clothes in record time and hit the door at a run. I didn't have a plan. I just needed to get the hell out of there. I let my legs carry me wherever they wanted to go, which was down the stairs and right out the front door to the porch.

The sun was climbing up over the horizon, swathing the land around me in a majestic glow. Beams of red peeked around the throng of trees that surrounded the house. The sky around me sparkled with moisture frozen right out of the air by the subzero temperature. Trees twinkled as the sun's rays reflected off the frost-covered branches. I stood there, watching the sun rise higher in the sky, hypnotized by the splendor of the wonderland around me.

Cold air pierced my lungs with each inhale, and my warm breath puffed out mini clouds on each exhale. A coat was wrapped around my shoulders.

"Maiz thought you might need this."

I turned to face Vex. The last time I had seen her was at my dad's funeral. Looking at her now, there was no resemblance between her and Maiz that would indicate they were sisters. Vex was a few inches shorter than me, and her voluptuous figure was something desired by men all over the world. Her hair hung down to her shoulders in blond, cascading waves that shone with silky softness. The opposite of my processed hair, which looked and felt like straw.

Her sharp blue eyes always sparkled with joy, and her long lashes were the envy of women everywhere. She was always bubbling over with happiness and an attitude that was always looking on the bright side of things. When we were younger, her happy-go-lucky attitude was annoying as hell, but she was hard not to love. She was not the type of person I'd expect to see out on battlefields, taking the lives of others.

"You're trying to figure out how Maiz and I are sisters and how you missed it," she said.

"Crap, you can read my mind, too?" I asked.

"Shit no," she said, sounding like Maiz. "You've been checking me out for the last five minutes. It's not frowned upon by Greek god standards for siblings to get together, but ew. I know you well enough to know you don't swing that way, anyway. So, I figure you're going back through the years, looking for a sign. Like we would make it easy. If that were the case, we would have used Maiz's twin."

"Maiz has a twin?"

"Yeah, Mona. She's way cooler than Maiz, in case you were wondering."

I looked forward to getting all of this behind me so I could meet all my sisters. It dawned on me that Vex might be here because of a problem with Raven.

"Is Rae okay?"

"Other than the fact that she married that waste of space, Dan, she's fine," Vex said.

Talk about a knife to the heart. I hadn't even been invited to my own sister's wedding.

"I wanted to tell you that first night you were here," Vex said. "But Maiz didn't think you'd be ready. I left before you saw me. It wasn't until later that I found out about what happened with Marc. I am so sorry, by the way."

She wrapped her arms around me in a tight hug. She might be small in stature, but what she lacked in height, she made up for in strength.

I had forgotten about my first night. The night I thought Maiz was losing her marbles because she was talking to herself in different voices. It felt like that had happened ages ago. I'd learned so much, and so much had happened in such a short period of time that the days were blurring together. With all I'd learned, I still felt ignorant of the secret world around me. Now, I'd have to save it if I wanted to learn anything more about it.

"Your eye is doing that twitchy thing," Vex said. "Do you wanna talk about it?"

"What's there to talk about? I was born to kill the unkillable. There are werewolves, demons, and spirits, oh my. This beautiful world we live in is in danger of being destroyed. I may have killed my boyfriend. I haven't seen or spoken to my son in ages. The last time I saw him, he died in my arms. Raven hates me. She didn't even invite me to her wedding."

"First off, that was a nightmare, meant to weaken and scare you. Don't let it. Second, Rae did invite you. You never responded. She told me that she's reached out to you many times over the years, only to get no answer. She thinks you hate her."

"What? I never got anything from her after I went to the funeral. This must be Marc's doing. I'll kill that asshole the next time I see him."

Marc had done his damnedest to isolate me from everyone I loved. And I had pretty much let him succeed. I'd pushed away friends, ignored family, and let him walk all over me. He hadn't known what he was up against when he went up against Maiz, trying to push her away from me. It was a miracle she hadn't ripped his balls off years ago. I sort of wished she had.

Vex looked nervous, reluctant to say what was on her mind.

"What is it?" I asked.

"Marc is already dead. His body was discovered last night. We're pretty sure Apep killed him after he failed to kill you before your power was released. The cops aren't sure if you're dead or alive, but they're looking for you."

"Oh," I said reeling from the news.

I hated Marc but I also loved him. He had been a major part of my life for many years and now he was gone. I'd never see him again. Never be able to hug him for not killing me. Or punch him in his face for almost killing me. And then there was Lake. He had lost his father. They may not have been close, but a boy should have his father.

Vex wrapped an arm around mine, steadying me on my swaying legs.

"Does Rae know?"

"No, she's on her honeymoon in Hawaii. Don't worry about her. I'll protect her. From all of this. From Dan. He's a lazy ass and makes her feel like shit, but she takes it in stride. Never lets it get her down. She still thinks she's happy."

Eerie how similar our life choices were. I hoped for her sake that her path didn't go the same way as mine.

"If things start to escalate, please get her out of there," I said. "Kill him if you have to. If you can't because of the rules or whatever, I'll do it. Don't let him hurt her." Vex nodded. "If I make it through this, let's all plan to get together."

Vex smiled wide. "I have something for you." She reached behind her back and plucked an odd-looking sword out of thin air. "This is a kopis. My personal kopis for battles and wars. It's made of adamantine, a metal found only on Olympus, and was forged by Hephaestus himself. I've tainted it with hydra poison, so be careful not to cut yourself. I don't know what it will do to Apep, but I didn't think it could hurt. I'd have added some of Typhon's too, but after Zeus defeated him, he made sure he was locked up good and tight in Tartarus."

A story that Lucian had told me in a dream came to mind. It was about a ferocious mountain of a monster named Typhon. It was said that his head touched the stars when he stood, and he had wings that obscured the sun when they unfurled. Below the waist, he slithered on two snake tails instead of legs. Above the waist, he looked human, except for scales as strong as armor covering his torso. His hands were as strong as vice grips, and he could grow one hundred snakeheads from his shoulders. Each snakehead was capable of spitting viper venom.

Like Apep, Typhon wanted to be king of the heavens. It was Zeus' throne being threatened, and it was Zeus who would defend it. He was the only one formidable enough to take on such a beast. The battle that followed nearly split the earth into pieces. Zeus won by the skin of his teeth, sealing Typhon in the pits of the hell realm, never to see the light of day again. Gods willing.

"If Zeus was capable of taking down Typhon, why can't he fight Apep?"

"Well." Vex hesitated. "Zeus defeated Typhon, but he didn't kill him. He's only locked up in Tartarus. Zeus could fight Apep, but since he's not Greek, he can't be sent to our underworld. There is no other place strong enough to hold him. He needs to be killed. Zeus might be able to do it, but he'd rather have someone else do his dirty work. Little-known fact, Zeus is a scared little bitch when it comes to Nyx and the power she holds. She offered to fight Apep for him, but Zeus didn't want to take the chance of losing her and her power to the beast. Instead, they came up with 'fight chaos with chaos.' Enter you."

"Damn. Is he going to help at least?"

"No. He'll be in hiding. If Apep kills you, the world will be destroyed."

"I already know that."

"No, *you* will destroy it. If you die, a fail-safe will be activated, destroying the world before Apep has the chance to take your power. The Olympians will be safely tucked away in a bunker. They'll rebuild after it's done." She frowned at me. "You should have that eye looked at."

I slapped a hand on my trembling eye. "It's just the stress." I waved my free hand at her. "Forget the eye. You're telling me that if I die, I'll self-destruct, killing everyone in the world except the Greek pantheon?"

"Yes and no. You will self-destruct, and only the twelve Olympians and Chaos will survive. That's why they aren't here to help. They figure, why risk their lives when they'll make it anyway? And if Apep were to take hold of their power, it's that much more against you. Again, why risk it. You don't need them. You got this, girl!"

"Uh-huh, uh-huh. Me. It's me. Alone," I said, hand still held to my eye.

"You are so not alone. Maiz and I would be honored to stand by you. The wolves and demons have all volunteered to fight with you. And if I'm not mistaken, Lucian loves the heck out of you. I can tell by the way he looks at you, he wants to devour you." She obviously eyed my neck. "He's gonna protect his lady love, even if it kills him."

Kills him. No, I didn't want him to be killed. It was in my nightmare that he would die a horrible, painful death that I couldn't bear to witness firsthand. It was disturbing enough in my dream; it would be excruciating to see it in real life.

They said that dreams come true, and some of mine had. I felt blessed to have Lucian in my life. If something happened to him, or anyone else I loved, because I'd put them in danger, I wouldn't be able to live with myself. This fight was mine and mine alone. As much as it sucked, I'd do what I needed to do to release the rest of my power, and then I'd kick Apep's ass straight to hell.

Or wherever Egyptian gods go when they die. So long as he's dead and gone for good.

"I should get going," Vex said. "Things to do. I'm in the middle of opening a bar, ya know."

"No, I didn't know that. Congratulations."

I realized how little I knew about the lives of my sister and my—other sister. How strange to think that I had all this family now. I wanted to ask if Rae and I were really sisters, but it didn't matter. Whether we were related by blood or not, she would always be my sister, and I would always love her as such.

"Don't worry about Rae. I've got her covered," Vex said.

She handed me the sword. I took it carefully so as not to accidentally touch the blade or cut off a limb. It was heavier than I'd expected, probably from the custom metal it was made from. The blade was much longer than any knife but was shorter than a typical sword. It was only a single-edged sword, with a rather noticeable recurve toward the hilt. Looked like a perfect weapon for chopping heads.

I followed Vex back into the cabin. Adam and Maiz sat on stools at the island. Adam, with his advanced wolf hearing, turned as we came in. Maiz was too engrossed in the conversation they had been having to notice us. She was looking at her phone, too busy typing to see Lucian look up at us.

Lucian leaned against the counter in the kitchen, arms crossed over his chest. He had been watching us on the porch. I was nearly stunned off my feet to see him standing there, looking as if he hadn't been on his deathbed less than twenty-four hours ago.

"What else did Gideon say happened?" Maiz asked.

Gideon. The name Lucian mentioned when he called to check on Lake.

"Yeah, what else did he say?" I asked.

I looked at each face for any hint of an answer. Vex took a seat on a chair next to Maiz. Adam was looking down at his hands on the counter. Lucian looked unfazed.

"Fuck," Maiz said, looking rather pissed at herself.

If I were in her shoes, I would have done a palm to forehead. Maiz was much more graceful than I, obviously.

"Somebody better tell me what's going on, or I might practice with my new weapon on you all."

I held up the sword in what I thought was a hidden-dragon, fighting-baseball-player sort of way. Both Maiz and Adam looked to Lucian. He pushed away from the counter. Favoring his right leg, he limped toward me. Putting a hand on either side of the blade, he aimed it down toward the floor. Up close, he looked tired. My blood had given him temporary strength, but it was fading, and so was he.

"No need to wield a weapon. I'll tell you, but I think we should sit," he said.

"Careful of the blade. Vex poisoned it. I don't need you sick in bed from two monsters."

"Yes, Butter, I know. Maybe you should hand it over to Maiz for safekeeping."

Was that because he knew I'd want to use it on him or because he was worried I'd hurt myself? He let go of the blade and braced himself on the counter. I did as he suggested, handing over the sword to Maiz. Then I wrapped Lucian's arm around my shoulders and helped him over to the couch in front of the fireplace. It blazed to life, presumably by Lucian's doing.

We had relative privacy away from the kitchen, but I knew by the quiet, the three supernaturals were listening. Vex said she needed to go, yet she still sat in the chair. She must have decided that this would be much more interesting than arrangements for her bar. Lucian wrapped a hand around mine. It was cold yet calming. I took a deep breath.

"An alarm went off at my house. Where Lake was staying," he said quietly. "My brother, Gideon, went in to check it out. He found Sandi."

The only Sandi I knew was the sweet waitress from the hotel restaurant.

"I'm confused." Like always. "Sandi broke into your house?"

"No, I entrusted Lake to her care at my house on the island."

"Is she okay? Is Lake okay? Did Gideon find him, too? Where is he? Lucian, please tell me my son is okay."

"They should have been safe. I can count on one hand the number of people that know how to find my island."

"You're avoiding my question. Tell me where my son is."

"I can't. After you left the room, I called Gideon back. He told me there was a significant struggle, but there was no boy. All the blood was Sandi's."

I was fighting a losing battle against the tears welling in my eyes.

"How does he know it's all hers?" I asked.

"It was all ethereal ichor, like mine." He placed a cold hand on my cheek, wiping away a tear with his thumb. "I didn't lie when I said he's okay."

"How can you be so sure when you don't know where he is?"

"Because we're connected. I can feel his life force; he's a strong kid. I'm his—" He stopped for so long, I thought that was the end of his sentence. "I'm his dad."

"No, you're not. No. You're not. It's not possible," I said, jumping up off the couch.

"It's extremely rare for a walker and a mortal to conceive in the dream world, but not impossible if circumstances are right. A little more common for two deities," he took a long wheezing breath. "It's one of the reasons we aren't allowed to keep the dream stone."

"My son—is your son. My son. My son is missing. I let you keep him from me. You told me he would be safer away from me. I trusted you."

"I promise I will get him back."

"All these promises," I was shaking my head in disbelief. "I can't with you right now."

No one tried to stop me. No one followed me as I went back to my room. I wanted to scream and cry and throw things. That would make me feel better, but it wouldn't bring back my baby. It was unimaginable that I would never see him again. Hear his sweet voice. Watch him sketch one of his pictures. *His pictures.* He'd known what was going to happen. He'd known who his real dad was. Is that who he was referring to when he made the random comments about his dad protecting us?

Acid rose in my throat, and I had to make a run for the bathroom. I wretched the contents of my stomach as images of my dying son cracked my heart. When the last bit came up, I collapsed in a heap on the floor. The cool tile felt good against my feverish skin. I felt like I had purged some of my emotions from my stomach. I was still upset, but not blow-up-the-house level upset.

"Rose," Adam said from outside the bedroom door, "can I come in?"

Pulling myself off the floor, I grabbed the hand towel to wipe away any remnants that may have been left behind. I went to the door and opened it. Doing a quick peek around the hallway to make sure he was alone, I let him in. The sweat that coated my skin from being sick was now evaporating at an alarming rate, causing me to shake uncontrollably. Or maybe it was the situation. Probably both.

Adam had plopped himself down on the corner of the bed.

"You look like hell," he said.

"Way to make a girl feel good."

I walked to the other side of the bed, sliding under the covers, and pulling them all the way up to my nose. Adam turned to face me.

"Looks like I finally got you in bed."

"Not the right time, Adam." He looked like he was about to say something, but I stopped him. "I don't want to talk about it. If I talk about it, it becomes real. I need to believe this is a nightmare. This is all a nightmare. My son is fine, still hidden away, where no one can hurt him. I can't think about how he might be with some lunatic who is torturing him or who may have—"

I couldn't finish that thought. He was an extremely smart boy. There was a good chance he was hiding or had gotten away. Lucian's home was on an island, surrounded by water that went on and on, but I hadn't seen the whole thing. There could be a boat docked somewhere. A life raft sitting on the shore. A random door that led to Olympus. Anything but the other option.

"I don't want to talk at all," I said, laying my head in my hands.

Adam scooted closer to me, leaning back against the headboard. He pulled me close with an arm around my shoulder. His body was abnormally warm. I was still chilled, so I wasn't going to complain. The warmth helped to stop my shivering, and his thumping heartbeat eased my racing mind.

I thought of Marc and what his reaction might be if he found out about the mind-blowing, power-releasing sex I'd had with Lucian. Or if he could see me now, cuddled up in my bed with another man. *I forgot; he doesn't have reactions anymore.*

It was nice to be with someone who wasn't berating me for overreacting. Telling me that I was crazy for getting so upset when I didn't know that anything had happened. Adam listened when I said I didn't want to talk. He wasn't prying or trying to get me to open up. He was just holding me, being an emotional support. Though I knew for certain he would listen if I ultimately wanted to spout on about Lake, or Lucian, or whatever life problems I might have been having. And there were many.

It was a new concept to be surrounded by people who truly cared about how I felt or what I had to say. Everyone here might have been a little *too* worried. They were all trying to keep me in the dark because they were afraid I might break. I knew they were doing it out of love, but dammit, they were going to have to realize I was a grown woman, and I could handle my shit.

Adam's cheek rested on the top of my head. It wasn't the most comfortable position, but I could tell by his steady breathing that he was asleep. I wasn't the only one who'd had a rough few days. Adam had lost his entire family. We both needed a little cuddling. I followed his lead and let myself sleep.

Sometime later, I woke up alone. The room was quiet and dark, a chill in the air sent shivers down my spine. Outside my window, the sun hung in the sky, but the bright rays weren't making it to the room. I slid out of the bed, grabbing the throw blanket to wrap around my shoulders on my way to the door.

In the hall, there were no voices or wonderful smells drifting from the kitchen. The sitting room and kitchen were both empty. I had that odd feeling of something being an imitation. The whole house was swathed in shadows. I walked outside, and even though the land was still blanketed in snow, it wasn't cold. Chilly, yes, but not cold like late December warranted.

There was no movement. The world around me was still, the air stagnant. Everything looked fake, like a backdrop to a play. The peculiar state must be part of a dream. Or a nightmare, since they'd been coming regularly each time I slept.

Please, God, or whatever higher being I was supposed to pray to now that I was part of the Greek pantheon, let this be a pleasant dream. I didn't have to wait long to find out.

"I've found you, my sssssssweet."

I turned to the man standing beside me on the porch. He was shorter than me and I had to look down at him. His skin had an odd red tint to it, as if he'd spent a day too long in the sun. His long black hair was pulled back in a loose ponytail. What caught my attention most, though, were his yellow eyes with black slits for pupils. Snake eyes.

"Apep," I said confidently. "I am not your ssssssweet."

"Ah, a ssssssassssssy one. I would have thought Marc beat that out of you." He smirked at me, a shit-eating grin, as Maiz would say. "I'm sure you'll tassssste plenty ssssweet when I sssssuck the life out of you." A black forked tongue flitted from between his lips. "Your little boy toy thought he was sssso clever hiding you in the most obviousssss place."

"If it was so obvious, why did it take you so long to find me?"

"I wassss preparing. I've sssshown you exactly what I have planned for your friendsss. That'ssss nothing compared to what will happen to you. Unlessss. You join me. We can rule the new world together. I'll even sssspare your little boy."

"It's hard to take you seriously when you're barely taller than my boy."

"Bitch!" His face turned as red as a cherry. "I'm offering to sssspare you, yet you talk to me like that. If you want to sssssave your ssson, you will meet me at noon at Paintbrush Canyon. And you will come alone. You follow these sssimple inssstructions and I may sssspare the child. I've taken a liking to him—there'sss a darkness in him that intriguesss me. He can be molded."

"I've never been here in my life. I have no idea how to get to Paintbrush Canyon."

"Oh, come now, you're a sssmart girl. I'm sure you'll figure sssomething out." His forked tongue flicked out again, then he laughed at the look of loathing on my face. "Be there or be square."

It was my turn to laugh. "Seriously, you're making it so hard to see you as the monster I've been told you are."

"Isn't that what the kidsss are ssssaying these days?"

"You're a few decades off."

"Time fliesss when you're having fun. Doesn't matter what the little sssscumbagsss are ssssaying, because soon enough, they won't be sssaying anything. They'll be dead. Wiped out. Exxxtinct."

"Yeah, yeah, I get it. You have to get through me first."

"Indeed, I will. Noon. Alone." Then he was gone. Disappeared in a cloud of smoke.

"Are you a magician, too? That's so old school. Better learn new tricks, but I guess the saying is that you can't teach an old dog new tricks. You're old! I'm new and I will kick your ass!"

I didn't know if he could hear me, but yelling made me feel better. Ready or not, it was time to save the world.

***

When I woke up, for real woke up this time, Adam was sleeping next to me. He had managed to move under the covers while his arm was still wrapped around me. I maneuvered out from beneath his hold to check the clock. It was already a few minutes to ten. I had two hours to release the rest of my power, learn to use it, learn to fight, and get to the meeting place. Which, by the way, I had no idea how to find. It could be anywhere in the world, literally. Shit, shit, and more shit.

I considered saying "screw it" and going back to bed. Not like Apep could destroy the world without me anyway. But if Apep had Lake, his life was at stake, and I couldn't risk it. Tiptoeing to the closet, I considered what to wear. I'd never been in a fight before and wasn't sure if I should go comfy slacker, or more get-down-to-business.

I decided on a pair of black leather pants and a loose black sweater. Figured it was a smart mix. I wouldn't trip over baggy pants, and the top was loose enough that I could hide my weapon. I pulled my hair back in a tight bun, then swiped on eyeliner and mascara. Checking myself in the mirror, I looked kind of badass. If looks alone could win this war, it'd be over already. Leaving the bathroom, I peeked at a still-sleeping Adam before I slipped out the door.

In the kitchen, I found Maiz staring blankly at a frying pan, a spatula poised above.

"Where is everyone?" I asked, making her jump.

"Dammit lady, you're getting good at sneaking up on me. The wolves came in late, so they're still in bed. Should be down soon, though. Lucian went to his room after you left. I haven't seen him since, and I didn't see where Adam went."

I grabbed a cup out of the cupboard, poured some coffee, and took a sip. If Adam hadn't told anyone he planned to go to my room, it wasn't for me to say either. Nothing had happened, but I wasn't about to get anyone in trouble. Even if he was a king.

"Fuck, Rose, I'm sorry about Lake. This shouldn't have happened to such a cool-ass kid. If anything happens to him, I'll destroy the world myself."

"Thanks, Maiz. I feel the same way."

"Do you need to cry? Throw stuff? Shoot someone? I'm sure Lucian would understand. Hell, he'd understand if you shot *him.*"

"That's exactly what I wanted last night. I've calmed down, but I still need time away from everyone. Especially him. I think I'll go out today, do some soul-searching, scream at the heavens, that sort of thing."

"It's not safe out there," Adam said, coming down the stairs.

I gave him a perplexed look. He gave me one right back. How he'd managed to sneak upstairs from my room, I had no idea. There must be a hidden staircase somewhere that I hadn't discovered yet.

"It's not safe anywhere," I said. "Lake was supposed to be safe on another plane and now he's missing. Or dead for all we know. If I want to have a day to myself, I think you all should understand. I'm surrounded by gods and demons and wolves. How much trouble can I get in?"

I tried to tone it down toward the end so as not to raise suspicion.

"I guess you're right. I can show you how to drive the sled," Adam said.

"You're going out by yourself?" Lucian asked from the stairs.

He looked better than he had yesterday. In fact, he looked absolutely delectable in his dark-wash jeans and tight black shirt. My blood was really doing the body good. There was even a faint glow in those beautiful eyes of his. I had to remind myself that I was positively pissed at him.

"I've already had this conversation," I said to him. "Yes, I'm going out alone. I need this. And you owe me this."

The room fell silent. Maiz went back to flipping pancakes.

"When did you want to go?" Adam asked, breaking the tension.

"I think now would be best. I've lost my appetite."

I sent a glare at Lucian, whose eyes were now a blazing red color.

I moved to the door, saying hello to the men coming down the stairs. Pulling on my snow gear, I could feel the sword slipping with my movements. I had loosely tied the blade along my spine, hoping along the way that it wouldn't fall out or accidentally pierce my butt cheek.

Carefully, I tried to adjust without drawing attention to the moving bump at my back. Boots, snow pants, coat, hat, gloves…*damn this cold weather.* I forgot about this when I'd planned my outfit. It'd be difficult to fight in such bulky clothing, but I'd manage. I had to. Lake was relying on me. My friends were relying on me. The world was relying on me. I could practically hear billions of people screaming in my ear, begging me to save them.

"Stop it," I demanded of the ghostly voices.

I realized I said it out loud and not just in my head. Looking around, all eyes were focused on me. I gave them an awkward smile.

"Sorry. I thought I heard—I thought—I had a bad night, okay? I have to go," I said, making my escape.

I quickly exited the cabin, Adam close behind. We headed over to one of the smaller snowmobiles. He showed me how to turn it on and off, how to turn the throttle, and where the brake was. By my good fortune, there were no gears to deal with.

My dad had tried to teach me how to drive his old stick shift when I was learning to drive, but I couldn't get the hang of it. The car would jump, clunk, and stall. I couldn't get it going faster than fifteen miles per hour or make it farther than a block. My dad was so patient, always encouraging me, always believing in me. He never yelled or got angry. He just laughed. His laugh wasn't directed at me, but with me. He had to have the transmission replaced by the time I was done with it. It was quality father-daughter bonding time.

"Thank you for everything," I said.

I hugged him tight. It could be the last hug I gave anyone. Ever.

"I just showed you how to drive a sled. A toddler could do it."

"For last night, too. Staying with me. Being my friend."

"Are you sure it was me? I think I'd remember if I got to stay with a hot lady."

"Damn it all," I said, releasing Adam from the hug. "It was Lucian, wasn't it? He told me he could change identities. He knew I wasn't gonna let him in, so he used your looks to check on me. Did a pretty good job sounding like you, too."

"That's why you gave me that weird look when I came down the stairs. You expected me to come from the back hall. Shit, I missed my chance on that one."

"I have to go. Tell that jerk I'll deal with him if—uh, *when* I get back."

"What are you up to?" Adam eyed me suspiciously.

"Little ol' me? Why, you know I'm always up to no good." I forced a laugh, trying to ease the uncertainty that was written all over Adam's face. Getting serious again, I said, "I just need time."

"Yeah, so you keep saying."

I gave him a kiss on the cheek before pulling the helmet over my head. Straddling the sled, I sluggishly pulled away from the house. I drove that way until I was more confident in my ability to maneuver the machine safely to my destination. Lucky for me, when Adam took me out in the park, I'd grabbed a bunch of those little brochure things. One of them had a map of the park and surrounding areas. I knew that if I could get to the road Adam had taken that day, it would lead me anywhere I needed to go. Soon enough, I had found my way to the main road that would lead me out of Yellowstone and then into the Tetons. My speed was too fast for the snow-covered roads, but I had a lot of ground to cover if I planned to make it on time.

The powdery landscape looked pristine in all its glory. A pack of wolves was running along a river to my left. It was beautiful to see a family so close-knit bounding through the snow. I wondered if I knew any of them or if I'd get to meet any more of them. If I'd ever lay eyes on such an idyllic sight again. I tried not to focus on anything but the path ahead, letting the white land blur around me.

I exited the park at the south entrance, following the 191 to the Grand Tetons, stopping at a pull-out only to consult my map. I figured out where the "you are here" dot would be, then calculated the rest of my route to Paintbrush Canyon.

Chapter 9

Apep was waiting for me in a clearing devoid of any snow. The whole way there, everything had been cloaked in white. Even the mountains that loomed over us were glacial. But here I stood, inside a large swatch of unburdened ground. It had a midsummer warmth, like I had stepped inside an invisible bubble into a different ecosystem.

I stripped off my snow gear, tossing it outside the unseen edge of the bio-dome, then stepped over to where Apep stood.

"This is what the great Greek godsss came up with to defeat me?" He looked me up and down with distaste. "You can't even ussse your power to get from one place to another. You had to ussse a vehicle. You're alssso late."

"I could have used my power. Or maybe I wanted to give you the illusion that I'm weak. Guess you'll find out soon enough."

I tried to puff out my chest to make myself look bigger, but someone on the outside would probably think I was pushing my boobs at the small man. "Is that lisp thing you do fake? It seems like you choose what words you want to draw out. You should either drop it or stop saying words with s's in them."

If he were Lucian, his face would be pouring lava and his eyes would be snapping fire at me. Instead, Apep's tongue flicked in and out of his mouth in agitation.

"I'm glad I've chosssen to kill you over trying to rule with you. I'd never be able to ssstand you. Come forth, demons."

Creatures started appearing all around me. They reminded me of chameleons changing colors to be seen. These were the same beings that had chased me through the woods in my nightmare. Hunched, ugly things with only a mouth, their noxious odor stinking up the little biodome area. They must have been able to mask their nasty smell along with their ugly faces.

His army wasn't limited to the condom creatures, there were "humanlike" demons that materialized. Their features were sharp, like an actual pointy object that could poke an eye out. Cheekbones, nose, chin, shoulders, each was different, but no less sinister.

"You said to come alone."

"I did. I never sssaid I would," he said laughing.

"She's not alone," a voice boomed out from behind me.

Apep's laughter was cut short at the sight of Lucian and his formidable army. He came in looking tall, strong, and glorious—a force to be reckoned with. Flanking his right were Maiz and Vex, and to the left, Adam, Kane, and Zane. Behind them, troops of wolves, demons, and demon dogs.

I could have cried at the sight of them. There were so many willing to stand up with me. Some barely knew me. Some didn't know me at all. They came for the cause, the save-the-world cause. Lucian winked at me, giving me a much-needed confidence boost. As Maiz would say, *let's do this shit!* This time, when I turned back to face Apep, I squared my shoulders and held my head high, demanding respect and feeling larger than life. Apep, on the other hand, was fuming.

Lake appeared at Apep's side. It had only been a few days since I'd seen him, but he looked years older. There were no visible marks that he had been harmed. He stood there looking serene, as if nothing was amiss about what was happening. As if he wasn't now wrapped in the clutches of a demon lord, determined to destroy everything.

"I know how this ends, and I'm not scared," Lake said. "I love you."

Apep moved a large cutting knife to Lake's throat.

"Aww, how very touching. He lovesss his mommy. Not for much longer."

He smiled wide, showing off a mouth full of long, jagged teeth.

"Dad won't let me die. He promised," Lake said.

"Your dad is rotting somewhere in the pits of hell," Apep said, referring to Marc. "It's time for you to join him."

He didn't know that it was Lucian who was Lake's dad.

Apep pulled the blade across Lake's neck from ear to ear. Red poured out of him like a faucet had been opened. I wanted to run to him so I could hold him as I had in the dream, be there for him so he wasn't alone in his last moments.

I was frozen in place, unable to move. It was hard to tell if I was frozen from fear or from another force holding me. It only took a couple of minutes for Lake to bleed out. He slumped in Apep's grip.

Apep released his hold, letting the small, limp body fall to the ground. Emotions bombarded my entire body. Rage first and foremost. For everything this man had taken from me. Lake was my world, and now he was gone. I hated him with an absolute loathing that I didn't think possible to feel toward another person.

That was our signal. A line had been crossed. A battle horn had been blown. Someone had thrown the first punch. We all switched into attack mode. I was ready to rip this man limb from limb. Before I could even take a step, a strong wind blew, swirling around me. My vision darkened, throwing the world into shadowland. Lightning snapped in my veins, and my muscles felt as if they were being torn apart. This must be how Bruce felt when he turned into the Hulk.

The pain became so intense, I felt as if I was going through a tree shredder. I screamed out—an ear-piercing, earth-shattering scream. A long crevasse opened in the earth beneath my feet, but I didn't fall. I hovered above it as others all around me scrambled to keep from being swallowed up.

Since I had no idea how to work these new powers, I didn't want to push my luck by staying over the crevasse. All I did was think about standing next to Lucian, and my body was moving on its own, landing me on solid ground right next to him. Whether it was me, or someone else helping me out, I took it as my first victory.

"You're running at full capacity now," he said. "Give him hell, Butter."

While I was busy transforming into my full power potential, the wolves became wolves, and the demon dogs became, well, demon dogs. They were black, blurred forms that glitched and twitched, their blazing red eyes contrasting with the coal-black fur. They held my attention because I had seen them before in one of Lake's sketches. He'd known this battle was coming.

Full-blooded demons crouched at the ready, waiting on my signal to commence attack. Fingers had changed to claws, capable of ripping and tearing apart anything that became trapped in their clutches. Some had claws that looked fiery hot, others had smoke rolling out of their noses, while still others' powers were yet to be seen. The only thing between us and the enemy was the crevasse I had created.

Apep leaned over, looking into the hole.

"Oh, good," he said. "I needed a place to throw my garbage."

He kicked at Lake's lifeless form until it fell into the abyss.

I pulled the kopis from my back and started running toward the charging enemy, swinging the sword at everything that came toward me. Wolves and demon dogs leapt through the air, faces pulled back in a snarl, teeth bared. Demons were rushing toward the onslaught, battling to avenge our fallen comrade.

Bodies collided in a mass of flashing teeth and claws. Guttural screams of rage and pain filled the air. In all the chaos, I had lost track of Apep. I scanned the crowd of combatants, seeing red, green, and black blood covering all of them. Towards the back, away from the melee, I found Apep watching. A determined Lucian was headed straight for him.

Apep's body began to bend, contorting in ways no human being could manage unless they were septuple-jointed. Bones moved, rearranging themselves as his body grew larger and taller. His face elongated to form a snout, and what used to be arms melded to his body, his legs becoming one to form a tail.

In only seconds, Apep had mutated into an enormous yellow-orange serpent with an intricate gold pattern running along his back. He towered fifty feet above us, another fifty feet of him still planted firmly on the ground. A large hood flapped out from the side of his head, with golden scrolling on the inside. His mouth opened to show us rows of jagged teeth, and that revolting forked tongue flicked out. I could hear him hissing. If I wasn't mistaken, I'd say he was laughing at us. Shit, I'd laugh myself if I wasn't so bowled over at the sight of his true form.

The Olympians honestly thought that a normal-sized person like me could take on a beast such as this? They were out of their freaking minds. Lucian had raised his hands in front of him, looking like he was about to cast a spell. Moving faster than my eyes could track, Apep had coiled around him, constricting tighter and tighter. Pain etched deep lines on Lucian's face.

Holding the kopis above my head, I ran at Apep. I swung the sword down as forcefully as I could manage when I reached his coiled body, only to have it clang off the hard-as-metal scales. I tried again with the same result. There were dents where the kopis had made contact, but nothing more.

I looked at Lucian, trying to hide the panic I felt inside. There was no way for me to save him. His eyes were beginning to bulge, and I could hear his bones snapping under the pressure of the constricting body.

"Bellll—" Lucian forced out, then he was still.

And quiet.

Apep uncoiled, letting Lucian drop to the ground like an unwanted doll. He used his tail to sweep the body down the same crevasse he'd kicked Lake down. I stood in horror and disbelief as I watched the mangled body disappear. Two of the most important people in my life were dead because of me. I had failed them. I wanted to scream, cry, feel sorry for myself, grieve their loss, but there was no time. Apep made sure I was aware of this by giving me a hard whack with his tail, sending me flying.

My landing was far from graceful as I hit hard in the dirt, scraping and sliding. Before I even had time to shake my head clear, Apep was coming straight at me. I held out my hands, envisioning an invisible wall that he would slam into, but it didn't work. He turned, swiping his tail in my direction once again, effectively punching me in the stomach, knocking the wind out of me as I flew off my feet. I flipped and slammed to the ground, pain radiating from multiple broken ribs.

Funny, I was supposed to be the most powerful thing around, but I had no idea how to use it. Or how to defeat this guy. While I figured out these new powers, I'd have to use my handy dandy brainpower, using the weaknesses of snakes against him. Apep wasn't a typical snake, but it was the best idea I had. It was my only idea.

My next hurdle: I didn't know jack about snakes. My parents thought snakes represented the devil, and we were never allowed to have one as a pet. Truth be told, after this shitshow, I was right there with them in that belief.

Let's see—sight. Snakes couldn't see well, especially at night. So, all I had to do was distract Apep until the sun went down. In other words, I'd be getting my ass kicked for the next five hours to make it to sundown. Next idea.

Duh. Snakes were cold-blooded. That was why we were inside some invisible terrarium, with no snow and no cold. Remembering that night with Lucian, when I could feel every cell in my body, I tapped into those senses. Concentrating through my pain and fear. Using them to reach out to my surroundings, finding the dome towering over us. I just needed to figure out how to break it.

"I can see the wheelsss turning, but nobody is home."

Apep was laughing at me again.

"That doesn't make any sense, you moron."

Before I knew what was happening, he had wrapped around me, squeezing the life out of me.

"I thought you were sssupposssed to be sssome big, bad bitch." His head dipped down to my level. His tongue flicking in and out. "I can sssmell your fear."

Smell, of course, another obvious one. Snakes smelled with their tongues. I had an idea; it wouldn't kill him, but it might prompt him to release me. Lucky for me, my arms were free of his coiling body. I waited for the opportune moment, summoning as much strength as possible to hold my body together just a little bit longer.

Apep flexed, constricting tighter around me. The pressure my body was under should have made my head pop like a grape. I supposed the power within me held me together, keeping me from snapping like a twig.

His tongue flicked out, right in front of my face. With lightning speed, I grabbed hold with my left arm, then swung my right hand over my head, slamming the blade of the kopis down on the strip of flesh. Not only did I cut the tongue clean off, now there was hydra poison coursing through his bloodstream.

As predicted, Apep released me, dropping me the height of a five-story building. I landed on my feet without any additional broken bones in a crouching position, ready to strike. Finally, something was going right. No mere mortal would have survived that fall. I felt a renewed spirit after the small win in that battle. The giant snake was slithering away, blood dripping from his gaping mouth. The hydra poison didn't have an immediate, obvious effect, but I still counted it as a win.

I was feeling powerful now. Not just in the formidable sense of the word, but I could feel it in my veins. Finally, I could harness and use what my momma had given me. It was as if my brain had been rewired with this new power information, and I just knew how to start wielding it. Regrouping, I focused on what else I could do to bring down the snake.

Forces beyond me, huge bodies, pulled at me. There were millions of them, all chaotic in nature, some stronger than others. I looked up at the clear sky. Closing my eyes, I blocked out everything around me. Using only my mind, I pulled at the closest of the massive forces, moving it slowly but surely until I was sure it would move into place.

Opening my eyes, I could see the moon on a direct path to cover the sun. The other masses were all the stars and planets in the sky. The better option would have been an early sunset, but if the sun suddenly fell from the sky in the middle of the afternoon, that would most likely cause widespread pandemonium. It was bad enough I had caused an unpredicted eclipse. I didn't have time to think of what other chaos may have come with moving the moon. I'd fix it later.

The eclipse would give me a few minutes of much-needed darkness to work with. I thought about my next move as the sun's light began to fade. The low light might make it harder for Apep to see me, but if I remembered correctly, some snakes could detect body heat. Between the adrenaline and the fight for my life, my body was running hot. That might be an issue. The leather pants I'd worn had saved me from ripping my legs to shreds with my falls, but they were also hot as blazes. All I could do was pull my sweater off to release some heat. The moon made its last inch into total solar eclipse phase, and the sun's light was blotted out.

Before I could make a move, another presence radiated all around me. I'd created enough darkness that I could feel Nyx, goddess of the night, and her power filling the air. Her radiance wrapped around me, connecting our souls, intertwining and uniting our powers. I'd been created with her power, so it might be more accurate to say that I was pulling her remaining power to use as my own. Her night essence cooled my body, giving me the stealth I needed against any heat-detecting glands.

I ran at Apep again—he had stopped and lowered himself down to the earth in the sudden darkness, waiting out the eclipse. Swinging my kopis like a crazy lumberjack trying to take down a giant tree, I tried to find a weak spot in his armor. Large dents speckled his scales but held strong against the onslaught.

Apep turned toward me, where he could feel me clubbing away. Not where he could see me. He attempted a hiss, and oily black liquid spurted from his wounded mouth, steaming and burning as it hit the ground. He opened his mouth wide, prominently exposing fangs that dripped with venom, then lunged for me.

Like a magician, I was flashed from where I stood to reappear feet from where I had been. Vacating the spot right before a fang the size of my body would have been jabbed into my face.

"I got you, baby girl," Nyx's voice said in my head.

Apep whirled and lunged again and again. Each time, I was flashed out of the way. I was no longer swinging at him, and so I was unsure how he was "seeing" me.

"We can't keep doing this. We're wasting the eclipse. The next time he comes at us, put me above his head."

With the next lunge, I was flashed above his head, hovering just behind his eyes. Apep stopped, listening, waiting for me to land within striking distance. That's how he'd known where to aim, he could hear my feet in the gravel.

I assumed Nyx could read my mind, the same as Lucian could. With my thoughts, I told her what I wanted her to do. I readied the kopis above my head, counted to three silently, and arced the sharp edge of the blade down as Nyx moved me into position. In perfect sync, the tip was shoved into the right eye as I'd hoped.

Apep reared up off the ground, bucking and whipping around like a wild bronco, taking me along for the ride as I held tight to the hilt of my still-buried kopis. His head was too wide for me to wrap my legs around, and the scales were too flat and slippery to stand on, leaving me nothing to do but flap in the wind. I was getting bumped, tossed, and banged seven ways to Sunday. There was no way I could keep this up for much longer.

Even with the thick soles of my snow boots, I couldn't get a grip no matter how hard I tried. How nice it would be to have sticky shoes. And just like that, my boots stuck to the scales as if they were magnetic. Good thing I had those dream surf lessons. Finding my balance, I pulled the blade from the ruptured ball and slammed it into the other eye.

Apep half-hissed, half-screamed with the new jabbing pain. I hadn't realized how high up we were until he began a nosedive for the ground. Having the minuscule time to plan my landing, I thought back to a shopping trip to Target with Maiz. After an unfortunate encounter running on an icy parking lot, she taught me it was best to tuck and roll when speeding toward the ground. Bidding my time, I waited for the right moment to jump for safety, leaving my magnetic boots behind.

Being smashed flat as a pancake beneath Apep might not kill me, but I would bet it would hurt like hell. As it was, by following Maiz's advice, I only came up with a few extra bruises. My ribs had seen better days, but much better than the alternative, in my opinion.

Apep was on his back, rubbing his head along the rocks. Probably he thought I was still attached to the boots, and he was grinding me to mush. Or maybe he was trying to extract the blade that was still lodged in his eye. A difficult task when you don't have arms. In any case, his belly was exposed. A smooth, pale-yellow belly that wasn't protected by metal scales. Suddenly, it hit me like a ton of bricks—Lucian hadn't been trying to tell me about a bell—he'd been trying to say belly.

Please let this work. I reached out to my sword, summoning it to my hand. This could go very wrong, and I could lose an arm. Or a torso. I hadn't made it this far to be cut down by my own sword. Thank the heavens the hilt planted firmly in the palm of my hand. Time to end this fight. This fucker was going down. I planned to gut him from top to tail.

Pulling from my cauldron of powers, I tied Apep to the ground with invisible ropes. Although I couldn't be sure it was me that had done it, I was relieved when he stopped moving. His body flexed as he tried to break free of his ties. I went to his unprotected belly, ready to lay open his soft underside. Raising the blade high, I faltered on the comedown.

Here's the thing: I wanted to kill Apep. I had to if I wanted to save the world, but it was easier said than done. I'd never killed anyone before.

The eclipse had passed. Warm sun was shining in on me again. I closed my eyes, raising my face up toward the heavens. In my mind's eye, I could see Lake and Lucian smiling at me, telling me I could do this. Their smiling faces faded into a black abyss, never to be seen again. A new face appeared—one I didn't recognize. His face was strong and stoic, while his eyes swirled with galaxies instead of an iris and pupil. My dad, Chaos. I wasn't sure how I knew who he was; I just did.

He reached out a hand to me, allowing me to tether his power to mine, giving me the ultimate trifecta with Nyx's power. And the willpower to do what I needed to do. I raised the sword up, slamming it down through the underside of Apep's chin. Running the length of his body, the blade slid through his skin like a hot knife through butter, opening a soupy mix of blood and guts.

I was no doctor, so it was hard to identify what was what, except for one thing. The heart. The most important organ in the body. Without the heart, there would be no blood flow, or whatever the black crud was that he was filled with. Without oxygen-rich crud, the brain couldn't function. No functioning brain, no functioning asshole.

I wrapped my hands around the heart. Dark, chaotic energy moved down my arms. The only way to describe it would be like what happens to molecules in steam. They were in constant motion, moving faster and faster as they heated up. The energy traveled through my fingers to Apep's heart. He arched and twisted, but my ties held fast. Had I known what was coming next, I would have stepped away. Unfortunately, my powers didn't come with the ability to see the future.

Apep's heart exploded, spraying crud and chunks of tissue all over me. Some even sprayed in my mouth, making me gag at the fetid taste.

Only then, when I knew he wasn't coming back from this, did I notice the quiet. Any fighting that had been going on before I started my battle had stopped. Or concluded, and I had no idea which side had won. Hoping for the best but fearing the worst, I turned to face the victors.

Bodies littered the ground. Ground that was covered in red, green, and black blood. Wolves and demon dogs howled, while the caldera demons hooted for our accomplishment. Every face I gazed upon was battered and bleeding. And unfamiliar.

It was all over. The world was safe. I should be happy, but I had lost everyone. Everyone I loved had died because of me. To top it all off, if I died now, I'd most likely still self-destruct. I had no choice other than to live with the grief.

I dropped to my knees, ignoring the jolt of pain from my battered body. Letting my heavy heart take over, I started to cry.

"Why so glum, chum? We won."

I wiped at my eyes to clear my vision, make sure I was really seeing him.

"Adam," I said, jumping to my feet and into his open arms. "I didn't see you in the crowd, and I thought you had been killed."

"I know, doll, I'm sorry. New title comes with big responsibilities. I had to attend to my people."

He cast a glance at the serpent that was still laid out on the ground.

"What the shit," Maiz said. "How does the wolf get the first hug?"

"I know, right?" Vex chimed in. "We've been around her whole life. While he's been here, what? Four days? That's bullshit right there, girl."

I released my hold on Adam. Jumping all the way to the girls, I wrapped an arm around each, pulling them in for a group hug.

"Holy hell, you stink, woman. You should go back to hugging the wolf," Maiz said.

"You don't smell much better."

"No, I think that's still you, honey," Vex said.

I laughed through my tears, pulling them in even tighter.

"Mom."

My breath caught at the little voice I'd thought I'd never hear again.

"Go get that boy," Vex whispered.

Dropping my arms, Maiz and Vex stepped aside. Lake stood next to Gaia, holding her hand. All that remained of the large cut across his neck was the dried blood staining his shirt. He let go of Gaia's hand to run to me, jumping in my arms. I squeezed him, promising I would never let him go.

"Mom. It's too tight. I can't breathe."

"Sorry, baby, I'm just so happy you're okay."

Gaia walked up to us.

"How is this possible?" I asked.

"Gramma gave me a present when I was staying at Dad's house," Lake said, looking at Gaia. She didn't look super enthused about being called a grandma. "Do you wanna see it?" He could barely contain his excitement.

"You know I do."

Lake walked over to where I'd left Apep's body. I nearly called him back for fear that the snake would pop back to life and swallow the small boy whole. Before I had the chance to say anything, Lake started to grow horns, ranging in size from small to large, on either side of his head. The horns continued down his back, all the way to the tip of his tail, which swung from side to side. Large, leathery wings sprouted from his back, and his smooth skin was replaced by shiny, garnet-colored scales. He had grown in size, much like Apep when he'd transformed into his snake form but was still very small for what I imagined a full-size dragon to be.

With a whoosh of his wings, Lake's dragon form took to the sky, flying up and down and all around. He dove back down, stopping just above the snake's lifeless body, grabbing him up by the tail with long claws. Struggling to get the serpent that was three times his size off the ground, Lake dragged the body over to the same hole he had been tossed into. He flew over the hole, dropping the garbage down the shoot where it belonged.

"That takes care of cleanup," Vex said.

"Fuck yeah, that kid is the shit!" Maiz said.

"Maiz, language. Little ears."

"What? I thought we were gonna be here all day cleaning that bastard off the ground, piece by tiny piece. Besides, he's too far away to hear me anyway."

She was right. Lake had flown about two miles in two seconds. I turned back to Gaia.

"What did you give him?"

"Immortality," she said simply.

"In the form of a dragon?"

"Yes. Lake knew his future and that he wouldn't make it to his twenty-fifth birthday, when his real immortality would kick in. To save him, I gifted him the dragon, something I took ownership of when my friend Tiamat, a Mesopotamian goddess, was killed and scattered among the earth and heavens."

"Is Lucian—Is he alive, too?"

She shook her head, her eyes filling with tears.

I knew the pain she was feeling over the loss of her son. Mine was only gone for an hour or so, but I still knew the heart-wrenching hole it left.

"The dragon is very powerful," Gaia said. "Apep would have known right away that it was inside the boy. We had to mask it until the time was right. If he didn't kill Lake, the rest of your power never would have been released in time."

Even with the masking, Apep had known something was different about Lake.

"If Lake really died, how is he here right now?"

"Lucian, he's always been Hades' favorite Oneiroi."

"He made a deal with the devil," Maiz clarified.

Gaia glared at her. "He bargained his soul for Lake's. When Apep thought he killed Lucian and dropped him down the hole, Lucian healed Lake's body, Hades released Lake's soul, and I released the dragon."

The dragon landed beside us, leaning his head down, close to mine. I tentatively touched its snout, feeling the hot, rugged skin under my fingers. Big, black eyes stared into mine. With my hand still resting on his muzzle, the dragon began to fold in on itself. It was like watching a weird virtual reality of origami. The color faded, limbs shrank, horns and wings retreated. He became smaller and smaller, taking on the shape of a young boy. My hand now rested on a beautiful head of hair, unruly as usual.

"I told you Dad wouldn't let anything happen to me," Lake said, smiling at me.

"He wanted to do this for his son," Gaia said. "And for you."

It was the sweetest, dumbest, most infuriating thing anyone had ever done for me.

***

Back at the house, I had a hard time letting Lake out of my sight. I didn't want to risk losing him while I took something as trivial as a shower. Once I had promises from Maiz, Vex, Adam, Kane, Zane, Sky, Star, Bram, and a few others I didn't know, I felt comfortable enough to retreat to my room. Not before I got an "Aw, mom, I'm not a baby" from Lake.

I started by throwing my clothes in the garbage, then tying the bag shut. In the shower, I washed my body a minimum of five times. Even then, I could still smell the stink of Apep in my pores. Because my hair had been pulled back, it had mostly been spared the spattering, and I felt it was clean enough after only three washes.

I slathered perfumed lotion over my whole body in hopes of masking any lingering smell, then dressed in a pair of comfy sweatpants, a tank top, and a sweatshirt. I brushed my teeth twice, gargled twice, and put on a little mascara. My shower had already taken longer than I wanted, so I opted to pull my hair back in a messy bun.

Heading back out to the sitting area, everyone was right where I left them. Lake was sitting on one of the couches, playing a game on a tablet. Adam was to his left, Maiz and Vex to his right. Lake was busy explaining to a fascinated Adam the best way to defeat the bumblebirb. Once the bumblebirb was defeated, the jungle dragon, Yharon, can be summoned. Sounded like my life. My life was a video game, complete with evil creatures, moon lords, and a whole world full of the unknown.

I sat on the couch across from them, watching what would be my new normal. Just hanging out in a room with werewolves, ancient spirits, and my son, the dragon. This was my new family, and no matter who—or what—they were, I loved them.

Epilogue

I put the finishing touches on my makeup and sprayed an extra spritz of perfume to hide my nervous sweat.

"Butter, it'll be fine. Vex told you Raven is excited you're coming," Lucian said.

He wrapped his arms around me from behind and nuzzled my neck.

Here's the thing about saving the world from a psychopath hell-bent on taking over: everyone owes you one. I took a page out of Lucian's playbook; I bargained for his soul with Hades. He's sort of a sucker for love stories. I suppose that has something to do with his own love life.

His body was more of a problem. The venom had done a real number on his insides. Now that I had a teacher to guide me on how to use my new tricks, I could heal him, but the venom remained. No matter how many times I put Humpty back together, the venom kept breaking him apart.

Amun Ra provided me with a type of antivenom to try to slow the damage until it either passed or we could get a more specific antivenom made. That meant we would need to find the demon that the toxin had come from.

She went by Vis, short for visceral, and she had disappeared after that first attack. According to Amun Ra, she wasn't even from Egypt. Many knew of her, but not where she came from. Or where she may have disappeared to. A lot of demons had escaped or fled our battles, now running freely through the general population. Reinforcements had been called in to help find and destroy the remaining enemies, but that wasn't my concern tonight.

Until Vis was found, Lucian fed on me when he needed a little boost. Today, Christmas, was no exception.

"Make sure you don't get any blood in my hair. I don't have time to wash and straighten it again," I said, pulling my hair to the side anyway.

"You can use your powers to do that girly stuff, you know."

"I forget. I'm still getting used to it. Plus, this makes me feel like a normal person."

"Do we have time for anything else?"

His hands were exploring their way under my shirt.

"You know, I wish we did, but we have to be there in five minutes."

His fingers were creeping across my panty line. "We could be fashionably late."

"Lucian. You know how important this is."

He healed the marks on my neck and flashed us some coats. Lake popped himself into the large bedroom of the Yellowstone house. As a child, he was learning how to use his powers a lot quicker than me. I held his hand, flashing us all to the front door of my sister's home in South Dakota, fourteen hours away. This new form of travel was amazing. I'd never be late for an appointment again.

I rang the doorbell, feeling my heartbeat speed up as we waited to be let in. Lucian squeezed my hand, giving me a reassuring smile. The door opened to an elated Raven.

"You're here. Oh, my heck, I'm so glad you're here," she said in a high-pitched squeal.

She practically threw herself at me, and we hugged. It wouldn't make up for all our years of separation, but it was a promise for the future.

"Holy crap, Rose, your guy is hot," she whispered in my ear, not knowing that both Lucian and Lake could hear her or that Lucian could pick up all her thoughts.

"This is Lake, your nephew." I paused for them to hug. "And this is Lucian. My—" I looked at him, hoping he'd fill in the blank.

"Fiancé." He held out his hand to her, but she wrapped him in a hug.

Raven invited us into her split-foyer home. We walked up the stairs that opened to a large, open room that included a living room, kitchen, and dining area, separated only by a small counter. The tall, vaulted ceilings echoed our voices back at us, making the room feel bigger than it really was. It was a modest house, but knowing that Rae had financed this all on her own, I'd say she wasn't doing too shabby.

Sitting in one of the high-top chairs at the counter was Vex.

"Vex, you remember my sister, Rose." I waved, and she winked at me. Of course, Rae didn't know that Vex and I were in contact almost every day. She also didn't know that Vex, Lake, and Lucian were acquainted. "This little cutie," Raven continued, "is my nephew, Lake, and this is Rose's fiancé, Lucian." Vex gave me a questioning look, and I just shrugged. "This is my bestie, Vexaria, but we all call her Vex. Over there on the couch is my husband, Dan."

The man on the couch was frumpy. Dressed in sweatpants and a baggy t-shirt, he sat drinking a beer while watching ESPN. I imagined that if we weren't here, he'd have his belly hanging out and a hand tucked in his pants. Without looking our way, he raised his bottle in greeting.

Vex and Maiz might not be able to interfere in Rae's personal life, but that didn't mean I couldn't. It wasn't too late to get her with someone better. She and Adam would be adorable together. Or any of the one thousand sexy gentlemen I'd come across over the last few weeks.

"Now that everyone is here, we have some exciting news," Raven said. "I'm pregnant."

Crap.